blood shinobi
revenge to redemption

by Edmund Kolbusz

outskirtspress
DENVER, COLORADO

Blood Shinobi
Revenge to Redemption
All Rights Reserved.
Copyright © 2013 Edmund Kolbusz
v2.0

Cover Photo © 2013 Edmund Kolbusz. All rights reserved - used with permission.

Outskirts Press, Inc.
http://www.outskirtspress.com

ISBN: 978-1-4787-1522-1

Library of Congress Control Number: 2012922693

Outskirts Press and the "OP" logo are trademarks belonging to Outskirts Press, Inc.

PRINTED IN THE UNITED STATES OF AMERICA

For Lisa,
Thank you for your constant encouragement and praise.
Your words buoyed me during storms of self-doubt.

For my present and former students of
South Forsyth High School and Lambert High School,
Thank you for enthusiastically accepting a manuscript in its
rough and rudimentary form. Your comments were heard
and your suggestions applied.

For Julie Scott,
Thank you for your support, your editing and your suggestions.
They were truly invaluable.

Prologue

Oda Nobunaga, the son of a minor Japanese warlord, came to head the Oda clan and Owari province at the age of fifteen (1551). Brash, bold and rude, it is understood that he was so wild and such an embarrassment that one of his father's loyal retainers, who was tasked with helping Nobunaga rule, committed suicide over his audacious behavior. However, these traits of arrogance, boldness and unpredictability were instrumental in conquering over one-third of the country. He is a controversial and enigmatic figure who forever changed Japan. Oda Nobunaga waged war, negotiated complicated treaties, committed heinous atrocities for thirty-one years in an attempt to subdue the entire country "under one sky"... his.

He was considered a tyrant: ruthless, cruel, and cunning, yet there were aspects of his rule which were deemed farsighted and progressive. He welcomed the newly landed Portuguese with their new faith, Catholicism, and their new weapons, the arquebus. He hated the Japanese faith, Buddhism, most probably because of the warrior Buddhist monks who were a constant source of irritation for him in that they were intractable, utterly uncontrollable, a constant thorn in his side, economically and militarily. He recognized that the world beyond Japanese shores was more sophisticated than feudal Japan and that the Portuguese were only the first of the Europeans who were to land upon the island's shores. There was much to be learned from the new world, but as the Japanese were firmly entrenched in their ancient traditions and political systems the provinces were constantly warring with one another. Treachery, subterfuge, deceit, murder, conspiracy, brother against brother, and nephew against uncle, these machinations were accepted as the way of life. Japan had fought against itself for over a thousand years and Oda Nobunaga was the first to try to unify and change the country, albeit not for altruistic reasons, but out of sheer arrogance, and desire for wealth and power. Nonetheless, his ambition was timely and ultimately Japan did change, although not exactly as Oda Nobunaga had planned.

During his conquests he murdered brothers, kidnapped children, held them for ransom, married his siblings to the daughters of his enemies, forgave assassins, waged warfare against astronomical odds and won, tortured, slaughtered, wiped out entire villages, towns and monasteries.

He hated ninja. He had no use for them, and he hated the warrior monks, especially those of Mt. Hiei, just north of his capitol in Kyoto and the Ikko monks of Ise.

The warrior monks of Mt Hiei and the Ikko of Ise were constant sources of irritation for Oda Nobunaga. He could not control them. They were autonomous and militarily fierce. They resisted his dominion and plagued him as much as they could. He hated them.

He hated them as much as he hated ninja. He refused to use them although they were used against him. They were clandestine families, clans, headed by a Jonin, an "A" level ninja, one who knew how to contact the Chunin who orchestrated ninja assaults upon whomever the Jonin decreed. They were assassins, but what was more important was they were spies, and the best spies were females, as they posed as concubines and uncovered many secrets during drunken pillow talk. Ninja were skilled acrobats, martial artists, performers in song, dance, haiku; they knew how to kill and to heal wounds. They were talented people well versed in a variety of skills ... and all for sale. There was one drawback to the tradition; it was lethal, but then that was Japan 1600.

Chapter 1

Nakamura leapt from the stony compound wall and landed softly on a gently sloping buttress. Nearby, in the garden, a company of resting carrion crows startled by the intrusion raised a racket which resounded throughout the fortress grounds. Silently, Naki cursed himself; despite his stealth, he would be caught. He would fail. Abbot Kosa warned him, "Nakamura, do not attempt this." He forbade him. "Only a beetle-headed fool would attempt to single-handedly invade Oda Nobunaga's citadel. Wait patiently," he said, "the time will come." Was the master correct? Was this truly folly? On the other hand, he was ready was he not? He believed he was; he trained hard, much harder than the others. He was superior to the others … ah, but was he a fool? Would he fail and die because of his need for revenge? After this first noisy foul misstep, he shamefully conceded that he would be caught, and he was nothing more than an ill prepared rogue. Even if he somehow succeeded in assassinating Nobunaga, he would place the monastery and Mt. Hiei in peril.

Fear fueled another wild exertion and he leapt onto a

low hanging branch of the nearest and largest tree; hidden by the branches and the black of the night, he waited for the inevitable investigation by the warrior guards.

He did not have to wait long. Terse commands from the men-at-arms penetrated the night's still air. Through the leaves he could see black and lightly armored shadows searching for the cause of the midnight disturbance. Again, the crows created an indignant ruckus and flew up into the branches of the very tree which concealed the hapless assassin. A soldier approached the massive trunk of the tree where Naki waited - where he waited for his eventual discovery. Rather than looking up and easily detecting the intruder, the foot guard looked down, raised his flap and relieved himself on the tree. With a grunt, he finished and shouted deep guttural orders for the others to return to the palace.

At least an hour passed before Naki deemed it safe to spring back to the ground. What had he been thinking? His passion for revenge possessed him. Now, what were his options? Calmly, he reasoned. Surely, the monks would have realized his intentions, to disregard their wise counsel. Surely, they must believe he had been discovered. Surely they fear that a dreadful revenge for the assassination attempt would be forthcoming. How could he have been so irresponsible? How could he have been so selfish? He cursed himself; he cursed his impatience; he cursed Oda Nobunaga, and he cursed his life. Again, he felt the despondency which first engulfed him thirteen years ago, deeply ... and darkly.

With disciplined control, he compressed his ribcage expelling fear and troublesome air from his lungs and the blackness from his soul into the inky night. He deeply breathed clear air fresh, free of the demons of his misguided venture. He had not been seen. It was not too late to turn back. Shame awaited him upon his return, perhaps punishment. However, he had not jeopardized the lives of the monks or the villagers. For that he was grateful. With unnatural strength and agility, he bounded onto the rampart and swiftly scrambled to the top of the stone wall and crouched silently, hidden by the darkness of the night. In the distance, somewhere Nobunaga slept safely. A fire of rage burned within.

Clearing his mind, he turned and leapt; silently, he landed on the ground and in one fluid, perfect motion was on his feet padding back to the village and the fate that awaited him.

—————⫸⫷(◉)⫸⫷—————

The black of the night was vanishing, a gray dawn was rising, when Naki entered the village. He paused by a stream to cleanse … his thoughtlessness away. A voice startled him.

"Nakamura, you are up so early."

It was Abbot Kosa. Nakamura stood up and slowly turned towards his spiritual advisor and mentor in the art of *ninjutsu-zukai*.

Hoping that his absence may have gone undetected, Naki answered, "Master, I walk to clear my head for it is full of misgivings."

"You walk? … because of your dreams?"

"Yes, Master. They have intensified. They are fiercer than ever before."

"Have patience, my son. Remember fast ripe, fast rotten."

"But, Master, my anger is intolerable. If I wait any longer I fear I will rot from the waiting. I must act.

"By yourself?"

"My pain consumes me. Master, I can end my pain. I can end Japan's pain. I am ready. I am unparalleled. How many times have you said so, yourself?"

"Your skills are formidable, agreed. No one matches your dexterity with the yari. In your hands the katana sings resonant and your opponents only hear the dirges of their impending death. But, you must wait."

"Wait!"

"Yes! You can not do this alone. A single arrow is easily broken, but not ten in a bundle. Had you continued with your foolishness you would have been killed."

"Master, what do you mean?"

"Do not shame me and yourself in denying what you attempted last night! You must wait. If you wish to free your-self from the torment of this devil you will only succeed if you heed the wisdom of the gods."

"Forgive me Master."

"A fog cannot be displaced by a fan. A great wind will blow and this pestilence will pass."

"When?"

"I have forgiven your impetuousness, and now I grow impatient with your insolence! Leave me!"

Humiliated, Nakamura bowed and left. Abbot Kosa knelt down and dipped his hands into the cold mountain brook. He cupped some water and splashed his face. The sun rose over Mt. Hiei and the gray morning sky was now a cloudy confusion of color.

Nakamura entered his quarters. The others were at prayer. They were presently in communion chanting and meditating. He looked at the rows of plain cots, neat and orderly; they spoke of austerity, commitment, and especially obedience and … where was he? … alone, alienated, troubled and tormented.

In the middle of the doorway, he prostrated himself. He sought to cleanse his mind … his soul. On his knees, with his arms outstretched, he arched his back and pushed his chest to the ground, and then with a focused stretching he exhaled deeply trying to relieve his muscles of his self-inflicted tension. Sitting back on his heels he moved into Child's Pose and remained still until he found a semblance of calm and tranquility.

After a while, he rose and walked to his mat to lie down. With closed eyes, he prayed the demons of his sleep would not return. A gentle breeze passed through the open windows easing him to sleep.

Unfortunately, the dream began … again. At first, there was a rumbling, horses at a gallop. Hundreds and hundreds of black horses racing against an evil sky, all furious with maddened eyes, snorting flames from hell. Their violently flared nostrils torched brown bordering grasses. Bushes burst into blazing fireballs consuming young trees and ancient timbers. Ashes and soot swirled upwards and formed masses of black columns in the sky. A maelstrom of death pounded a path of hellish fury towards the sleepy village where only a few old women were stirring … gathering water for tea. Grudgingly, the gray dawn succumbed to the meancing black clouds darkening the day and the hellish doom thundered closer.

Hot bitter blood pulsed through Naki's veins. Asleep, he, his soul, was again fouled and his spirit blackened. The dream continued. He heard screams, frail, weak … abruptly … they were silenced. Men's voices clamored in confusion. Arrows whistled through the morning air. Flames licked wooden doorways and roofs. Smoke and searing heat forced everyone, young, old, strong and feeble into the courtyard. Flaming feathered shafts greeted them. Shrill shrieks of agony. He smelt burning flesh. Swords were hurriedly drawn from their scabbards. Men rushed forward.

Tightly packed ranks of blackened armored devils wielding long *yaris* advanced, dispassionately cutting down opposition. Left and right flanks separated searching, stabbing, slicing, anything that was not black, masked and heavily protected with leather armor.

Naki restlessly turned in his bed and the dream continued. The air was putrid with the stench of blood and death. Yet, they were not finished. Once the specters from hell were satisfied they had accomplished their mission, they began to play. Squads were dispatched to flush out any children who were hiding in hopes of escaping the massacre. Gales of laughter and approval greeted those who returned with innocents found cowering under steps or behind walls. They were herded into a pen and contained until it was his or her time. One by one, children were selected depending on the game. Infants were tossed into the air and lanced before they fell to the ground. Older children were ordered to run for their lives and were shot down by a volley of arrows and spears. When the devils tired of their amusements, they simply dispatched the few children that remained with the flick of a sword. A final razing of any structure left standing completed their mission, and they carelessly rode away.

Naki awoke drenched in sweat. He rose from his bed and shivered uncontrollably. A violent spasm turned his stomach and he wretched a small pool of yellow bile onto the ground. He stood up, and raised two clenched fists into the air and deep from within roared a fierce cry of unimaginable anguish.

Every muscle flexed; he exploded. Unconsciously, he sprang up to fight the phantasm, the enemy invisible. His feet kicked the phantom foe, hard; his fists pounded the foe's face and body. In his mind, Naki envisioned Oda Nobunaga and his minions, and somehow in the midst of his fury he found a sword, and the air was victim to a swirl of slashes and stabs. A final cascade of lethal blows embedded the blade into a supporting post.

Exhausted and finally purged of his rage, Naki realized what he had just done. He looked about embarrassed trying to extract the weapon from the wood, but he couldn't; he fell to his knees panting for air.

"I think you won." Looking at the sword stuck in the beam, Ryu, Naki's trusted sparring partner, was standing in the doorway with a bemused smile. He had witnessed the last few moments of the display. "If you wish to spar I am always ready; you do not need to fight air." He grabbed the handle of the *katana* and gave a mighty pull. It would not budge. He yanked again and still nothing. He began to wriggle it upwards and downwards, back and forth, finally with a great shove the blade grudgingly bent, only to defiantly spring throwing Ryu back onto his ass. He landed hard. "Ow, damn," he bellowed. Standing up, he pulled down his cotton pants.

"*Kuso*, shit! Look at my ass, it's broken … it has a big … crack. Hah, hah, hah …, get it, a big crack … on my ass," he laughed again, amused at his own cleverness. Naki, despite his recent distress, gave in and laughed along. Eventually, Naki retorted, "It's not only your ass that's cracked.

Ryu lunged forward and began punching Naki in a playful mock attack. Instinctively, Naki grabbed a pummeling fist by the wrist and with one smooth deft maneuver locked his friend's arm causing Ryu to slap his chest in surrender.

"Enough!"

Naki released the arm. "*Fuzaken jyane--yo nande sonna koto shitan dayo-?*! Damn! Why the hell did you do that?" Ryu stood rubbing away the pain. "You never could take a joke."

Naki stood up and yanked the sword from its bondage. "Here, you can have your blade back."

"*Suteki*! Amazing! I could not have pulled that out, not with a dozen oxen."

"I am as stupid as an ox."

"No, you are not. You are amazing. You are an amazing warrior. You are a mountain cat in a young man's body; you have speed, agility … cunning."

"I am foolish."

"I wish I were as foolish."

Outside a stirring was heard.

"Enough!"

At that moment the monks filed in one after another calmly, serenely. Politely nodding to Naki and Ryu, they prepared for the morning's exercises. A bell tolled. Everyone shuffled into the court yard, including Naki and Ryu.

The sky was clear; the sun was hot. Following prayer, the monk's daily ritual was to assemble and practice. They lined the perimeter of the compound. To Naki, they were a block of Japanese humanity ready to obey whatever the Abbot decreed, whenever the Abbot decreed. They were creatures ready to agree, to fight, and to die without question for the cause … the cause? Did they understand the cause? Did they feel the cause, like he did? He was confused; he felt ashamed, again. How could they be so patient, so obedient? They were so loyal. He had almost betrayed them, those who nobly wait to fight. It wasn't his cause alone. How many thousands and thousands had suffered at the hands of the Oda clan? What made him, Nakamura, special? Why should he claim to be the vanquisher … the vanquisher of this … son of a minor warlord …who through audacity and treachery waged war … ceaselessly throughout the land? An adversary such as Oda Nobunaga is not going to be disposed by a lone rogue … a lone shinobi. For twenty three years Nippon has shed rivers of blood … lakes of tears, what dark specters possessed him to think that he might have succeeded in ending that misery and especially alone? The Abbot Kosa knew. He has the intelligence, the blessed chie. Again, he was deeply ashamed. What was he thinking? Why could he not be obedient like the others? Because! He was self-possessed and full of himself? Why did he not have more of the *bushido*, the way of the obedient warrior within him? Why could he not abide, like Samurai, by the code of honorable service? Nakamura answered his troubled spirit's questions with one enveloping response: his dreams.

The practice began. With the clack of two hardwood sticks everyone rose and bowed to the sensei. Gruffly, he gave the command for warm up. The monks quickly assembled into perfect lines of ten across and five deep. Each knew his place. Another whack signaled the first position: Mountain Pose with hands in prayer. Successive clacks led them through Crescent Moon, Proud Warrior, Front Lunge, Front Lunge with twist, hand to the sky, Downward Looking Dog, Upward Looking Dog. The drill continued for twenty minutes until every monk was limber. Then there were the *katas*. Front kicks, side kicks, low blocks left and right, punches to the head, chest, groin. Forward step shoulders level, block, punch retreat. On and on it went everyone moving in perfect unison. A healthy chorus of kiai's punctuated the mountain air.

A gong sounded; it was the hour of the Dragon, time for one to one combat. Servants trooped onto the grounds and lay down a bundle of wooden practice sticks: long ones for the yaris and shorter ones for the *katanas*. "Naginata first!" the drill master barked.

The regimen demanded that the less skilled fight first. Two young warrior monks stood and chose their weapons. They proceeded to the center of the circle. Forty eight men sitting in Diamond Pose circled them as they prepared to exhibit new moves. The two warriors respectfully bowed to one another and extended their weapons. The youngest one immediately lunged forward and delivered a succession of furious downward strikes which were easily blocked by his opponent. The older one, only by months, established his balance and with elegance and ease slipped inside and landed a blow with the short end of the long stick to the chin of his comrade. Down he went like a freshly felled fir. Leaping backwards the older one correctly estimated the severing length of the naginata and smacked the ground with the stick inches away from the ear, neck and collar bone. Had it been real, the blade would have sliced his neck, broke his clavicle and severed his esophagus. The perimeter sat silently as the winner offered the loser the pole to lift himself up. Both bowed to the master and took their place. The winner pleased with his performance knew that next time he would not be the first to enter the circle.

The practice continued. Pair after pair entered and fought, with long poles and short sticks. Every combatant finished feeling a sense of victorious pride or defeated humiliation, yet each ensured his feelings remained hidden. Every display was greeted with a stony silence from the impassive crowd.

Eventually Naki was called. The best went last. His opponent was Zatoichi, a middle-aged ronin, a master less samurai, formerly of the Kitabatake clan. He had only recently sought shelter with the monks of Mount Hiei. His prowess in all aspects of the Samuri, the sword, the horse, the bow were impressive and he had rapidly earned the respect of the monks; some feared him; however, the Abbot Kosa curiously accepted him even into the inner sanctuaries of the monastery.

Both chose their weapons: the long swords. After the customary bow to the referees the rivals faced each other and bowed. Naki stood spiritually centered, sword positioned forward and up. He tried to still his thoughts, his emotions through *fudoshin*, unmoving mind. However, his mind would not be still. It wasn't any uncertainty about the competition which disturbed him but something else. He sensed darkness, a black void of space, an absence of light in the sunlit courtyard. He heard low menacing whispers from deep within a dark hole, evil, sinister.

A fierce "*Kiai!*" dislodged him from his delirium and a bamboo stick smacked his head, a glancing blow. The shaft soundly struck his shoulder. His eyes winced from the pain. He needed space. He bounded backwards. Breathing deeply, he cleared his head and readied himself. This time he saw the plunging thrust; he sidestepped his charging assailant. Naki dropped to his knee and swung his *bokken* low at the back of his competitor's legs. Surprisingly, his blade passed cleanly under the leaping samurai's feet. The ronin landed, well balanced; he twirled about and struck heavily downwards at the crouching youth. His practice sword angled precisely, Naki blocked the blow directing the descending shaft to the ground throwing Zatoichi momentarily off his balance. Sensing the advantage, Naki rose and smacked his opponent's back sending the experienced warrior hurtling face first towards the ground. Instead of landing heavily, the samurai acrobatically spun parallel to the ground and counter struck at Naki's sword preventing another blow. Using his left arm he broke his fall and landed harmlessly. Instantly, he was back on his feet sword poised for an annihilating strike to Naki's head. It was blocked. Naki then stepped inside and neatly locked up his arms.

He found himself face to face, nose to nose with his opponent. Naki looked into two cold and condescending black eyes. A vengeful sneer snaked over the samurai's lips. His face flushed dark red and an inhuman hiss came from his core. Outrageously, he spit into Naki's eyes momentarily stinging them, and with an incredible strength he twisted free. A torrent of violent blows followed, high and low. Some landed, powerful and painful. The yard exercise had now turned into a brawl. A combination of serious and decisively injurious hits rained upon Naki, and he lost his balance and fell. The warrior towered over him whirling his shinai for a final and unrestrained strike. Naki lay on the ground entirely vulnerable. But before the stick struck, Naki hooked a leg and dropped Zatoichi forward onto his knee. The move momentarily delayed the impending punishing blow and gave the young shinobi time to bring his sword crashing into the forehead of what was now not a competitor but an adversary. The strike dazed him. He salvaged a moment. Two quick cracks: right temple, left temple and he toppled, limply, face first onto Naki.

Rolling him off, Naki leapt to his feet. No more was needed. Zatoichi's eyes were glazed; his face was slack and blood trickled from his nose. It was broken. Naki stepped back and assumed Mountain Pose. Slowly recovering, Zatoichi rose, staring angrily, vehemently at the now passive youth.

The crowd applauded the display. The exercise concluded, a gong sounded. Everyone stood then dispersed. For a few moments Naki and Zatoichi remained in the yard facing each other. With a disdainful swipe at his bloodied and broken nose the older contender left the field leaving Naki alone.

He won, but he felt no satisfaction. He was confused. The sky had clouded and darkened in the meantime, and now it began to rain. Naki stood letting the warm shower thoroughly soak him. Somehow he was hoping it would wash away the ashes of his troubles.

Chapter 2

Ryu jumped the three steps and onto the veranda. He peered into the shuttered common room where Naki sat alone sipping *cha*, tea. He said, "Abbot Kosa-sama wants to see you in the Lotus Hall."

Naki's eyes shifted from the small cup he held in his hands to his friend in the doorway. "Thank you, Ryu-dono. I come at once."

"What does he want, Naki-dono?"

"I don't know," Naki lied.

"You had better hurry."

"I will."

Ryu turned and proceeded across the compound. Naki sat for a moment. He thought he had gotten off too lightly this morning with Abbot Kosa. His renegade actions were shameful, and then he tried to lie to the all knowing Abbot. He knew it was his karma to be punished, but how: expulsion from the sanctuary, public humiliation? He sipped the last drop of tea and stood ready to humbly accept whatever fate awaited him.

Across the courtyard, he walked to a path, well maintained, that lead to the temple. Bordering shrubs were neatly trimmed, and the flagstone walk was swept clean of all fallen foliage. The temple stood in the distance, elegant and serene. He mounted the steps. The ornately carved, highly polished, heavy wooden doors mysteriously swung open before him. As he nervously crossed the threshold, he espied two monks who were awaiting his arrival. After he removed his sandals, the guardians of the door motioned him to the large room on the left. Apprehensively, he stood before the Lotus Hall. The shoji, rice papered latticed doors, opened.

"Enter, please Nakamura", a sonorous voice invited. Abbot Kosa sat cross-legged on the dais, alone. "Please leave us", he uttered to the attendants. When the doors closed, the Abbot invited Nakamura to come close and sit before him. Naki settled within whispering distance of the platform. The Abbot Kosa in a soft voice counseled, "You can never be too careful. Even here in the sanctuary of the temple there are ears listening." Naki nodded.

"*Hai*,"yes. His mind raced. Why the secrecy? He thought he was to be chastised for his dishonorable actions and his disregard for the monastery and its inhabitants. Public humiliation was his due. Why was he alone with the Abbot?

"Your sojourn last night was premature," the Abbot reprimanded in a controlled tone. "I am mindful of your motivations; however, your recklessness would have endangered us all. It is not time for "The Devil Incarnate" to die. That time will come soon and then we will be free of the plague which ravages Nippon. You must persevere and act accordingly to the will of those who fathom the greater good.

"*Hai*. I understand."

"It is good that you do."

"No one knows of your foolishness last night other than me and my informers. Your delinquency is safely guarded. Had it been anyone other than you I would have banished them for their rashness in endangering the monastery. However, you are the exception."

"Master?"

"Zatoichi is a formidable opponent and you defeated him today. Unfortunately, he has a long memory and he will not forget his humiliation easily."

"Yes, Master, I sensed his *jaki*, evil spirit; I felt it powerfully."

"You are right, but that is of no consequence, for he is valuable to our struggle; his anger will be turned against the Oda clan and they will feel his strike. He is ronin, landless and master-less. He came to us desperate, poverty stricken. A proud samurai reduced to wandering and engaging in menial labor just to survive. He was employed by Lord Kitabatake for one hundred thousand koku a year before The Evil One devastated his master's territory. Rather than serve Nobunaga or commit *seppuku*, honorable suicide, he went ronin hoping one day to avenge Kitabatake's disgrace, moreover his own. His hatred for the despot burns deeply and that is why he is useful.

"So, I have two special instruments for Oda Nobunaga's destruction, equals each to be used in his unique way. His ferociousness and prowess in battle will serve as a model to inspire those who openly fight; he will marshal the battles. The monks of Mt. Hiei will restore him his honor. You, however, are to be used differently. You are ninjutsu. You will be my eyes, my ears, my hands. You will strike silent, lethal blows at the enemy to destroy them."

"*Hai*", Naki responded.

"Yet, you are not ready. Your impulses are not controllable. Last night was proof of that. Nobunaga has unsettled your spirit. You witnessed the horrors of his vile ambition. Your village was laid to waste. Your father, mother and sister were defiled before your innocent eyes. You suffer dreams of unspeakable dread."

"*Hai*", Naki responded.

"You are a man with an arrow in his eye. Your pain is so strong it blinds you to the truth: to the way. You have seen his evil and this painful arrow leads you to desire his immediate ruin. You seek retribution for them and for yourself. You wish him to die, now, along with your dark dreams. But, you face a monster, a monster that can squash you like a gnat. If you cling to this desire, it will only destroy you. So then, how do you see clearly enough to be able to destroy the fiend? To vanquish what seems indefeatable. First, you must remove the arrow. You must suffer and endure the healing. When you are ready, you will create a new consciousness with which to see. To see the way and what must be done."

"Hai," Naki spoke softly. For a moment, his word of comprehension hung gently in the air before it landed hard with understanding. It would be agonizingly difficult to wait to heal; he would rather act. Nevertheless ... deep within he knew it was the correct and necessary thing to do ... to wait. The Abbot was right. First, be rid of the dreams; free from the blinding vengeance tormenting his soul and clouding his judgment. Once he possessed clarity of vision then he could fashion a way of satisfying his desire to see his enemy dead? Struggling briefly with the thought, he determined he would comply with the sagaciousness of the counsel.

"Shortly, I will give you an authorized assault, not against Nobunaga directly, but one which will bring you closer to your desire. Meanwhile you must prepare your mind and your body to do what is humanly impossible, but yet possible. Do you understand?"

"Hai!"

"Good, you are dismissed."

Naki bowed deeply, rose and left. His spirit was ambivalently confused, heavy and light, fraught with doubt, full of hope. Could he pluck this shaft from his eye? Did he have the fortitude to vanquish the demons that infested his spirit and create a new consciousness? Could he really help rid the land of this vermin and restore peace? He wondered.

———◦《◉》◦———

Naki politely excused himself from the others. They insisted he join them in sake, song and pleasures of the night, but he wasn't in the mood. He defeated Zatoichi today, a notable accomplishment. If any other warrior had done as much, he would be drunk and in the gentle pleasurable care of a prostitute that his companions would have cheerfully procured for him. However, Naki declined the proposal. Rather, he wanted to think about what the Abbot said. About having to wait and that he said, "*You are the exception,*". Why not just an exception? Why "*the*" exception? What exactly made him so different? He knew his martial skills were excellent, but there were many talented and skilled warriors at the monastery. Why was he *the exception*? For him, today was just a win. He felt no satisfaction, no pride, no glory and certainly no sense of superiority. Why was he empty of the joy and natural feelings of accomplishment? His feelings were dark, brooding, lonely and unatural. He had felt like this his whole life ... then it burst upon him.

"I am exceptional because of my dreams," he heard himself exclaim. That is what the Abbot meant. I have the night visions. I am who I am because of my dreams.

The darkness - deep. Blacker than black. In the distance a red glow. Trees bursting into flaming torches. Hooves, pounding, nostrils flaring, eyes glowing. Horses from hell. Riders mounted. Blades glistening, swords swirling. Long spears pointed. Thundering, thundering. Crying, wailing, and screaming! Arrows - agonizing. Flesh burning. Long swords, slashing. Faces twisted. Eyes insane. Blood proliferating, sizzling from the heat. Roofs ablaze, beams burning. Steps afire. Slaughter, screaming, laughter.

Naki's eyes opened wide but he could not shake the images. The agony continued. A little boy in the woods witnessing. Monsters in black swarming. Everywhere, black devils spilling red blood. Vomit, putrid stench. Men pissing in fear. Feces. Women ripped naked ... torn apart. Bowels spilling. Birds fluttering squawking, flaming. The dawn breaking, a little boy hiding, helpless in the woods. Petrified. Laughter. Spears impaling infants. Laughter. Arrows whistling at older children. Finding their mark. Shrieks of pain. Laughter. Swords decapitating. Laughter. Stabbing the still. Kicking the dead. Torching what was not on fire. Hooves thundering, pounding, receding into the distance. Leaving, leaving, leaving nothing but a small boy's eyes wide open in terror. Naki rose up on his cot and puked over his quilt: rice, fish, and bile, soiling and fouling.

The oppressive odor repulsed him. He looked around. Everyone was still asleep. Quickly bundling up the quilt, he slid open the latticed door and stumbled outside to immerse his revulsion into the nearby stream; to immerse the evidence of the night into the crystal water of the morning. He sensed the Abbot, watching.

———◉———

Naki ignored the feeling of his being watched, and he struggled to attend to the beauty that surrounded him. The dawn was magnificent. A few clouds reflected the burgeoning morning light and glistened resplendently gold in the eastern sky. The air was fresh. Burbling gently, the sound of the brook soothed the tension he had suffered short moments earlier. Still struggling slightly, he focused on the water which had carried away the vileness of the night, now clear. A scent of nearby hibiscus wafted mildly in the breeze. See the beauty of the Earth he told himself. Smell, hear, and touch. Come out of the night and into the day. Suddenly, the Abbot's words echoed in his head. "You must prepare your mind and body to do what is humanly impossible." Nimbly, he scooped up the soggy quilt and wrung out the water. He hung it where the monastery servants launder the other's *kosode*, the kimono undergarments.

Satisfied that the quilt was clean, he returned to the stream and looked northwards into the mountains from where the stream flowed languorously. He reasoned he would follow the water and do whatever impulses moved him and what fate had in mind.

Loping, his strides were at first short and labored. Quickly and not to his surprise his pace eased into a comfortable rhythm. The length of his steps stretched into a satisfactory sprint. He veered into the stream to cool his increasing body warmth and to battle the resistance of the water. A stony bed challenged his footing and he struggled to maintain speed and balance. His eyes focused on every step making sure they were true and effective. He did not stumble. Even against the flow of the water he surged forward swiftly, faster and faster. He forded the widening stream and crossed over onto the opposite bank and continued with his run. The terrain took a sudden upward incline and Naki extended his gait to accommodate the new test. He continued his pace pushing himself harder and harder: he must do what is humanly impossible.

Ahead of him stretched low hanging branches. He scrambled to shore and leapt onto a large extended limb. Grasping another suppler bough he swung himself deep into the tree and came to rest nestling against the trunk of a giant ginkgo tree. He squatted; his back pressed into the massive deciduous and for a moment he struggled for his breath.

Once recovered, he sprang down and continued bounding through the trees and the water. Soon, he stopped again and rested, but only briefly upon a rocky outcrop of stone, and then he pressed onward, unrelentingly, now walking, briskly, upwards, over every obstacle strewn in his path. Through stands of pines, over water weathered boulders, across slippery algae covered stones. All manner of ground was observed and dominated. He felt alive.

Ahead of him just across the stream was a monstrously flat rock face that jutted vertically from the embankment; it hosted a lush canopy of ferns miraculously growing out of a stony wall. The arch of greenery formed an eye brow across the rock's surface. He stopped, and he marveled at how life could spring so beautifully and plentifully from such seemingly barren conditions. Naki nestled under the foliage and admired the tenaciousness of Mother Earth's issue and its will to live and thrive under such severe conditions. The ferns grew directly out of the rock face, abundant and indomitable, refusing to give in to the hostile conditions afforded by the rugged mountain soil. They were large, leafy, green and vibrant, seeming to defy the very laws of nature. Where did they root? In the rock? How could they survive let alone flourish?

<hr />

Fixedly, he studied the anomaly; resting against the rock, he struggled to understand this contradiction of the natural world. The ferns were doing what was naturally impossible. Is the impossible, possible? His chi lifted and he thanked Buddha for the sign. Was the Abbot right? Could he pluck the shaft from his eye and see the essential? For the moment, he witnessed the magnificence of nature, powerful and significant; he heard it speaking subtly and encouragingly.

With new resolve, he vaulted a mossy rotting log and landed back into the stream. He felt no fatigue. His gait was powerful, his footing sure. The water offered no resistance against his determination; he was preparing his mind and his body to do the impossible. Whatever that may be.

Naki wasn't sure how long he had been running uphill. He left the river, for the shallows had deepened and the water flow had strengthened. The narrow shore between the mountain's watercourse and the mountain's encroaching vegetation was beset with boulders of varying size. He sprang between some, leapt over others, and vaulted onto the ones he could not clear in one movement. Periodically, he paused on top of one of the larger rocks to catch his breath, resting on his haunches, his hands flat on the rock, his diaphragm pumping violently. He counted how long it would take for him to recover natural breathing. Thirty counts, thirty five counts. He didn't know what a rapid recovery was, but he knew at least that he had a marker and that he would remember.

Overhead a peregrine falcon screeched. Naki looked up to see the fowl speeding after a high flying swallow. An explosion of feathers ensued as the indisputable master of the air plucked its prey from the sky and disappeared over the tops of the giant pines. A few feathers fluttered aimlessly earthward and Naki followed their course. They wafted meandering with the currents of air falling gently; the remains of what was once alive and vibrant but vulnerable to the forces stronger than them.

They fell gently, moving to and fro, towards their final destination. Tenderly, they alighted on an unsuspecting target; a black panther, leisurely stretched across a large oak bough. The feathers sprinkled his head, tickled his ears and fluttered across his massive black nose. The flutter was sufficient to awaken the predator out of its mid – morning rest and it swatted a massive paw to displace the intrusive matter. A low disgruntled growl followed along with a sudden shake of its immense head. Its triangular ears flicked forward listening for danger or prey. Naki froze. It was no more than twenty *shaku*, feet, from where he was sitting. He was entirely vulnerable; he was an easy kill should the beast see him as a threat. It yawned. A massive maw exposed gleaming white conical teeth; the two on top were one and a half time times the length of Naki's fingers and twice as thick tapering to a lethal end. A long, wide, tongue curled upwards and wet a prodigious nose also triangular in shape consequently giving the creature a magnificence of symmetry only the gods of nature could endow. Its head sustained the motif of triangulation; powerful jaw muscles layered a widening royal face. This surely was the king of cats. Set on either side of the muzzle were two massive yellow eyes, almond in shape and amber in color. Their richness brilliantly contrasted against the silky sheen of a glossy black coat. Thick muscles in the neck gave way to powerful shoulders and to a torso created for speed, agility, and death. It unfurled its tail casually swaying it from side to side.

Naki dared not move. Any stir would draw the animal's attention. The monks had trained him to remain still for hours, to blend into the blackness of the night. But this! He was perched upon a giant boulder at mid-morning in full view of an enormous beast. This he had not trained for. He tried to remain calm, but he knew it would be just a matter of time before the animal sensed his presence. What was he to do? He looked for shelter. There was none. He looked for a weapon. There wasn't any. He checked the direction of the wind. Ah, at least the gods favored him with a gentle breeze downwind of the creature. Naki looked back at the beast on a branch and to his horror he saw the yellow eyes fixed directly upon him. His body twitched in terror. The royal monster, still as stone, gazed at him with expressionless eyes. He wanted to scream. A sound so terrifying even this cat of cats would think twice before it dared to consider him an unexpected morning meal.

However, Naki suppressed the impulse. The expected snarl and the sudden leap did not come. The muscles were not taught It was still, entirely tranquil. Its expression was placid. The tail flicked leisurely left and right. Naki wondrously understood that he was neither a threat nor a banquet. It seemingly held no interest in him, yet its eyes did not leave him.

It proceeded to groom itself; the substantial crimson tongue licked its fore paws which were three times the size of Naki's hands. Naki imagined the claws hidden within those pads. The cat's eyes never left him. Even with the grooming the leopard never took its eyes off Naki. It was as if it were speaking to him in some animistic manner. It was conveying a message which Naki could not comprehend. He understood he was not in mortal danger, but beyond that it was a mystery.

The cat seemed to comprehend the confusion and with astounding suddenness it leapt to the ground. It landed softly away from the miserable Naki, and with a knowing turn of its head it looked back at the human on the rock. Again their eyes connected for a moment; then it launched itself into the woods disappearing amid the undergrowth.

Naki dropped his head and sighed relief. Exhilaration overtook him. What had just happened? He, just moments ago, was staring into the yellow orbs of death, and now he was still alive and giddy with excitement. His head was light; his limbs were numb; he experienced a sense of detachment from his body. If he tried to move he would would fall off the rock. He closed his eyes and breathed deeply until he felt a sense return to his limbs. He looked about. All was still. All was calm. However, the forest green was unusually verdant. The brook chattered all too clearly. The air smelled new. Butterflies burst in proliferation; Tiger Beetles with large bug eyes and fearsome jaws marched with relentless purpose gleaming in their metallic colors; a Giant Wood Spider spun a glistening web of gossamer death - seeing a spider during the day was considered lucky, but unlucky at night. Dragon flies fluttered amidst the foliage. Never had he undergone such a heightened state of sensation, such acuteness of sight, smell, and hearing. The wind, gentle, light caressed his face stealing the sweat upon his brow cooling him with a comfort he had never encountered before. He pondered, had he unconsciously performed some meritorious deed and was now being blessed by the spirit world with extra ordinary sensations? What was going on?

Naki climbed down from his rock perch and squatted beside the boulder leaning his head against the soft moss which grew at the base. He looked about to see if his heightened awareness was still acute. It seemed to be subsiding and he was returning ... to ... what? Humanness? For a moment he had the eyes of an eagle, the nose of a wolf, and the ears of a deer. When he stood up his human muscles reminded him of the exertion he had put them through. They revolted and screamed indignantly at having been so abused. He ached terribly. For a moment, he regretted his zeal. His descent from the mountain would be torturous. Philosophically, he reasoned he must do what is impossible. He began to run.

———◦《◦》◦———

It was late in the afternoon by the time Naki returned to the monastery. Ryu was in the common room poking the embers of the fire looking for life in the ashes with which to boil water for tea. A small flame burst alive and he fed it coals. Its flame increased and he was pleased that he would not have to relight the pit.

"Tea", Ryu inquired? "You look as if you could use some. Where have you been? Zatoichi has been asking for you?

"What did he want?"

"Nothing good, it was better that he didn't find you."

"I suspect he wants vindication."

"He will have to wait." Ryu was Naki's number one devotee. He was a few years older, squat and solidly built. His face was round and full of amusement. The corners of his mouth curled wryly upwards giving the illusion of a face in perpetual delight. Large bright eyes, the corners of which were similarly turned up, illuminating a demeanor of laughter and joy. However, the jovial features were counter punctuated by a thick neck and powerful shoulders. They spoke of strength and menace. A broad barrel chest was bordered by arms of immense size and authority. His hands were small yet strong. His knuckles, heavily calloused, had been pounded into lethal weapons by his habit of breaking hemp bound boards. He squatted, gently poking the fire, on shanks of formidable size. Small feet incongruously balanced this enigma of menace and mirth.

Ryu was Naki's closest companion. Naki, naturally solitary by nature, did not trouble himself with any of the others, but it was Ryu's congenial demeanor and open faced honesty that won Naki's trust, eventually. It was a trust which had not been betrayed.

He only trusted two people: Ryu and the Abbot.

Chapter 3

The next morning Naki rose earlier than usual. Miraculously, there was no sensation of the soreness from the previous day's outing. On the contrary, he felt invigorated, joyously alive in body, mind and spirit. It was an unaccustomed feeling. Furthermore, his sleep had not been disturbed by hellish visions. He flippantly attributed his well being to the fact that he had so exhausted himself from running in the woods that he would have slept through an earthquake. He vowed to continue to train in the mountains as it seemed therapeutic.

The others were still deep in slumber. Silently, he gathered his *kinu,* a large, long sleeved shirt, and his culottes and stole outside. Naked, except for his loin cloth, he headed for the stream to wash up. The air was fresh, easy to breathe. The rising sun splashed the sky with hues of scarlet and gold above the black mountain peaks. Naki looked forward to another romp in the woods.

He felt a strength and agility which he never sensed before. What mystical insights did the Abbot possess? How did a subtle suggestion manifest itself into a magnificent sense of indomitable power? Elated he chose not to question the wise one's wisdom but to categorically follow his superior's plan.

His strides were easy, brisk, long, coordinated and balanced. Rough terrain was effortlessly controlled. Fallen pines were hurdled with facility. Ancient willows which offered branches low and sturdy enough for Naki to leap onto were clambered effortlessly. He climbed to the very top of one and it offered a view of a spectacular mountain stream. In the distance he observed a six tiered waterfall gracefully falling into a placid pool. The pond was bordered by lush purple and green flora. Massive mossy rocks jutted from the banks presenting a perfect place for a cool tranquil break from his exertion. He was exhilarated.

Excitedly he slid down the tree and hurriedly proceeded in the direction for his well deserved rest. Suddenly, he became aware of a presence, something large, powerful and dangerous. He stopped and listened. Silence. He knew the entity was close by-watching. He could feel it. Not tangibly but via his innate sense for detecting danger. It was an ability he had discovered at a very early age. It was a unique survival instinct. It had spared him when Oda Nobunaga's hordes razed his village. Somehow, well before anyone else, he knew he was to hide. He didn't know why he just did. It was his salvation and his damnation. He survived a massacre, unfortunately only to become a witness to the murder of his father, his mother, his sister, Keiko, his uncle and the entire village. He hid in his secret sanctuary between the boulders at the edge of the village behind the bushy azalea. From there he saw everything. These images haunted him his entire life.

His eyes searched for a weapon; branches, rocks, stones anything so he wouldn't be defenseless. He heard it move. It was approaching. Then it stopped. Silence. The forest was quiet. Naki was still. He was being studied. Naki's eyes looked deep into the woods. Green, brown, black shadows blended confusingly making it impossible to discern anything. Then he saw them: two large yellow eyes embedded in a mass of blackness. It was the cat. How could he have been so foolish as to forget his encounter with the beast the day before? He was spared an attack yesterday, but today he would not. Slowly he knelt down never taking his eyes off the gold almond shaped orbs staring at him. He picked up a flat stone and a round one the size of his fist. Smashing the round one against the flat one he hastily fashioned a sharp edged weapon. Optimistically, he hoped the noise would startle the animal against an attack; however, the eyes remained steadfast. Smoothly, Naki slid behind the nearest fir tree and positioned himself behind the trunk hoping to use it as a buffer between him and the creature.

There was something on him. He glanced down to see a monstrously large, black and yellow wood spider exploring his foot. Naki superstitiously reasoned, ... lucky ... a spider during the day! He hoped it wouldn't bite. It moved on to its massive web in the tree.

Then, he felt another sensation: cold,wet. He saw a large chalky, dirty blot of greenish brown on his hand obeying the laws of gravity, dripping ... dropping to the ground. He looked above him and saw a great spotted woodpecker; it had just unloaded its morning meal. Naki groaned.

He returned to the eyes watching him. They were gone.

He looked in disbelief. They were gone. Amazed. What did this mean? He dropped his makeshift weapons and sat down. Straight away, he jumped up swiping thinking there might be more surprises for him. Realizing there were no more alarms, he flung the feathered deposit off his hand with a quick flick and then wiped the rest of it across a tree trunk, but only to replace the wet mess with tree gum.

"Oi!"

He laughed. Vigorously rubbing the sticky matter off his hand, he laughed again; it felt good.

The image of the falls broke into his thoughts. "A swim is what I need now," and he raced up the mountain.

It did not take long before he heard the soothing cascade inviting him to drown the mishaps of the day. He stood upon some mossy rocks and breathed in the beauty: a riot of rich purples, pinks, and greens. Six ledges towered above him spilling crystal splendor from one level to the next. The falls initial turbulence was quickly dispelled and manifested itself into a pond of serenity and calm, a tranquil pool of blue, grey magnificence. He stripped off his shirt, culottess and loin cloth and dove naked into the water. A natural swimmer, he dove deeply. Curious sculpins investigated the intruder and swam harmlessly around him. Playfully Naki chased his inquisitors, but was unsuccessful in apprehending anything.

Surfacing he shook his head free of water and gazed at the glory of his discovery. For the moment, he felt peace. He pulled himself up onto a rock and checked for any unwanted creatures. He stretched out to bathe in the sunlight, and it wasn't long before he was asleep.

He dreamed of Keiko, his sister. Two years younger than Naki. She was the epitome of joy for his family. Her black eyes were always full of glee and awe of the world around her. He recalled no matter how inquisitive, mischievous or annoying she was she was always patiently tolerated. Her timid smile and charming innocence dissolved any frown her parents or brother could ever hope to sustain. When she giggled, she laughed the sound of tinkling wind chimes. She was the little sister, who was always pestering her big brother, getting in his way, playing coy; he loved her. He couldn't save her. After they had gone, he found her. He lifted her broken bloodied little body out of the puddle of crimson mud and cradled her and cried so hard he believed he was going to die. He didn't let go of her. He lost consciousness with her in his arms and when he finally came to, he was being carried by the Abbot towards the safety of the monastery.

A fish splashed and awoke Naki. He heard soft female voices tittering. Confused, clearing his head, he tried to remember where he was. Finally he did, in the mountains, by the waterfall, on a mossy rock … naked. He looked up to see three girls convulsively hugging each other in fits of gentle laughter. Somewhat ashamed, he rolled off the rock and into the water.

"What are you doing here?" He shouted.

His annoyed tone stopped their laughter and paralyzed two of them into a fearful silence.

The third, unaffected by his chauvinistic air of superiority, brazenly strutted forward and challenged him.

"What are you doing here? Naked!"

Unaccustomed to such boldness from women let alone girls, he shouted again.

"I say, what are you doing here?"

"This is our pool. I say, what are you doing here?"

Disbelieving his ears and the audacity coming from the oldest and the prettiest he smacked the water and charged towards the shore, unmindful of the fact that he wasn't wearing any clothes.

With surprising speed the eldest snatched his cotton trousers and loin cloth from the rock where they lay and teasingly waved them in air, scampering a short distance up an incline to relative safety. The others quickly followed enjoying the game of putting a young man in his place.

Infuriated Naki climbed out of the water and grabbed his *kinu*, and wrapped himself up.

"Let's see how they like you in the village," she shouted and disappeared with his clothes and his dignity into the woods.

Aghast, Naki couldn't believe what had just happened.

By the time he climbed down the mountain, he was too tired to care.

The villagers he passed were polite and tried not to stare as he made his way, almost naked, back to the compound.

Ryu on the other hand exploded with his typical mass of mirth. Naki stood stone still and waited for his companion's convulsions to subside.

Finally, Ryu asked, "What happened? Where are your clothes?

Naki refusing to answer calmly found some more and put them on.

"What happened to your clothes?" This time, Ryu asked with a little respect and smattering of genuine concern.

"They were stolen."

Ryu knew better than to continue the questioning and said, "I will help you find these thieves and we shall teach them a lesson."

Ryu left him alone. Naki was sure he heard a final snigger from his jovial friend as he disappeared into the compound.

The embers in the fire pit were still glowing with life and it didn't take much prodding to entice the coals to burst into flames. Naki swung the cooking arm over the flame and hung the iron tea kettle to boil water. He gathered his tea tools, knelt humbly and waited. With a long wooden spoon he placed some green tea into his simple ceramic bowl. Using a bamboo ladle he transferred the hot water into the cup. Obeying the traditions of the *cha-no-yu*, the tea ceremony, he stirred the leaves and the water with his straw whisk; when the brew was properly mixed, he placed the tool directly in front of him. He let the tea steep a moment or two and then picked up the cup and ensured that he did not drink from the front but spun it in his hands a few times as was polite and proper. He raised it with elegance and tranquility to his lips and swallowed the brew in three sips. He savored the bitter but acquired taste. Sitting back he allowed the medicinal properties of the tea to take effect. He anxiously sought the serenity enjoyed earlier before being disturbed by that annoying girl. He closed his eyes and dozed.

A messenger pounded up the steps, stopped at the doorway, summarily bowed and shouted, "Nakamura-san, Kosa-sama wishes to see you now! *Iku!*" To go now, please.

He departed as quickly and loudly as he arrived. Naki gathered up his instruments and left to see the Abbot.

In the Lotus Hall two figures sat respectfully before the dais. The Abbot had not yet entered. Naki recognized one of the two, Zatoichi. The other was smaller, and diminutive next to the Samuri. He took his place on the floor and waited. He did not look at or acknowledge the presence of the other two but stared straight ahead of him. A lattice door opened; Abbot Kosa entered and knelt before them on the raised platform. All three bowed in respect before he spoke.

"Yoshida Zatoichi, Ito Nakamura and Tomoki Sai, you have been summoned to assist in the next assault against the vermin plaguing our land."

All three bowed in humility and honor for having been chosen. Each looked sideways at each other and to Naki's shock the tiny figure beside the samurai was the girl from the woods, the one who stole his clothes. Wisely, Naki quickly averted his gaze and looked at Zatoichi who was glaring at him with cold superior eyes. He must still be angry from the other day, he thought to himself.

The Abbot continued, "It is understood that Nobunaga is gathering forces. His brother-in-law, Azai Nagamasa, has broken allegiance with him; returning to his senses, Nagamasa resumed the age old alliance between his family's clan and that of the Asakura. The Asakura, till now, have been temporizing; they have neither openly opposed Nobunaga nor whole heartedly sided with him. Nobunaga grows impatient. He wants the northern territory; he needs it; he will get it either through diplomacy or war. Now that the Asai, his brother-in law's clan side with the Asakura the demon feels diplomacy is lost; he feels they are now a threat, so we believe he is gathering forces, amassing strength, to spread north into Asakura provinces. We suspect war, but we must make sure.

"We must send the demon back to hell before he becomes too strong. So, we conduct attacts upon his allies: his brother's stronghold and castles of other cowardly lords that have sided with him ... rather than resist him. We must weaken his resources before it is too late.

"Zatoichi-san, you will have command over our best warrior monks, ten thousand *Sohei*. You will train them in the ways with which you are most familiar and have been most successful. Should we need to fight conventionally, we will be ready.

"I understand the Ikko-Ikki, our rebel brother monks in Nagashima, also wish to fight, so our numbers will be formidable. However, we do not have much time. We do not know if he is planning to spread north, nor do we know when, so our time is short. Be efficient; be effective; train the monks well and quickly. I surmise that we may have one month to prepare. Zatoichi-san, can you be ready?"

"Hai! I ... we will be ready!"

"If he chooses to fight the Asai/Asakura he will do so with fewer men than anticipated, certainly with less spirited men. If we can thwart him, demoralize him, we will have succeeded in our first step in routing him out of existence. Nevertheless, for now, we know that Nobunaga, firmly rooted in Kyoto, is a threat to everyone.

"Sai-chan, you are your father's emissary. You are to discover if these rumors of forces gathering in Kyoto are true;

furthermore, find out if the Asai and the Asakura are indeed ready to challenge the monster. Once we know these things then we can proceed accordingly. Sai-chan, I warn you, these missions will be dangerous; Nobunaga is cunning, as are his allies; his castles are full of traps. Prepare well. You will have little time. Nakamura-kun, you will abide by Sai-chan's instructions."

"*Hai*," Zatoichi thundered, "I will be ready."

Naki and Sai remained silent.

With that the Abbot rose and left. The samurai stood up and towered over the two still kneeling before the dais. He issued both of them a cold stare and then strode across the hall floor sliding aside the rice paper door, insolently leaving it open. Naki and Sai waited a few moments in silence before leaving, politely sliding it closed.

Outside along the garden path leading to the village buildings Sai spoke. "Would you like your clothes back Nakamura-san?"

Naki ignored her question and said, "Abbot Kosa-sama trusts you. Why?"

Sai said nothing.

"You are quick. Where did you learn to move like that?"

"I have trained for many years Nakamura-san."

"Where?"

"The Enryaku-ji monastery is very large you may have not noticed me, but I know of you Nakamura-san."

"How? I do not visit the village or mingle with the others."

"You are known as the quiet one ... the deadly one."

"Deadly? I have never killed anyone."

EDMUND KOLBUSZ

"Ah yes, but everyone sees how lethal you could be. I have never actually seen you before, but I know of you, so I humbly apologize for being so rude at the waterfall. If I had known who you were I would never have been so insolent."

Naki fell silent. He never realized that because he ignored the others that they did not ignore him. Is that why Zatoichi is hostile? He must know of me too. He must have believed his honor and reputation had been tarnished by some son of a simple farmer or even an *eta,* the lowest class of creature. Outside the monastery Zatoichi could have lopped off Naki's head with his magnificent samurai sword; however, since he is ronin and under the control of the Tendai monks his status does not allow indiscriminate killing, and he has no rights to behead anyone who offends him. He must abide by the laws of Shinto and bear allegiance to the Abbot.

Surely, now, he knows I am important to the Abbot, and no matter what my background he will put aside his pride and fight with me against the Oda clan. This idea dissipated as quickly as he conceived it. I must be careful of him, he concluded.

"Nakamura-san? Where do you wish me to deliver your clothes?"

Naki returned his attention to Sai.

"Who are you? How do I know I can trust you?" he asked sharply without reserve for politeness or propriety.

Offended by his brashness, Sai brusquely dismissed him and vanished into the village as swiftly as she had in the forest.

Chapter 4

The next morning Naki awoke to find his culottes and loin cloth beside his mat. They had been washed and folded. Between the clothes, barely visible was a small piece of paper. Puzzled, he slipped it out and went to the stream: "Go to the falls." It was signed "Impudent girl." Without hesitation he returned to the barrack, dressed, slipped a knife through his sash and grabbed his *bo*, a six foot long hollow hardwood staff and his sword. This time he remembered the cat. If I am to be in the forest, he reasoned, I shall not be unarmed.

He ran with intention. There were no leaps in the air, flips over boulders or swinging from branch to limb. His strides were even and measured, and as he warmed to the run they stretched to a steady sustained sprint. Despite the increasing pitch of the mountain, he gained speed. He followed the stream and only ran through the water when the bank disappeared. Naki was so intoxicated with the spirit of his running he did not notice the animal loping along with him on the other side of the bank. It remained in the shadows of the woods and never ventured into the clear along the river bank. It leapt over fallen limbs and charged through the undergrowth. It was invisible to Naki.

Before the sun was at its highest point in the sky Naki reached the falls. The black specter that mirrored his mountain run had disappeared into the deep greenwood. Winded and wet from sweating, Naki intently surveyed the halcyon of gently cascading water, the calm fish filled pool and the abundance of wild flowers, ferns, bushes and majestic trees. Had he arrived too early? He didn't see anyone. Was he late? He heard a tiny splash, almost imperceptibly, from behind one of the large mossy rocks that jutted from the shore. He looked to see, and crouching behind the stone peering over the lichen was the impish grinning face of Sai. She pushed off the rock into deeper water. "Do you swim?" she asked before she dove out of sight. Naki stood dumbfounded. Who is this girl? He thought to himself. When she surfaced some ways out he could see even through the refraction of the water that she was naked. "Do you swim?" she asked again.

"Yes", he said.

"What are you waiting for? Again she dove beneath the surface of the water only to resurface a considerable distance from the shore. She is part fish thought Naki. Unashamed, he stripped and plunged into the water. The cold mountain pool immediately rejuvenated him. He swam into deeper water and allowed the buoyancy of his body to let him float freely on the surface.

"Where did you learn to swim? She was beside him treading water.

Startled by her sudden appearance and so close to him

he harshly asked, "Who are you? Why does the Abbot trust you?"

"All in good time Nakamura-san. First you must answer me my question. Where did you learn to swim?"

"I learned in the streams and rivers by the monastery."

"You swim well," she said.

"Thank you Sai-chan; however, I believe you are part fish."

"I can swim the width of this pond under the water in one breath."

"I should like to like to see that".

She disappeared under the water and moments later appeared near the opposite shore.

"Over here, Nakamura-san, I am over here."

Naki looked to see her emerging from the water quite a distance away. He could make out she was lithe and strong. She clambered onto the stony ledge where her clothes lay and dressed. Even from such a distance he sensed her strength and her attractiveness. A fish's gentle nibble to his toe startled him out of his mesmerized state. He blindly kicked at the curious intruder. When he returned to look for Sai again, she was gone. Confused, he turned, swimming back to his clothes. He reached the shore and by the time he dressed she was approaching him along the bank.

"How did you get over here so quickly from over there?"

"There is a rock ledge behind the waterfall; you can easily cross from one side to the other."

"How did you know that?

"You forget, Nakamura-san, this is my terrain. I know everything about this mountain, the woods and the water.

"You are a curiosity, Sai-chan. I have never met a woman like you before."

"*Arigato*, thank you, Nakamura-san. Now, come we must go."

"Where?"

"Follow me" And with that she was scrambling up the slope and into the forest.

Naki rushed to keep pace. Again she disappeared. He scoured the green black wilds and saw nothing but fir, pine and beech trees.

"I am here." Out from behind some large leafy ferns she appeared, almost beside him. "If I wanted to kill you, I could have," she said. "You did not see me. I could have slit your throat and you would have bled a silent death on the forest floor."

"Thank you for not killing me."

"You're welcome. This region is our training ground. We learn to be invisible here. We learn to swim, climb, hide and kill without being seen."

"We? Who are we?"

"My brothers and sisters, my revered father and the other families. Come you will meet them. It is rare that an outsider is permitted to enter the clan, but the Abbot decreed it and so it shall be."

She took him by the hand and led him through a thicket that ended at a rock barrier. A narrow fissure cracked the face of the wall and sideways she slipped through it pulling him along. No light penetrated the crevice and they slid forward in complete darkness. The fracture opened into a larger area. Naki could tell by the echo that he was in a large cave.

The ground rose as they proceeded and soon above him he saw a shaft of light. She held his hand tightly to ensure she wouldn't lose him. "There are some sharp drops so be careful. Hold onto my hand and stay close to the wall." They continued to climb towards the light. The rocky walls narrowed again but the ground flattened, and when they reached the opening and she led him onto a rocky outcrop. "There is our camp," she said as he looked down through a leafy canopy of trees to a camouflaged group of wooden structures with grass roofs well below him in a narrow valley.

"How do we get down?

"We climb." To the left of the ledge were thick tenacious vines that adhered to the mountain's face. She swung onto the solid woody tendril and slid gracefully downwards. Naki followed wondering if it would support his weight. It did, and soon he was standing on level ground at the edge of the compound. Sai preceded him into the complex of huts and houses. Two large dogs with wedge shaped heads and small upright ears charged towards them. When they reached Sai they danced and circled her happily. Their tails curled up over their backs wagging a warm greeting. Sai gave each one a gentle scratch on its head and then they scampered off behind one of the structures. Silently, she led him towards one of the more domesticated buildings among the rustic constructions. "My father is *Chunin*. He will help train you for your task."

They entered the simple quarters. Seated upon a square of tatami mats sat what Naki surmised was Sai's father, the *Chunin*. He was an imposing figure. Tall and angular with high cheek bones and strong sharp chin. His charcoal hair, streaked with gray was pulled tightly up onto his head samurai fashion. From his face, weathered and taut, peered two black piercing eyes. His black kimono hung from him with a noble elegance incongruous to the plainness of his surroundings. Sai knelt and bowed at the entrance platform as did Naki. Without a word he gestured for them to sit with him.

"Father," Sai spoke, "I bring you Ito Nakamura."

Naki bowed again at the introduction.

"I am Tomoki Konnyo. The Abbot Kosa-sama has ordered that you join our family. This is most unusual. Our existence hangs upon our secrecy. To issue an outsider into the clan is, I am sorry to say, somewhat troubling for me, but Kosa-sama decrees it and so it must be. I hope his faith in you is wise and that your loyalty to the secrecy of our ways is as unshakable as this mountain.

"I assure you Konnyo -sama that Kosa-sama's faith in me is firm. I am your humble and loyal servant."

"It is reported that your skills are impressive. However, that remains to be seen. You must demonstrate excellence in all ways of ninjutsu. Regrettably, you have little time, but if your reputation proves to be true, you will be ready for your first mission. Sai will show you where you will be housed."

Naki bowed and Sai backed out of the room. Outside, Naki surveyed the compound. The village looked like any other village. Numerous buildings surrounded a large open earthen training ground. Some were single family dwellings, small neatly maintained homes with polite porches. Others were larger, obviously designed to house many individuals. Nothing seemed out of the ordinary other than the community was tucked in a valley hidden from the rest of the world. Mountain walls, lush with vegetation circumscribed the entire setting. Curiously, there didn't seem to be an obvious access in or out other than the way he and Sai entered down a sinewy vine. How did they build the whole complex? How did they get food and supplies into the area? Konnyo-sama said their existence depended upon secrecy. What secrets were there to learn? What was hidden? Naki's curiosity was piqued.

Sai motioned him to follow her. She led him to a large gray, wooden, rustic shelter. It seemed very old, yet well maintained. Inside was a sparse open living area hosting a massive cooking pit. Beyond the common area were the sleeping quarters similar to what Naki was accustomed to at the monastery. Naki was eager to learn.

"This will be your bed. This is your special place. Only this area is yours. Every spot belongs to a family member. The sleeping area is where we rest, meditate, and visualize our missions. It is an important place. Our habits and patterns of life have helped us survive for many generations. The life of a ninja is short, but our clan has succeeded in living longer and accomplishing more assignments because we are well trained, highly skilled, and extremely disciplined. The sleeping place is where our people see their task in their mind's eye. Every fortress wall, doorway, hall rafter, ceiling tile, trap is seen beforehand in the mind and soul of an agent. The path of the mission is drawn on the memory like ink on the skin. We train physically outside, mentally and spiritually here, inside. I know you will accept and respect our practices, if not it will cost you your life, or someone else's."

"Hai," Naki said, impressed by Sai's seriousness and sincerity. Up till now he had perceived her as an athletic and mischievous girl, but now he saw a depth of spirit and nobleness to her which he admired. "Hai," he said again thinking that a repetition of the word would convince her of his commitment to their ways.

A terrible thought stabbed the moment. "Sai, the Abbot told me I am unique and that I am the exception. I believe this may be true because of my powerful night visions. They are so strong that they affect my sleep. I am afraid I may disturb the others. In the monastery I was partly secluded so I would not bother anyone. Ryu was nearby and he was not troubled by my fits, but here I do not wish to jeopardize anyone's life.

Sai nodded. "The sanctity of the quarters must be maintained. I will speak with my father, perhaps there is another way. But your exception is not limited by your dreams. You have skills which we can sharpen; you have abilities which are now asleep, but which we can waken, and you have this passion which manifests itself in your dreams. I do not share my father's concerns about you. I believe you to be a member of this family already. You have always had the spirit of ninjutsu although you have not been trained entirely in its secrets. You will be ready for our first mission. I will see to that. Come we begin immediately."

Naki followed. She led him to a sheltered grove on the periphery of the compound. Nested among the trees was a small wooden shrine with a plain bench seat sitting atop a smooth cut stone. Roughly hewed beams supported a protecting wood shingled roof. Flowering *jinchoge* bushes graced the fringe. A spirit of peace and serenity emanated palpably from the hallowed sanctuary. Naki felt a sudden release of tension from the excitement of his new exploit. His nostrils widened. He breathed in the scent of the bushes and his mind swirled deliriously as if intoxicated by the bouquet of flora bordering the tiny church.

"This is a powerful place," he whispered.

"It is where we come to enhance our *chi*. Sit."

He sat and she beside him. He looked out and the training camp was obscured by the trees and bushes of the grove. The air was still and sweetly perfumed. They were encased in a miniature heaven.

"Clasp your hands so." I will show you the nine finger cuts of *Kuji-In*. It is the way of concentrating the mind. They can work on many levels. First, you will learn *Toa:* to live in peace with man and animal. It is being at one with you. It is for harmony with the universe. Clasp your hands together. Extend your last two fingers and form a point. Touch your tips. All other fingers are interlocked. Thumbs are together pointing forward. Close your eyes and breathe deeply. Remain still."

Sai demonstrated; Naki mimicked. They sat in silence, eyes closed, breathing evenly and deeply. In the calm and spirit of *Toa* Naki settled even further into a comfortable state of being. However, out of the serene blackness, a shape began to emerge, an ebony form initially indistinguishable against the black canvas of darkness. Naki felt a spasm of anxiety, but he fought to suppress it and managed to sustain his breathing. The image continued developing. It wasn't until Naki saw two yellow eyes peering at him did he realize

EDMUND KOLBUSZ

he was staring into the face of the panther. It looked at him with the same countenance as it did when they first met. It was telling him something, but Naki didn't understand. He wasn't afraid; he was puzzled. Was this cat real or had he just been imagining it? No, he didn't imagine the meeting. That was real. This is imagination, but what does it mean? The vision brightened and now he was able to make out the full form of the animal and he sensed the essence of the creature: magnificent, noble, royal.

It began to run, easily at first and then it opened up its stride. It bounded across an open valley with a power Naki had never witnessed before. It continued to run increasing in strength and determination then its running turned into charging; it leapt into the air at an unseen prey: its back was arched; its body was stretched, and all four limbs were extended as if it were flying through the air; its paws unsheathed their deadly arsenal and its fangs revealed themselves in a stupendous snarl. Then it vanished. Blackness once more. Naki emerged from the trance. Sai gently touched his arm.

"You saw something. What did you see?" she asked delicately.

"I saw a large cat. One I encountered in the woods before I met you. It seemed as if it were trying to speak to me, tell me something. I saw it run and then attack. It was very powerful."

Sai said nothing. She only smiled.

"Come," she said, "let us see about where you are to sleep."

They returned to the compound. Naki waited outside her father's house while she went in to discuss the arrangements.

She emerged smiling again. "It is settled. There is a comfortable place in the stable with the animals. They surely will not be disturbed by your fits. You will have your solitude and you can focus on your mission. It is good."

Naki nodded in agreement. As they walked across the training ground, they met members of the village, cousins, distant and close, in-laws, and friends who were considered family. He noted a certain deference given to her. Perhaps, it was because she was the daughter of Tomoki-sama and she was entitled to a greater degree of respect than was usual for a female. Naki would soon discover that her revered status was not only based upon her relation to the *Chunin* but because of her gifts.

He was led to the large communal area where some of the clan wre eating. She instructed him to sit, and she fed him trout, vegetables, rice, cakes and tea. She was a model of propriety during the meal attending to his every need. Her social skills were equal to any high priced concubine that Oda Nobunaga might have in Kyoto castle. She flattered and amused everyone with her charm and witty banter. After the meal, a *koto* was brought out; she sat upon a cushion in the *Ikuta* style of playing and strummed and sang more sweetly than Naki ever thought possible. Every so often she would demurely look up from her playing and catch Naki looking at her with a mesmerized look upon his face.

When the socializing concluded, she led Naki to the stable where in spite of his *sake* soaked brain he still had the capacity to find the lodging pleasantly acceptable. Someone prepared a stall to suit his needs. The earthen floor had been packed, swept and cleaned. Tatami mats had been placed on the ground. Futons, pillows and blankets were laid out. Small paper lanterns illuminated the room and dividers were positioned to separate him from the livestock. Fresh clothes lay on the cot. The barn and the animals had been well maintained and there was no overpowering odor to assault his senses. The animals were penned and quiet. A nearby door led to the outside and just beyond a lazy stream trickled and soothingly burbled. Naki felt entirely comfortable in his new surroundings. There was plenty of room, a comfortable mat, clean clothes, and fresh water just outside the door. Sai told him she would see him first thing in the morning. Shyly he uttered, "Time spent laughing is time spent with the gods. You have made me smile."

She turned and kindly said, "One who smiles rather than rages is always the stronger. Now get some sleep we have much to do tomorrow," and then she was gone.

Ready for rest he extinguished the lanterns and lay in the dark listening to the animals rustling and breathing. He could hear the stream outside quietly chattering to the rough edged rocks it was rounding and smoothing with its infinite patience. He closed his eyes, saw Sai's beautiful face, and fell asleep.

As she made her way to her father's house Sai contemplated upon how best to deal with this neophyte shinobi. He is already attracted to me. On the one hand this is good for he will accept my training, but I must be very careful. He must not fall in love with me. It will distract his attention and retard his progress. He must be absolutely clear in his mind and his soul. He is already clouded by his thoughts of revenge upon Nobunaga. He must not have any other diversions. However, he is unique. He learns quickly; his animal spirit appeared immediately, so he will develop rapidly. I must be careful with him, nurture him well. I must not make a mistake.

Curiously, the thought of her guiding Naki's development titillated her. Suddenly and uncontrollably an impish impulse overcame her and she lost the mature and sophisticated demeanor demonstrated earlier during the evening's entertainment and started running full gait across the yard. Leaping into the air, arms extending in swan like fashion she flew six feet tucked and tumbled. When she landed she transferred her momentum to springing upwards turning and kicking in mid air. She landed solidly on the ground facing the opposite direction. She giggled at her skillfulness and spontaneity. Soberly she realized, I must be careful, for I am a woman.

"Excellently done," said her father who was standing on the porch of the house and had seen the acrobatic display. "But Sai-chan, what is the reason for this sudden display of your talents?" Embarrassed that her father witnessed her less than dignified approach to the house Sai honestly replied, "I am not sure father. Something overtook me and I had the urge to fly."

"Your body travels through the air as if it was a bird, light and free, but does your mind root in the seriousness of this venture? Are you firm in your understanding that we must not fail? You must not fail. Lightness of head or heart has no place in your being now."

"Whatever do you mean father?"

"My child, ever since your mother died trying to prevent an unholy alliance with Nobunaga and the Shogun Ashikaga Yoshiaki, I have vowed to teach you, to prevent you from committing the same fatal mistake she made. She died because of a lapse in discipline. You know, she learned of a trap, that I was in mortal danger, and she acted uncharacteristically. She made a mistake, did not exercise her customary caution … discipline. Her concern for my life clouded her ability to recognize the dangers surrounding hers, and her concern for me cost her life. I lost my wife and Nobunaga succeeded in ensconcing himself in Kyoto.

I do not wish you to go on a mission with a clouded head. Your faculties must be acute and your judgment precise. Do not let this boy distract you in any way. You are to train him as you would any of the other members of the family and of the clan. His life is in your hands and most importantly yours is in his. We have survived because we are disciplined, Nippon first, ourselves second."

"*Hai*, father, I will not fail you. He will be well trained and I do not wish you to worry about my discipline; he means nothing to me."

He studied her with his deep black eyes. "Good, go to bed."

Sai bristled at his curtness and his treatment of her as child, but acquiesced and respectfully followed his command.

As she lay in bed staring at the wooden rafters she reflected upon her father's words. She remembered her mother, a beautiful elegant woman full of laughter, wisdom and gentleness. She remembered her athleticism and her skills in the fine arts of being genteel. She had the sophistication and the softness of a courtesan and the steel of a ninja. She died trying to save her husband. She remembered her father's dictates: strong focus, steely discipline, vigorous commitment to their life and causes. Sai became very sad. What a life I have inherited she thought to herself.

Shaking her head in self chastisement, she refused to succumb to her melancholy and immediately put it out of mind. She closed her eyes and went to sleep.

Chapter 5

"Good morning Naki-san. Did you disturb the horses with one of your fits or did you sleep well?

Naki opened his eyes. It was still dark. Sai was kneeling at the foot of his cot. It was a moment before he remembered where he was. He shook off the cobwebs and realized that he had slept through the night without one of his nightmares. Sai was sitting in Diamond Pose, looking at him placidly and serenely, a cool pool of crystal water, fresh and flawless as only nature could fashion. It is curious he thought to himself how such a delicate creature could possess such strength of body and of mind.

"I slept well, thank you. No visions that frightened me or the horses."

"That is good. Are you ready to learn more of the secrets of the Tomoki clan? We have many."

"*Hai*, let us begin."

"First, refresh yourself in the stream behind the stable. Then meet me at the sanctuary. I will be waiting for you."

She prepared tea. "Sip some *cha*, soothe your soul, refresh your body in the brook and come meditate.

She rose and walked out of the stable. As she left, the horses, now fully awake, flicked and shook their heads, anxious for some of her attention. They were not denied. She greeted each one by name and gently stroked and scratched its nose. When she finally disappeared out the main door their necks were craned, watching her leave. It was as if they were sorry to see her go.

Naki drank some tea, invigorated himself in the brook and hurried to the little shrine. When he arrived, Sai was sitting on the wooden bench. Her eyes were closed, and her hands were on her lap clasped with the fingers interlocked inwards towards the palms. Her soft, deep breathing arrested Naki's advance; he stopped at the edge of the tope and waited quietly.

Softly, she said, "Come, sit," her eyes still closed.

"Did you hear me?"

"No."

"Then how did you know I was here?"

"I sensed you."

"You sensed me?"

"Which finger cut were you meditating upon?" he asked curiously.

"*Jin.*"

"Show me."

She raised her hands and showed Naki how to interlace the fingers and turn each inwards.

"This position of hands increases the ability to feel the thoughts of others," she said. "I was meditating upon you."

"Me?"

"Yes."

"And what did you feel."

"Many things. Please, understand, I must be certain I can trust you. You will learn ancient secrets which only a few are privileged to know."

"And can you trust me?

"Yes, I can, although you have demons that will try to destroy you and perhaps us. We are an ancient clan of shinobi that has survived for many generations. It would be unwise for us not to take precautions; we can allow nothing to jeopardize our existence. We do not accept outsiders; however, we have permitted you to enter our family. You are an exception. Abbot Kosa has decreed that it be, yet I must make sure that you are worthy to use what we teach you without endangering yourself or us. You must face your demons and vanquish them if you are to survive.

"Demons? What demons?"

"Anger, hatred, revenge. Demon influences that will hinder your development, impair your ability; evil beings that can take any number of forms: hallucinations or dreams, and they will poison your mind to cloud your judgment. They will try to prevent you from your destiny.

"My destiny is to kill Oda Nobunaga, to rid the land of this pestilence, to avenge my father, my mother and my sister."

"Perhaps, ... and yesterday, you learned the *Toh*, harmony with the universe, peace with mankind and nature. You had a vision, a cat. You achieved a consciousness many never attain. Others, who are blessed, must meditate months and even years to connect with their animal spirit. I believe your destiny is more than just a vanquisher of this demagogue. The gods have more in store for you. You must not let your demons impede your way. You must fulfill your fate. The cat will serve as your ally; it will guide you."

Naki was dumbfounded. He never conceived that there was more to his existence than being Nobunaga's nemesis. What has fate prescribed for him? He wanted to know. And, what of the cat? It could have killed him twice, yet it didn't. Why?

Sai folded her hands and motioned to Naki to do likewise. "This is the cut of the *Sha*. It is the position of healing oneself. Begin."

Together, they sat silently, breathing evenly and deeply. A warm sensation tingled upon the tip of Naki's spine; it spread soothingly throughout his body: hips lower back, shoulders, with every breath he took. His muscles relaxed, and his angst eased as he willingly succumbed to the force coursing through his body. Subtle exhilarating vibrations reverberated gently penetrating deeply into his muscle tissue taming and calming his anxiousness. His nostrils flared widely to allow even more of the crisp mountain air to make way into his lungs. Each breath fueled a fire of soothing energy which in turn delightfully eased his aggravated psyche. Astounded with the power of this meditative cut, Naki interrupted his position and squinted sideways at Sai.

Reposed, she was beautiful, captivating. Eyes closed, face relaxed, she was somewhere far away, unaware of his intrusive stolen glance. Embarrassed, he directly returned to his own meditation, continuing to free his mind of all distraction and disquiet.

The darkness became his bastion of tranquility. A smile swelled upon his face and his tense brow relaxed. The blackness deepened taking on a luxurious texture of rich velvet. He felt elated, euphoric, excited ... but that was to be short lived.

From within the center of his euphoric oblivion two small red, hot coals began to burn the lustrous pile of his rapture. They ignited the fabric of his tranquility and they burst into flame. Quickly the ebony cloth of serenity became a nightmarish vision of two hellholes of fire. Thick crimson fluid seeped from out of the orifices where the conflagration began, oozing, spreading, quenching the combustion, leaving only ash and soot - a ruin. Through the charred holes of his velvet cloth, in the distance, he saw himself, a small frightened boy hiding behind a bush watching the annihilation of his universe: his father, his mother and his beloved sister. Paralyzed with fear, impotent and ashamed, he watched as dear Keiko was forced to run for her life. A spear deftly launched penetrated her back and emerged angrily from her tiny chest issuing forth all the blood her little body held. She fell forward only to have the javelin impale itself on the darkly stained ground. Obeying the laws of gravity she slid the downwards the length of the lance and came to rest. Her tiny form twitched once and then she was still. Naki heard gales of laughter. He watched a demon plant a foot upon her back; he watched him extract the missile that perforated her precious figure. He watched him wipe her life's blood from his bloody shaft to the cheering of a crowd. Naki saw himself, a powerless older brother, struggle for breath and then collapse into a heap behind the bush. Little did he know that his immobility saved his life.

"Naki? ... Naki?

Naki emerged from the trance.

"You are perspiring. What did you see?" Sai asked anxiously.

"Fiends, demons, hellions.

"You saw them?"

"Yes."

"Now, you must vanquish them."

"How?" Naki asked plaintively.

"Meditate upon the *Sha*. Your questions will be answered - even the ones you haven't asked.

Naki shuddered, stunned. He had never dreamed of his sister before. He had witnessed the specter of his mother and father far too vividly and far too frequently; he had seen the village decimated, but he never had a vision of Keiko's death.

"Do you regret what you saw?" Sai asked.

Trembling slightly, he said, "Yes ... no... I am not sure ... perhaps... I don't know."

"Do not be afraid of the ghosts in your mind. They will not hurt you; however, they can thwart your destiny. The gods spared you for a reason. Do not question; only learn. You have all the instruments needed to crush the forms that press upon you."

Naki fell silent. He did not wish to think any more upon what he dreamed during his waking moments. Sai sensed that the morning's reflection had come to an end, so she took him by the hand and said, "Come you have more to learn."

"Will it be as painful as what I just discovered?"

"No," she said comfortingly.

Inside one of the rougher structures on the complex a wizened old man with ancient eyes mixed powders of ash, talcum, dust and thin slivers of nettle thorns. Nearby lay hollowed eggs which had been covered with a black lacquer.

"*Metsubushi*," Sai said. "They are sight removers. Ya-San will fill the egg shells with powder and then seal them with wax. When there is danger and a need to flee these bombs, thrown at an opponent or to the ground, will burst into a fine cloud of black smoke. They will rob the enemy of their vision. It is very irritating to the eyes. The thorns ensure lack of sight after the dust clears."

Ya-san looked up from the table, politely smiled and nodded at Sai then resumed his work. "We carry nine in a bag hidden within our clothes. Nine is a lucky number."

Sai led Naki deeper into the building. "This is where we store our weapons." The furthest wall was a neatly arrainged set of cubicles extending from the ground to the roof beam. "We call this our wall of war." Inside rectangular wooden niches were *yaris, katanas, bos*, staffs, of varying length, short swords with square guards called *tos*. Sai chose one and reached into the adjacent box and drew a scabbard. "Look, the sheath is longer than the sword. Blinding powders, poisons or secret documents can be concealed within the tip. Place the sheathed sword into the ground and you can use the *tsuba*, the guard, as a step. With the *sageo* cord you can pull the weapon up after you. The rope can be used to choke an opponent or to bind blood flowing from a wound. All our weapons have many uses."

She showed him the *shoge*, a wooden handled sickle with a long weighted chain attached to the bottom that can be used for climbing or swinging and slashing. From another wooden box she pulled numerous discs with varying numbers of blades. "*Shuriken*," she said. "Death stars. Dagger hidden in the palm. This one," she handled very carefully, "is covered in poison. It burns and smokes. "Here," she pointed, "these balled barbs: they are for the feet. Throw them on the ground while being pursued and your foe will cease chasing and begin dancing, a painful dance, sometimes it is the dance of death when the ends are poisoned." She showed him short bows and arrows which could be concealed in a tube and the *fukia*, a blow pipe used to fire poison darts.

"It can be hidden in a cane or it can look like a flute carried by musicians." The *kusarifundo* was a short chain with weights attached to the ends and when aimed and swung skulls cracked like water chestnuts. She whirled one around and struck a nearby beam leaving a mashed dent in the wood. Naki could only imagine what it would do to a head or a chest.

She led him to the far left side of the wall of war and pulled out steel claws with straps. Some looked as if they could attach to the hands and others looked like they were fashioned for the feet. "*Shuko*, they are used for climbing castle walls, but when necessary, with them on your hands you can catch a swinging sword or rake an opponent's face. "Come," she said excitedly, "we begin today's exercise. We mount castles."

Naki looked up. In front of him, embedded into the face
of the mountain were large stones similar to those of a castle
wall. Sai slipped the *shuko* onto her hands and the *ashiko* onto
her feet. She leapt onto the rock face and clung to the wall
like a spider. In a matter of moments she had clambered to
the top of the façade. She carried the *shoge* with the chain
draped over her shoulder. Whirling the sickle blade she
hurled it above her and neatly hooked it onto a top ledge.
She let the weighted chain fall to the ground, and then using
the dangling chain and the claws on her feet and hands she
descended. Once on the ground she handed them over to
Naki and said, "You try Naki-san."

Hesitating for a moment, Naki asked, "What if I fall?"

"You die," she said.

Nervously, Naki laughed, but he strapped the instruments onto his hands and feet nonetheless and slung the
chain with the hook blade onto his shoulder. He closed his
eyes, breathed deeply and began to ascend. Surprisingly, he
found the ascent easy. The talons gripped the stones se-
curely and he was confident his natural abilities would take
him to the top safely. He was right. He successfully scaled
the wall. When he reached the pinnacle he mimicked Sai's
maneuver and secured the blade to the edge and let the
chain fall. His descent, however, was not as simple. It took
some adjustment to free the claws cleanly in order to slide
quickly back to the base. Part way down one of the prongs
of his foot claw, caught a protruding stone. Before Naki

could react, his head bent forward and his chin smacked his knee. An explosion of stars burst in his head, his vision doubled and he lost his grip on the chain, falling limply and landing solidly.

"Are you alive?"

Opening his eyes Naki saw two faces peering at him; both were Sai's. He lifted his head and groaned.

"The ground here is soft," she said. "At castle Kyoto you would not have been so lucky; there are only stones, large sharp stones."

"I am lucky then," Naki said. For a second time that day he did not feel quite so fortunate.

Gingerly, he got up and checked to see what was broken. Nothing was. He was whole, bruised, shaken, but whole.

"Good. Let us now go on to our next adventure, water exercises."

Naki couldn't wait.

———— ((○)) ————

Seeing the falls, however, was spiritually uplifting for Naki. The scent of hydrangeas wafted heavily in the air, and the splashing of the cascading water soothed his disquieted spirit. Thickly covered mossy rocks provided an unexpected pleasure for his feet. He began to strip in anticipation of a whirl in the cool crystalline water. "What are you doing?" Sai inquired.

"Preparing to swim," Naki said, "We are here to strengthen our water skills, no?"

"Yes, you are correct, but why are you removing your garments?"

"I am sorry, but I do not understand."

"We swim clothed. You must learn about the difficulties with swimming moats clothed, heavily weighted with weapons."

"Oh!"

Sai handed him the *shuko* and the *ashiko*. "Put these on please. Take the *shoge* and sling the chain over your shoulder." She reached down and snapped a tall reed growing by the pond's edge. Blowing sharply, she made sure the pipe was sufficiently hollow that air could easily pass through it. "Breathe through this. You will swim on your back. The shuko, shoge and the ashiko will weigh you down, but only so much. When you choose a breathing reed of correct length, you will be able to swim underwater without being seen. Hang the weapons from your shoulders. That leaves your hands and feet free to swim."

Naki looked at her skeptically. The weapons were heavy. He believed he would sink.

"Now go. Swim, across the pool!"

Obediently, he slung them over his shoulders and flopped gracelessly into the pond. Holding the pipe with one hand, he kicked out into the deeper water. Sai watched him pump his legs like a frog, and she laughed as he fought with his free but weighted arm to keep afloat. The tools were heavy, and he sank; the pipe fillied up with water which he swallowed. Panicking, he spit the reed from his mouth, and flailed his arms and legs miserably, trying to surface. Mercifully, he felt hands removing the heavy shoge from his shoulder; whereupon, he thrust for the surface. Emerging, red faced, violently coughing thick, milky white mucus, gasping for breath, he struggled to keep buoyant but sank again. Finally, Sai lifted him and dragged him to safety. Heaving spasmodically, chest straining for air, he gasped. Recovering, he realized she was straddling him and laughing.

"You have some work to do."

The ground never felt so good.

"Perhaps we began too quickly; next time you must swim with only the shuko and the the ashiko. Later, when you are strong you will carry the shoge."

Naki nodded.

"Now, we just swim. Get the pipe!"

It was floating lazily in the middle of the pond … mocking Naki's aquatic efforts.

Sai stripped off her culottes, shed her cotton shirt and carried them to a branch where she hung them up. "Our clothes will dry while we work," she said and dove into the water. Naki sat motionless enchanted by her charms. "What are you waiting for?" she yelled from the middle of the pond, "get the tube. You need to learn how to swim with the pipe before you carry anything."

He rose shakily, stripped and dove in to retrieve the reed.

"Swim across, "she advised, "on your back. Do not use your hands to hold the pipe. Let the reed drop into your mouth and then clench it between your teeth; do not crush it."

Naki got used to swimming with the hollow reed. He learned how to dive just deep enough for it to stick out the water and not let water into his lungs. He mastered keeping it just out of the water so that it would not be easily observed moving across the surface.

On shore, as she was dressing, she said, "You have learned well, today, Naki-san."

Naki was silent. Indeed he had. He learned that he could not destroy Oda Nobunaga single handedly; he learned how naïve and foolish he had been, and, thankfully, the gods guided him safely away from that night. He learned he was a misguided ninja capable of almost little. He now knew he was nothing: only a foolish orphan, hell bent on revenge, and he realized he was not even a ninja; but Sai was.

≈((()))≈

Dinner that evening was cooked *fugu*, the poisonous puffer fish. It was this blowfish which provided the toxins for the tips of the darts and the s*huriken*. Sai told Naki that one fish contains enough poison to kill thirty men, but not to worry about eating it because the cooks know how to cut it. Naki had never eaten so nervously. Thankfully, the rice wine was plentiful and the pains of the day were erased by its intoxicating effects.

The entertainment was also a welcoming distraction. Everyone performed. Women danced, and Sai sang to the *koto*. The most brutal and ruthless of men would be transformed, turned into sheep, softened ... seduced by theirr exquisite charms.

Acrobats flipped and tumbled across the hall floor with such speed that any man in pursuit of them would have difficulty catching them. Jugglers flipped knives, four and five at a time with remarkable dexterity. Actors dressed as beggars, samurai, merchants and monks played out realistic scenarios with astounding wit and cleverness. Sai whispered to Naki that every nine days the family gathers and performs. It was both play and practice.

Upon returning to his quarters, Naki ruminated over the day's lessons. He concluded that physically he was capable enough to accomplish any task assigned him. He was confident in his combat skills. The sword, spear and sticks were domains he just needed to maintain, and if he happened to improve in these areas within the next few weeks so much the better. He knew he would master the knives and the shuriken quickly; however, the climbing and swimming were matters that warranted attention. Also, the nine cuts of the *Kuji-In* would require daily diligence. He elected to begin training his spirit at that moment.

With some trepidation he recalled the vision induced when he deliberated upon the *Jin*. He did not wish to risk witnessing the execution of his sister again; however, he remembered the words of the Abbot. "You are a man with an arrow in his eye. Your pain is so strong it blinds you to the truth. First, you must remove the arrow. You must suffer and endure the healing." Naki was beginning to understand this mystic message. Sai showed him how the demons tormented him. They were the arrow. They needed to be removed, and only then would the truth, his destiny, be revealed. His hatred must be destroyed. But, then he thought anxiously, it was his bitterness and his anger which were the core of his being. It was this spirit that made him *the exception*. It was this energy that made him fight better than any other man at the monastery. If he freed himself from the arrow in his eye would he be as potent? He thought of Sai. She certainly is potent. She is more skilled than most men I know. She is not haunted by ghosts. Naki let go of his doubts. Trust the Abbot. Trust Sai. Trust the ancestry secrets of the Tomoki family.

He chose to work upon the *Toh*, harmony with the universe. Learning to live in peace with mankind may end the horrifying specters. He smiled wryly for he found it amusing that he endeavored to learn to live in peace with the animal kingdom and with mankind in order to be one with himself when his goal was the annihilation of Oda Nobunaga. He laughed at his own confusion. He had so much to learn, so he began.

A flat rock by the side of the brook behind the stable was a perfect place for beginning his journey of self-discovery. Assuming the Lotus position he began with his breathing; interlocking his fingers he focused his mind's eye upon something safe, his animal spirit, the panther. The cat will guide me. The cat will help me? Again, he laughed in cynical disbelief. The cat, the king of cats, the cat that could tear me to pieces, how will it help me, he thought? However, from somewhere deep within his being reassuring thoughts welled up and suppressed the rebellious skepticism. Do not doubt, have faith, believe. Shocked by his spirit's resolve to follow the way, he contritely continued.

He closed his eyes and the dusky darkness intensified from shady gray to inky ebony. Eventually, even the soothing sound of the trickling stream receded into silence. He managed to nourish the blissful oblivion for quite sometime.

The toxic effects of the sake had worn away and the aches from the humiliating fall earlier that day no longer reminded him of his bruised body. His spirit was light, ethereal. He felt his body could lift and whirl and transport him in any direction he chose. Then, disconcertingly, he heard a familiar beat. The ominous thunder of racing hooves he heard only in his dreams. He panicked. He desperately did not want to see the slaughter of his mother and father again. He did not want to see Keiko's body explode from the impaling spear, so with a tremendous exertion he focused his center and continued breathing, determined not to succumb to the demons descending upon his serenity. Fortunately, no visions appeared this time, but the deafening sound of the horses from hell continued in the darkness. The pummeling thump of hundreds of black leather clad riders resounded in his head. Then, wickedly the reverberations changed into heinous shouts of maddened men: crazed yells, screaming war cries, insane whoops and shrieks of glee. Naki struggled to retain the meditation. He cursed he would not surrender to the hungry spirits of his runaway mind. He recalled Sai's words: "Do not be afraid of the ghosts … they will not hurt you." Resolute, he endured the torturous clamor assaulting his inner force. The noise continued growing reaching deafening dimensions. Naki believed he would go mad. Then unexpectedly almost imperceptibly, he heard a roar in the distance, underneath the din; it resounded a second time only more powerfully and clearly. The third time was distinctly clear; it came from a wild angry animal, a large cat. The noises from the murderous men ceased. They disappeared. All was quiet again.

Naki opened his eyes. Across the stream, in the darkness, he saw the beast. It was taking a royal sip from the stream calmly lapping the cool water with its impressive tongue. It lifted its head and saw Naki; turning, it bounded up the embankment and vanished into the night.

Chapter 6

The following days were extremely strenuous for the house of Tomoki with all the training and conditioning. The days began well before the sun up and ended much after sun down. A providential momentum seized the entire familial tribe and it was sweeping them towards destiny. Time flowed as if it were a torrential tributary rushing to merge with a watercourse of fate. The exhilaration was palpable. Everyone was ready; even the horses and dogs were unusually responsive to commands and executed their duties remarkably, as if guided by some benevolent spirit, marshaling them to aid their human masters.

Naki excelled; his swimming strengthened to where he could cross the pond invisibly, fully clothed, at night, weighted with a variety of weapons. Some said his skills exceeded Sai's; he was an otter to her fish. When it was time to scale the wall the family clan excitedly gathered to watch Naki climb. They called him *Tokage*, the lizard, as he was able to not only traverse vertically but horizontally as well. On horseback, no samurai exceeded his prowess. The family's fighting tricks only added to Naki's arsenal of martial abilities. When the clan visited the monastery's village disguised as entertainers, many dwellers entirely familiar with Naki did not recognize him, even Ryu. On one occasion, when the troupe was performing in the square, he stopped a moment to watch the antics. Naki noticed him in the crowd. How Naki wished he could have secretly taken him aside. Naki felt sad as Ryu was a good friend with a big heart. He must wonder what happened to his young sparring partner. In due course, Naki knew they would be reunited; for the moment, he was on a mission.

———◦◉◦———

Then the decree came, a strike upon Oda Nobuoki, Oda Nobunaga's younger brother. Tomoki –san mandated a scouting mission. Monks, herbal medicine men, artists, ronin and concubines were to map streets and structures, detect points weakly guarded, determine the numbers of samurai and most importantly uncover any intrigues.

Typically, monks venture first. Buddhist monks are feared for their mystical peculiarities, they are free to do as they wish, go where they want and are generally not questioned or challenged even by the most arrogant of samurai.

Merchants of medicine are always welcome and generally not suspect; regularly, they are privy to discussions of the most corporal nature.

However, it is the concubine who is the most successful in uncovering important information. Concubines elicite vital intelligence from intoxicated nobles bewitched by their charms.

Entertainers provide the commoners with feats of juggling and tumbling, humorous improvisational theatrics, impromptu haiku, and spectacular fireworks; they are a distraction.

The ronin, on the other hand, nefariously, probe the depths of the underworld. As disgraced samurai, they are easily able to enter the domains of the disgruntled and the vindictive to disgorge plots of impending treachery and sedition.

Martial engagement was forbidden. A dozen family members were to conduct this foray. In order not to arouse any unwarranted suspicion, the monks traveled first followed later by the entertainers, concubines, merchants and the ronin.

Naki was to pose as a young monk and Sai as a concubine: he for his intimate knowledge of the ways of the monastery and she for her porcelain beauty and exquisite talents; this notion unsettled Naki . He struggled with the idea of her consorting with the demons; however, he kept his feelings buried. They were unimportant he reminded himself, a little bitterly: "Nippon first".

Day had not yet broken and the monks were on their way through the mountain pass heading east. They were an innocuous lot. Plainly clothed in loose fitting brown and orange robes tied at the waist with a large sash, heads shaved and feet clad with simple sandals; they were pious men on a pilgrimage. Dust encrusted their feet and tinged the hems of their garments. Any where scouts might be have been watching, they would not have drawn suspicion.

A large black ox pulled their cart filled with provisions

for the journey. No one spoke as they trudged towards Ogie castle, a day and a half journey. Only during the night, around the fire was there any guarded discussion about the mission.

Entrance into the city would be easy. The guards would not question them as Ogie was a traditional place of rest for religious travelers. Once inside, they were to disperse and pray at the various shrines within the mosaic. Ears were to be open to anything that might prove significant. They were to be unobtrusive, invisible yet, acutely aware of everything. Maps of the complex were to be etched into minds. They were to remain only for a few days.

The small blaze the brave monks cooked over was dwindling and the eight eagerly bedded down for the night. They prostrated themselves around the fire in the figure of the Eight Spoked Wheel, a symbol of Buddha, the Wheel of Truth. They conducted prayer in hope that the intelligence they gathered would be advantageous.

The fire provided little in the way of warmth against the cold mountain air and the ground was hard. Any discomfort the austere conditions inflicted was accepted as the Suffering of Suffering, characteristic of true monks: comfort and happiness are transitory and suffering is an acknowledged tenant of life. Since these ninja were in the guise of monks they mimicked their behaviors.

Naki was concerned he would have a fit. His close proximity to the others would certainly disturb them should he be visited by his hellions. Many days passed since his last lurid vision, yet he was not certain they had vanished. Uncertainty plagued his spirit. He determined to meditate upon the cut of the *Sha*, the healing of self, in hopes that his sleep would be peaceful and that he and the others would be well rested.

Rhythmically, mole crickets sounded their nocturnal clamor, lulling Naki from his meditation into a semblance of sleep which was neither sound nor deep. Semi-consciously, Naki was aware of all the night noises.

With alarm, he opened his eyes widely to sound of an intruder. He sat up, reaching for his bo stick. Expecting bandits or spies, he looked deeply into the darkness. The vestiges of the camp fire emanated a dull orange radiance, barely enough light to distinguish the bodies around it.

Naki listened. The ruckus of the crickets had ceased. Silence assaulted his ears, then a sound. He was about to shout a warning when he saw them. Two almond eyes reflecting the dwindling light of glowing embers. The cat. It was here. Naki distinguished two yellow jewels peering at him, but he sensed no danger. The cat was just watching … him. It was not going to attack. The intensity of its gaze was stupefying. Again, the cat was trying to communicate something, but what? In the blink of an eye, it was gone. Only the soft rustling of foliage was heard as the creature returned to the forest, leaving the sleeping wheel of bodies, oblivious to what had just occurred.

Naki decided not to tell the others. They would not understand. The cat came to see him, only. Why? What was it telling him? Sai said it is his animal spirit, his protector, but it is alive, massive muscle and bone. What does it want from him? Naki's intuition told him there was no risk; however, the reoccurring encounters were definitely puzzling.

He fell into a deep sleep and woke refreshed to the sound

of the ox snorting and shuffling restlessly. It was hungry. Hisao-san was tending to the animal. The ox belonged to him. Naki was sure that it was as old as the long lived man, yet it was still powerful and useful, just like the old man.

Hisao-san had risen early, and was now taking care of his animal, the fire, and the tea. Naki smiled and nodded. The venerable old man did not speak much, but one knew there was a deep well of knowledge and wisdom beneath the taciturn demeanor, experience which would undoubtedly be advantageous. Suddenly it dawned upon him; Naki wondered why the ox did not create a commotion when the panther appeared. Surely, the old ox would have sensed the danger, and raised a noise, yet it did not react. Was he dreaming? Bewildered, he became busy and put it out of mind.

The rugged mountain terrain softened to gentlly rolling foothills, and the road wound through meticulously tended farms and peaceful villages. As they neared, the castle could be seen prominently atop a monstrous, rocky, mountain outcrop overlooking the valley below. Even from twenty, *ri*, miles, it dominated the landscape. Hotaka -san, the mountain man, estimated it must be *cho*, four hundred feet, above the village below, and the terrain approaching the castle was flat for miles. Ken-san, noted that guards posted atop the castle structure would have a perfect view of anything which approached the village and the castle. The plan was to arrive by sunset.

It was dusk when they finally reached Ogie village. This night, they would spend at an inn, and at in the morning visit various shrines including the one atop the citadel.

The shops were closed, but the inns and tea houses

were open, swarming with samurai. Jiro-san wondered why. Boisterous bullies were everywhere drinking liberally and consorting with the tea house girls. The atmosphere was palpably dangerous, intense.

Yellow lanterns lazily hung outside these inns and were the only source of light along the dark winding roads. If one did not intimately know the village or have a guide one could get lost. Hisao-san told the others the castle grounds were probably similar in their confusing maze of avenues. Further, he warned that there are many false paths that lead nowhere. Finally, they found lodging.

"War is in the air," Hisao said. "Nobunaga has summoned the samurai of the surrounding provinces. He is assembling forces and they are here now, on their way to Kyoto. It is imperative we discover what is going on, quickly. Isamu-san, courageous warrior, and Kato-san you will visit the inns and listen, to loose-tongue, drunken ramblings. Kichiro-san, lucky one … find a shrine maybe some of the rabble will pass by; watch and listen. Naki and I will visit a bathhouse. Hotaka-san, Jiro-san, Takeo-san, and Yoshio-san wander the streets; note the routes to the castle gates, and count numbers of men. We reassemble at the Hour of the Tiger."

Obediently everyone dispersed. Hisao-san sat down and closed his eyes. Naki did likewise and waited for the old man to finish his reflection. When he was done, Naki gently asked, "Hisao-san, may I humbly inquire as to why we go to the bathhouse?"

"Are you not tired from the journey? A bath and a massage will be good for you. Besides, samurai enjoy the houses and talk freely."

The old man was correct. The Tatami house was teeming with samurai. Young Naki was not aware that only nobles, samurai and monks were permitted entrance to the natural hot springs. Young female attendants in light white cotton kimonos were busy washing, scrubbing, and entertaining their guests in the anteroom as they prepared them for entry into the steaming baths. The atmosphere was lively with the flirtatious tittering of the attendants hoping to engage their customers with more than just a massage after the bath. Naki's attendant coyly inquired if he would like some company after he relaxed with his massage. Delicately, to her dismay, he declined. She endeavored to hide her feelings but was not entirely successful. Naki felt flattered and somewhat sorry for her disappointment, but she was sweet and demure and would undoubtedly find pleasure and not to mention profit with another.

Numerous rectangular stone tubs lined the walls of the bathing room which looked out to a magnificent garden, lit by many lanterns. A dark pond filled with lily pads glowed orange reflections. Surrounding the pond, a garden of flowering bushes, stunted trees, and elegantly arranged rocks flowed out almost to the mountain itself.

In the bath, Naki tried to eavesdrop. However, the warm mineral water soothed his tired muscles and he succumbed to the relaxing ambiance. He fell asleep. Hisao – san kicked him. Snapping out of his reverie and giving his older companion an apologetic look he began to listen again. Hisao-san subtly nodded and forgave the carelessness.

Closing his eyes, this time his focus was on the low mutterings of the conversations within his tub, but the six samurai that shared the bath with them were suspicious of the two head shaved monks silently soaking with them, so they suspended their discussions and quietly indulged in the rejuvenating effects of the thermal springs. Naki redirected his attention and strained to listen to the discourse of the adjacent baths, but he was not able to understand anything coherently.

He recalled the first meeting with the panther and re-membered how his senses had become intensely acute. Underneath the surface he interlocked his fingers and formed the cut of Toh, harmony with the universe and with the animal kingdom. He visualized his encounter and how he was able to hear with the ears of a deer. Presently, a deep calm settled his mind. He heard the relaxed breathing of the men beside him. He heard the giggles of the attendants in the washing area outside. He opened his eyes and fixed them upon a ferocious man intensely engaged in a heated dialogue.

"Forget her. We leave here in a few days. Fool, how long did you think you could stay? Forget her! Since Asakura has refused to conference in Kyoto, his refusal is an undeniable defiance, a definite declaration of war. We will be fighting the Asakura, and the ungrateful brother - in – law within a month.

The hostile samurai berated his love sick companion a little more before leaving. Naki didn't know who Asakura Yoshikage was, but he did know the men stationed here would be leaving for Kyoto in a few days and then to war after that, against the Asakura, but when? Why was this samurai so angry? Was there some dissention?

Hisao-san whispered to Naki, "Come, we go now." The

words spoken softly, boomed like cannon fire in Naki's ears. Recoiling sharply, Naki reeled and violently smacked his head against the back wall.

"*Kuso!* Shit!"

"Nakamura-san! Are you all-right?"

"Why are you yelling in my ear? Are you trying to deafen me?"

"Nakamura-san, I did not speak loudly; I whispered."

Naki vigorously shook his head to quell the ringing in his ear.

"What do you say? You did not scream in my ear?"

"No, Naki-san, I spoke very softly. Are you feeling fine? You look like you are in pain."

"I am fine, thank-you." However he wasn't. The explosion in his ear and the bang to the head had him dizzy and sore.

Hisao-san deferring to Naki's discomfiture declined the customary massage after the bath, and the two left immediately. As they walked back to the inn, Naki's throbbing head improved, and apart from a subtle ringing in his ear, he was ready to talk.

"Is there something you wish to tell me, Nakamura-san?"

"I overheard a name: Asakura Yoshikage. Asakura openly declared war against Oda Nobunaga, and these troops here will be leaving for Kyoto soon, in a few days."

"So, Nobunaga is planning to fight Asakura, and no doubt his treacherous brother- in law.

His brother - in - law returned his allegiance to the Asakura after being wooed away by marriage to Nobunaga's sister. Did you hear when they plan to attack?"

"No … yes …within a month?"

"It is of no consequence. We will find out. If Asakura openly opposes Nobunaga, then he must have the support of the Asai; surely, they must be joined.

"There is one other thing, Hisao-san. The samurai was upset about having to fight. This puzzled me. Samurai are loyal to their masters and their master's plans, no? So, why the hostility? He must feel his Lord is making a mistake … something is amiss.

"Very astute, Nakamura-san, something must be amiss. We shall find out."

Naki thought of Sai. She might find out, but at what cost? What will she have to do to discover the reason? She would arrive in a day. These many desperate men will surely seek the comfort of pillowing, with a beautiful companion. She definitely will be consorting with one of these monkeys. He couldn't cope with the thought. His head ached anew.

The *Machia House* was quiet. The others had not yet returned. In the meantime, Naki and Hisao began to prepare tea.

Kichiro, excitedly slid open the latticed door and hurried into the room. "Hisao-san, I have news."

"Hai, we too, but wait for our brothers."

It was not long before the entire company returned. Hisao began. "We understand that Asakura Yoshikage wars against Nobunaga, and perhaps he has assistance from the Asai. Still their chances of destroying Nobunaga and dislodging him from Kyoto and the province of Ise are remote. Might he have help from someone else?"

"Perhaps from the monastery of Ikko-Ikki at Nagashima, "Kichiro suggested. There were other monks at the shrine, rough looking ones. I surmised that is where they were from; they had a coarse look about them."

"If Kichiro-san believes that these men are Ikko-Ikki from Nagashima, I am sure Nobuoki will suspect the same. This puts us in peril. They will be watching us closely. We may be circumspect or even attacked, but remember we are not to fight."

"Isamu-san, Kato-san, what did you learn at the inns?"

"There was much dissention, many arguments with raised voices. It was difficult to hear any one conversation. We did determine, however, there was a concern about numbers."

"So, Nobunaga thinks his impudence will result in victory again. Eight years ago he defeated Imagawa Yoshimoto with three thousand men against twenty-five thousand. Smugness, bluster and audacity along with the forces of nature granted him a victory which should not have been his. He should have been squashed then, but his arrogance and boldness saved him. For upon hearing of Lord Imagawa's plan to lay siege to Kyoto, he summarily rode out with an inferior force to cut off the impending attack. Craftily, he lay in ambush. Imagawa and his men rested at Okehazama Gorge, a deadly mistake. Positioning his men at the mouth of the canyon, Nobunaga blocked him in - there was no retreat from the gorge. Nature lent assistance as well. A storm hindered any detection of their close proximity. When the thunderstorm passed, Nobunaga's men rushed in, surprising everyone. Darkness, wind, water and mud added to the calamity. Furthering Nobunaga's good luck, Imagawa's men were drunk and tired from a night of celebrating, and so penned in they were decimated. Imagawa Yoshimoto, regrettably, was oblivious to what was happening, and it was only when he stumbled out of his tent did he realize he was under attack. He was easily captured and subsequently beheaded. All of Nippon was in awe of Nobunaga's victory.

"He will fail this time, Hisao-san. The samurai were unsettled; their spirit is weak".

"Do not underestimate Oda Nobunaga. He is infinitely clever. He turns the down side up. Out of adversaries, he makes allies; out of villainous traitors he makes loyal retainers; in battle he rallies his weak and inferior forces and leads them to victory. Do not be deceived; the samurai complaints are not sign of vulnerability. The Demon is wily, impetuous, irreverent, and consequently successful. He is afraid of nothing and all of his men are in fear of him.

"What do we do, Hisao-san?" Kichiro asked.

"We carefully continue with our plan. We enter the castle and study defenses. We assess weakness. We attend to any traps, as I am sure, there are many. For now, we sleep and rest."

Chapter 7

A day after the monk's clandestine departure another caravan left the Tomoki compound. Several wooden wagons bounced and rattled over rough mountain roads. A motley crew of actors and performers held tightly to side planks trying not to spill off. Behind them, a splendid carriage negotiated the rough mountain terrain.

Despite the colorful appearance of the group, it was a somber band of entertainers that travelled the treacherous road to Ogie. Venturing across central Nippon's highways was a dangerous undertaking. Marauders would find such an unprotected spectacle an invitation to murder and plunder.

The lawless of the land knew the terrain intimately and steep vertical rock faces presented plenty of caves and ledges from which to scrutinize unsuspecting travelers. It was their territory, and they employed the landscape effectively and with impunity. Ronin samurai together with murderers, thieves, and outcasts accosted wayfarers too often, rarely showing mercy. Seemingly vulnerable, the gay caravan was effortless prey. Wisely, the company scrutinized the narrow passes for signs of bandits.

The day passed uneventfully. Initial rough paths out of the mountain lair smoothed into better roads. Sai rode in the *jinrikisha*, a carrigage of comfort and modertate luxury, with her cousin, Yoshi, who was her mentor in the art of entertaining and pleasuring. Yoshi knew it would be delightfully obvious to any seasoned samurai that Sai was a neophyte. Her innocence alluringly transcended her mature appearance. She would attract a powerful man. Yoshi was sure of this.

Artistically, Sai had no equal. Her singing voice was sweet and resonant, and she was accomplished on the *biwa*. Only seven, she charmed her artistically discriminating father with her improvisational haiku. She was clever, witty, talented and desirable. She was the perfect dissembler: a deadly flower. Only one thing made Yoshi apprehensive. Sai had never pillowed with a man; but she was an exceptional student, and she had been given elaborate training and proper accessories for her mission; so her mentor believed that Sai would succeed and elicit vital information. She believed that between the sake and Sai, no information was safe.

Eventually, from within the comfort of the coach Sai heard Saburo, the captain of the group, decree it was time to rest; Ogie was within reach easy reach the following day. Yoshi clambered down the one step of the carriage and stretched.

Sai, remaining inside the *jinrikisha*, sensed a feeling of foreboding. Trusting her instincts she whispered a warning to Yoshi. "Tell the others to be alert. There is danger near."

Yoshi, not nearly as intuitive, but highly disciplined reacted immediately.

"Saburo-san … beware!" Everyone heard and understood. Weapons were never far away, and the troupe was quickly armed and ready. They did not wait long.

Out of the dusk, three figures appeared. Silently and eerily, they approached Saburo. He feigned ignorance, pretending to be unaware of the danger they posed. He greeted them cordially, with buffoonish stupidity.

"*Konbanwa*, good evening."

"*Boke*," Idiot," spouted a menacing voice! A short blade waved in his direction. "Shut up and move over by the fire." Saburo paused momentarily and complied. "Gather the others," the rough looking brute shouted gruffly to the shadows. "Collect them all and let us see what Fortune has brought us this evening." Several more scraggly and lightly armed barbarians loomed from the pitch herding Yoshi, Kenta, Mikio, Raiden, and Hana.

"Is that everyone?" the leader demanded.

"*Hai*, Toro-san!" an obsequious little monkey-man answered.

"Are you sure? Did you check the wagon?"

"*Iie*, no."

"*Baka*, stupid idiot! What are you waiting for?! Do it, now! Go!"

The little simian bounded towards the carriage that still contained Sai.

"All of you sit close to the fire, so I can see what I have here," the ringleader arrogantly barked, cocksure that the hijacking was under control. Six vulgar rogues encircled their prey. It was dark now; the only light came from the small fire Kenta lit shortly before they were accosted by the renegades.

From the shadows, Saburo assessed their strength: seven men altogether with swords, knives and bo staffs. The captain was a samurai who had seen better times. His once proud warrior attire was weathered and worn. His hair was not even bound in the tradition of the samurai, but was hanging loose, long and dirty. His katana was still sheathed upon his back, and a short sword was all that was threatening him at the moment. Saburo waited patiently.

"Misfortunate!" he thought to himself. This once proud, powerful soldier was now leading a company of incompetent misfits. It was evident their past plunders had been meager. Obviously, they were not very successful and probably not skilled at combat. It was sad that his association with these miscreants would shortly lead to his death. "Perhaps I do him a favor," he thought. It was a wonder they had all survived this long.

Saburo waited like a snake before a strike. Kenta, Yoshi and the others offered the semblances of frightened compliant wayfarers willing to acquiesce to the demands of bullies and villains.

"What is taking that retard so long?" the head ruffian growled.

The monkey-man in the meantime had hopped towards the carriage. He stopped for a moment. Stunned by the auspiciousness of the conveyance, he imagined a handsome booty lay within. As he opened the door, he was startled by Sai sitting, waiting for him. With the speed of a pit viper, she grabbed him by the neck and puffed a poison blowpipe dart directly into his left eye. She squeezed his throat to ensure he didn't make a sound. Instantly paralyzing, the venom froze an eternal expression of stupefied shock upon his leathery face; a small trickle of blood slowly leaked from the corner of his eye and proceeded down his cheek - as if it were a sad tear shed for his own demise. Once his body had completely succumbed to the toxic assault Sai eased his corpse to the ground, and disappeared into the darkness.

Saburo heard an owl hoot. He knew Sai had disposed of the little creature the samurai sent for her and that she was now nearby ready to assist in the disposition of these intruders. He temporized. He addressed the leader. "Please, noble sir, do not harm us. We are merely court entertainers, poor in riches and rich in poorness. We have nothing to offer you but our talents. We will entertain and amuse but we cannot provide anything more for we have very little."

Surprisingly, with eloquence the vandal responded with, "Very little is better than the nothing we have. What is yours shall be ours; unfortunately, it will cost you dearly."

Upon hearing his threat, Sai launched a dart out of the night into the back of the neck of the ronin. He fell to the ground. Stunned, the remaining thieves took a moment too long to react. Subtly, in the darkness, Joshi, Kenta, Mikio, Raiden, and Hana had all maneuvered themselves into positions within easy striking distance of the remaining marauders. An eruption of feet, fists, and blades ended the encounter. Six bodies lay dead, necks broken, backs cracked and only a modicum of blood spilled.

The melee was brief. All were intact - except for the offending party. Saburo counted the corpses and then exclaimed in a quiet voice, "We are missing one. The leader is not among the dead. He has escaped ... find him!"

He hadn't gone far. The ronin somehow had managed to

crawl into a deep shadow. Saburo stood over him. Drawing shallow breathes, he managed to utter to some words.

"Don't let me die such a pathetic death. Let me die as a samurai should. As shameful as I am now, let me die nobly. I have served honorably ... mostly. Only recently have I been reduced to such behavior. Let me die as I should."

Saburo knew the man hadn't the strength to commit sepeku.

"Allow me to be your second," he said.

The man nodded and Saburo unsheathed his katana and propped him onto his knees. He gave him his own knife. The vanquished warrior placed the tip against his own stomach, but he did not have the ability to plunge it in and tear it up and across. Saburo deemed the gesture sufficient.

"May you return a better samurai," he thought and raised the sword and swung. The head fell to the ground, flipped over once and came to rest nestled against a rock; facing the stars, it wore an expression of peace, as if it had come to terms with its fate.

You should have done this long ago," Saburo thought.

"Dispose of the bodies! We cannot leave any sign of violence along this road."

The bodies were stuffed into a mountain fissure. Piled stones made the grave appear like a natural mountain heap. No one would suspect that the crack contained the vestiges of seven poor scoundrels who had the misfortune of challenging the Tomoki clan.

Calmly and efficiently, as if nothing had occurred that night, the travelers bedded down. In the morning, they were on their way.

The road approaching the castle was astir with the excitement of economic activity. Merchants, farmers, men, women and children, burdened with heavy and cumbersome goods, trudged and wheeled carts and wagons toward town.

Toothless travelers smiled and informed the entertainers that their arrival at Ogie was most opportune. There was need for their distractions. When people saw Yoshi and Sai wry smiles and nods of approval abounded. "You will make much money," they said. The samurai are wild in their spending. Such beauties as you will entertain Oda Nobuoki, himself."

Yoshi smiled at Sai, yet Sai was impassive. Later, when the two had a moment Yoshi said, "Sai, you do not have to perform this matter. You can assume the role of one of the acrobats. I can conduct this business on my own."

"No, I will perform my duties."

"Are you certain?"

"Yes!"

Yoshi looked at her askew. Nothing more was said.

The townspeople greeted the entertainer's afternoon arrival with enthusiasm. Large crowds gathered even before the troupe was ready to perform. Once they began, reactions were riotous. Laughter and applause reverberated throughout the town, to the very walls of the castle itself. It was precisely this commotion which drew the attention of the guards and they were dispatched to investigate the source of the fuss. Upon seeing that the excitement was over a band of talented entertainers, word was sent that some amusements were taking place outside the walls.

———⸺⸺◎⸺⸺———

Sai was just beginning her final song when the performance was halted by a pounding of taiko drums. Belligerently, a contingent of guards beating a martial rhythm forced their way through the crowd. Soldiers surrounded the performers. A moment of confused silence passed before the captain of the guard officially announced that they, the performers, were to gather their things and proceed to the castle. Murmurs of dissension rumbled amongst the spectators before they were tersely silenced by the captain. "The *Kugyo*, the high court of nobles, commands the presence of this company to entertain the regent, his lord Oda Nobuoki this evening." Shocked gasps and surprised whispers gently purled through the thrilled knot of peasantry.

"Yes, yes, immediately," Saburo replied, as he began gathering instruments and props. The performance was over; the crowd dispersed. Yoshi nudged Sai and smiled; however, Sai was unresponsive.

"Are you sure," she whispered.

"Yes," said Sai.

The soldiers waited impatiently as the properties were quickly packed, and then everyone was abruptly marched through the town to the castle gates.

A line of guards preceded the performers while another flank followed. They were led over a narrow bridge which spanned the outer moat. Sai calculated sixty feet from the bridge to the first gate. Further, a second gate, larger, two stories high, reinforced with iron, lay ahead to the right. To the left she noticed a long open area bordered on two sides by high wooden walls which ended in a dead end. Chillingly, she realized it was to trap invaders. Ahead, another gate had hour glass openings on the rampart above where arrows or stones would inhibit intruders. As they passed through the wrought iron portal Saburo overheard the captain of the guard say, "Take the direct route the daimyo is waiting."

It was getting dark and everyone focused on memorizing this path, the most direct to the inner castle. A trudge of at least a mile down narrow avenues, up steep stone steps, over narrow water bridges and under stone covered passages eventually finished before two heavy, very ornately decorated doors reinforced by yet another iron gate. They entered a lower level room of dark, heavy post and beam construction. Torches lit the way up several narrow, steeply inclined staircases which were also fortified at the top with iron trap doors to shut out invaders. When they arrived at the fifth level, the hallways finally opened expansively. The walls were richly decorated and the floors were brightly varnished, although they creaked. Everyone understood why, and as they proceeded down the hall they became boisterous, laughing, playing, pretending, excitedly wandering about the hallway ... stepping to find places that would not announce an enemy.

Escorted into an antechamber, they were told to prepare; at the Hour of the Dog, they would perform ... for Oda Nobuoki and his regents. Three guards remained to monitor their preparations.

Everyone readied themselves: instruments were tuned; props were organized; Sai and Yoshi dressed in their most elegant silk kimonos tied with long obis in the form of butterflies. They applied powder to their faces and pinned their lustrous, black hair high upon their heads.

Sai perfumed herself with rose water. Despite the mature attire, her youthful innocence transcended the presentation and she seemed the image of a budding flower.

Yoshi looked at Sai with admiration. "You are beautiful," she said. "Everyone will adore you, and when you sing, all will be in awe."

"I do what needs to be done for Nippon."

"Are you prepared?"

"I have told you I am."

"Tell me, why you are so reluctant?"

"What do you mean?"

"Your face is not calm."

"I am sorry, I will relax."

"You must."

With the admonition Sai transformed herself into the epitome of tranquility. Her tense features softened and she became the quintessence of contentment.

"How is this?"

"Good," Yoshi said. "That is perfection. Sai," she continued, "I have never known one as gifted as you."

"You are too kind."

"It is truth. Now, let us see what we can find out."

"Hai!" Sai said with renewed spirit.

——————◉——————

An escort was heard marching down the hallway. Slinging
open the rice paper doors, a captain demanded the company
be ready for their engagement.

"Hai," Saburo chimed. "We are prepared." They were
rushed down the hall. Doors were slid open and they entered into a vast room filled with drunken, boisterous men:
powerful men. A hush fell as Yoshi and Sai were ushered in,
followed by the others. Numerous tatami mats were laid on
the floor to serve as the performance area. The audience sat,
casually, on three tiers facing the performers. Each level indicated the status of those assembled. On the lowest level were
generals dressed in modern colorful Samurai attire. Upon the
second level were regents, lords of their provinces, daimyo
supporting Oda Nobunaga in his quest for sovereign rule,
and on the highest level, in the middle of the room, was seated, the youngest brother of Oda Nobunaga, Oda Nobuoki.

He was a slight man of moderate height. He did not
possess the physical prowess of those surrounding him. The
heavily padded vest he wore over his kimono attempted to
give illusion of his being larger than he really was. His attire
was the brightest and most colorful, and the despised *mokkou*

insignia which emblazoned the Oda clan's flags and banners served as the motif on his vest and kimono. His face was narrow and sallow and appeared to be beset by many problems despite the festive atmosphere.

A chancellor stood up and officiously announced to all present that it was now time for some delightful distractions from a troupe of wandering entertainers that were discovered amusing the masses outside the castle walls. A raucous cheer erupted. He continued. "Let us hope they will be as stimulating for us." Whereupon he sat down and signaled for the troupe to begin.

Saburo had suggested that Sai begin the performance. Yoshi was to accompany her on the biwa. Carefully instructed on the proper decorum in such circumstances, Sai approached the discriminating audience humbly and shyly. She bowed, paused and waited for Yoshi to start. As her introductory notes were strummed, Sai sensed a palpable attentiveness from the nobles. She demurely looked up and saw every eye upon her eagerly awaiting her song. She began and she did not disappoint.

"I See Fields Of Golden Flowers,
Shine In The Evening Sun,
Above Are Misty Mountains,
It's So Beautiful
As The Wind Caress My Eyes,
Gazing Gently At The Sky,
The Moon Inside A Halo,
It's So Beautiful

There's A Dark And Lovely Forest,
In The Place Where I Was Born,
There's A Farmer Walking Down The Trail,
It's So Beautiful
I Hear The Sound Of Bird Song,
And The Echo Of A Bell,
Every Tree Is Wrapped In Moonlight,
It's So Beautiful

When I Think Of All The Beauty,
That Nature Gives To Me,
From The Flowers To The Mountains,
It's So Beautiful
There's Glory And A Wonder,
Far Wider Than The Sea,
I Say Yes To All This Loveliness
It's So Beautiful."

Yoshi ended the song with a few final delicate notes. The silence was nerve wracking. For what seemed an eternity not one warrior moved. Then a tumult of applause and cheers uproariously greeted her. Saburo silently whistled a note of relief. He thought now that the initial tension had been broken and they had been warmly received the rest of the evening should proceed smoothly. Yoshi continued to play the biwa, and she was immediately joined by the *Hagiku*, a thirteen stringed zither and the *Kinryu*, a side blown flute. The taiko drum sounded and Sai continued to sing and dance. She was soon accompanied by the others in the traditional form of pantomime. Old songs were played and new ones were offered and every performance was received enthusiastically.

Saburo wisely chose not to demonstrate any of their athletic acrobatics. Let them believe we are merely musicians so as not to draw any suspicion. As the presentation drew to an end, Saburo thanked the audience for their indulgence and hoped that their humble distractions were pleasing to all.

No sooner had he finished addressing the powerful patrons did Oda Nobuoki rise and speak. In a drunken slur he announced that the final performance of the evening had not yet been given. He stumbled down the three short tiers to the floor and faced his guests. He waved Saburo and his troupe away and they were brusquely ushered off to the side.

"My brother, General of Joint Army, Lord of Owari and Mino, Chief of the Oda Clan, extended a cordial invitation to Asakura Yoshikage to conference in Kyoto. The hospitality was rudely refused. Upon doing so Asakura Yoshikage declared that he was no longer an ally but an enemy to the vision of one unified Japan. We now gather to quash Asakura and declare to the world that we are 'One realm under one sword.' Our position is tenuous but, may, I remind you before the Battle of Okehazama my brother performed the Atsumori dance. Everyone thought he was a fool, dancing ridiculously at the shrine and then leaving Kyoto with only minimal defenses as he lead an army of only three thousand against twenty. But the gods favored the Lord of Owari and Mino and he slaughtered Imagawa Yoshimoto in his own camp. Tonight on this evening I too shall perform this revered dance and bless us with the same fortune.

Tension rippled through the party. Unsteadily, he poised himself to perform the same ritual. He began, shakily. With a step and a wave of the fan he wobbled through the motions as he recited his brother's favorite poem.

"A man's life of 50 years under the sky
is nothing compared to
the age of this world.
Life is but a fleeting dream, an illusion --
Is there anything that lasts forever?"

The assemblage was silent, clearly embarrassed that their host would drunkenly mimic what has become legend. Oda Nobuoki was not his brother's equal and Oda Nobuoki knew it. Even if the performance were to honor his brother and sincerely wish luck to those who were to go to war, the time and the place were inappropriate. Oda Nobuoki had let the sake get the better of his judgment and committed a social error. Everyone however, applauded politely not willing to further publicly embarrass their drunken host.

Feeling the estrangement he abruptly dismissed the gathering. "We are concluded," he announced and stumbled back to his position of honor trying his best to sit down with some dignity. The palace guards herded the performers and began to usher them out of the room.

Again Nobuoki spoke. "Stop, she stays!" referring to Sai. "The others may go." Without a look of protest the troupe left the room. Sai stood dispassionately off to the side and waited for the honored guests to depart as well. When they were alone, Nobunaga's youngest brother told Sai that she sings and dances beautifully.

"Thank you Oda Nobuoki-sama," Sai said demurely.

A panel slid open on the level behind the decorative artifacts. A young boy, appeared, Nobuoki's valet. "Master your room is ready."

"Come," said Nobuoki, "I need a massage. Are you equally skilled in the art of massage as you are in singing and dancing?

"Hai, Oda Nobuoki-sama, I am."

"Good, then follow me."

Sai sighed slightly, but betrayed no emotion and complied. She was led through the narrow passage behind the audience hall's wall. When another panel slid open, she found herself in Oda Nobuoki's bed chamber. Nobunaga's brother disappeared behind a dressing panel and began to undress. He indicated to Sai that she could hang her garments on the rack by the other latticed panel and that there was a white bath kimono waiting for her. Sai disrobed and donned the silky robe that he provided. She reappeared before he was finished and stood by the bed mat waiting for him. "Would you like some sake?" he said. She seriously considered having some as she would need some kind of numbing to get through the night.

"Thank you, no, Nobuoki-sama. It will impair my ability to give you relief."

"He appeared, "I believe I too have had enough for one evening. I do not enjoy these formalities, but I was asked to entertain, so obediently I did, and badly I might add. Forgive me, do not misunderstand, you and your companions were exceptional this evening; however, my final gesture caused embarrassment. I am not sure why I recited that poem. I was hoping to stir the men the way my brother can stir men to battle. They leave tomorrow for Kyoto and after that to the north to fight an army which may be stronger and better prepared than my brother anticipates. I do not share my brother's steely defiance of death and his, 'To hell with it all, we were born to die.' He says that a lot. 'We were born to die.' I am afraid I was born to live."

"Life is beautiful."

"Yes, you said that so eloquently in your song, and you too are beautiful, now come give me that massage."

"Would you like me to disrobe?"

"If you wish; I just want a massage. I don't believe I could perform as skillfully as you this evening. I just wish for a relaxing massage so that I may fall asleep to face tomorrow. Again, it will be full of formality. Should I fall asleep, you may lie next to me and sleep, unless of course you plan to kill me. You aren't going to kill me are you?"

"No, I am not going to kill you."

"Good then begin your massage and put me to sleep. My valet will escort you to your companions in the morning."

Chapter 8

Hiaso, Naki and the others took a convoluted route to the shrine atop the castle. Covertly, each spy assessed the castles strengths and weaknesses. At the shrine, during prayer, Naki tried to attend to meditations, but thoughts of Sai kept creeping into his mind. Later, they learned that a group of performers had entertained hundreds of people outside the castle walls, and that they were so entertaining and skilled that Oda Nobuoki, himself, commanded a performance.

Hisao was thrilled; Naki was not. He envisioned the worst. Immediately, he reprimanded himself. Sai can take care of herself. He wondered why he was so concerned. She never declared any interest in him other than as a student of the art of ninjutsu-zukai. Why should he be worried about her pillowing with the enemy? After all she is ninja, and it is war. All manner of deception must be employed for the greater good. It is a small sacrifice. However, his disquiet would not pass. He tried to use the meditations Sai taught him, but he wasn't successful. This is not good he thought. I

EDMUND KOLBUSZ

must take greater control of my mind. I cannot let my worry impede my mission. He distracted himself with menial tasks. Hisao told them they would embark for Kyoto, and then turn towards the mountain lair once it was safe. Naki prepared.

Nonetheless, he kept imagining Sai. He would not know how she coped until they returned to the Tomoki enclave. Kichiro asked Naki if he was alright. That he seemed sullen and distracted. "Yes, thank you, Kichiro-san. I am fine. I apologize if I seem troubled."

"She is very special, Nakamura-san, but do not worry. I have never met anyone as capable as her. She will be fine."

Naki was shocked to realize that his preoccupation with Sai's safety was so obvious, but did Kichiro or the others know that he was also concerned with her consorting, with devils or anyone else for that matter.

"You still need some work Nakamura-san. Your countenance is too open. You must learn to mask your feelings and make sure they don't appear so obviously upon your face."

"You are correct Kichiro-san. I will endeavor to be stone, wear a stone face."

"Stones crack and crumble. You must be water, still, placid, calm and cool. Water accepts, flows, finds its way. Your face and heart must be so."

"Hai," Naki said softly. "Arigato."

Again, he cursed himself, for being so obvious. I will not let the fire of my passion burn so hotly; I will be cool water; I will douse my fire, render it ash, wet and cold. He couldn't.

For him, the journey back was difficult. Sai kept figuring in his mind. He envisioned her lithe naked body lying next to Oda Nobuoki. He conjured her erotically arousing the demon's brother using her arsenal of carnal devises. She must please so she can deceive, he rationalized, but again his attempt to put things in perspective failed. He thought he would rather relive one of his heinous visions than endure the agony he was feeling now. Desperately, he recalled the pool where he first met Sai in hopes of freeing his mind and finding some tranquility from the pain he was presently feeling, but in his mind he only saw Sai, smiling, swimming and laughing, an image which just made his journey worse. He trudged towards the mountain lair deeply breathing in the thin air, and violently expelling the troublesome irritants to his spirit. He was wretched. However, he endeavored to keep a placid demeanor. His visage was pacific; his voice was modulated and his movements were minimal and efficient. He sought to be water.

He thought of the future ... of ... what was next? How his next mission might bring him closer to his destiny of destroying Oda Nobunaga? These thoughts were anesthetically effective in distracting him, numbing him, removing him from the pain of his preoccupation with Sai. Oda Nobunaga's decimation, he discovered, was the cure for Sai's alluring intoxication.

———«(◎)»———

The village was elated with their safe arrival, for too often, ninja never return. Surrounded by men, women and children, dogs, barking and jumping and wagging their tails, they appreciated their welcome. Respectfully but with a sense of urgency, the returnees were told to hurry and meet with the *Chunin*.

Inside the small church Tomoki Konnyo sat alone. His eyes were closed, his sword across his lap. Disconcertingly, his finely chiseled features were even further hardened with consternation. He presented a severe and somber image for the eight who hurried to acquiesce to his command. They all bent before him in obeisance.

Hisao-san spoke softly, "It is true. Asai Nagasama has turned on his brother-in-law and the Oda clan and rejoined the Asakura. Further, the Asakura declined an invitation to conference in Kyoto, a clear act of defiance; they are not foolish; they would not challenge "The Man on Horseback" if they didn't think they could win. Nobunaga now considers Asai Nagasama an enemy that must be punished; Nobunaga moves his men north … against the Asai … against the Asakura. Obviously, they believe their reunion will be enough to thwart Nobunaga's northward expansion, and Nobunaga would not rally against them if he did not think it highly expedient.

Interestingly, Naki-san overheard samurai who were very agitated and nervous," offered Hisso-san. "This may mean they do not believe they can succeed against the Asakura and Asai; however, may I humbly remind you, honorable Konnyo-sama, how devious Nobunaga is and how he can rekindle a victory from the ashes of defeat."

"Hisao-san, worry not. While he is preoccupied with the northern border we shall strike his eastern stronghold. We shall destroy his eastern defenses and tarnish his illusion of invincibility.

Shortly, my daughter shall return from Ogie; she will have more news. Oda Nobunaga's brother and his castle will be wiped from the face of the earth, and Oda Nobunaga will have a gaping hole in his Eastern flank. Now go eat and rest."

Naki's face blanched; he was stunned at how Tomoki Konnyo-sama could be so singular, so cold. He sent his only daughter into danger, to fraternize with the enemy, to dissemble, yet, he only seems interested in imminent intelligence. Was he not the least worried about her safety? The disengaged manner with which he conducted these affairs confused him. Where did his disaffectedness and strength of mind come from?

⸻ ✦ ⸻

As Naki and the others left, a distraught messenger arrived.

"Honorable Tomoki-sama, a message from the monastery! The herald handed Tomoki a rolled parchment, and waited patiently for the Chunin to read the report. A perturbed look contorted Tomoki Konnyo-sama's face.

"How long has the Abbot been ill?"

"Approximately two weeks," the envoy replied.

"Is it passing?"

"No, it is increasing in severity. Daily, it grows worse. He suffers severe aches of the head. He sweats uncontrollably. Often he retires to his chambers with bouts of nausea which are preceded by thick bitter salivations. When he is not sequestered in his chambers, when he tries to attend to his duties, he suffers stormy moods: one moment he is inexplicably euphoric and then as quickly his humor descends into despondency. Occasionally, he will lose his balance or fall into a terrible fit which, thankfully, eventually subsides. His affliction has raised great concerns among the people. He is unable to attend to his duties properly, so he relinquished trust to Daiske-sama, and the ronin, Zatoichi."

"What of the preparations against Ogie castle? How does that go?"

"Regrettably, not well. The samurai has taken advantage of the Abbot's delicate condition. He bullies Daiske-sama, and he forces the Abbot into acquiescing to questionable military strategies. No one is strong enough to resist him; he has usurped power."

"Nevertheless, Zatoichi, is being challenged, albiet secretly, by the elder monks. They disagree with his plans for open warfare; the elders prefer a covert night attack upon Ogie. We are familiar fighting against the enemy using the cover of surprise, and overpowering them in close combat. It is what we do and we do well. Zatoichi, however, relies upon his familiar Samurai techniques of warfare, meeting the enemy openly, head on. We are not prepared to fight in such a manner. If we do, Nobunaga's archers would decimate half our warriors before we could even begin to fight. Zatoichi sees the monks as fodder. It is not his concern how many die. We have twenty thousand men and he feels that is more than enough to ensure a victory."

"Thankfully, in a moment of surprising clarity and lucidity, Abbot Kosa-sama issued this directive. He wants to stop Zatoichi before he leads the monks of Mt. Hiei to slaughter;

he finally realized the mistake he made, and, he wants your clan, the monks of Mt Hiei and the Ikko-Ikki to assault Ogie castle … at night."

"Soon, I will know how to best conduct this matter. Tell Abbot Kosa-sama that I shall send communications to the Ikko-Ikki .We begin without delay."

"It is imperative we strike within a week. Zatoichi will not be ready before then, and if we ruin Ogie before Nobunaga fights Asakura, we may dishearten his troops and diminish his chances for success on the battle field."

"It shall be done. Reassure Abbot Kosa-sama that his wishes shall be fulfilled."

And with that he was gone.

The Chunin sat motionless with his sword across his lap, eyes half closed breathing deeply, breathing in the empowering chi from the heavens above, and searching for clarity and a solution to the present urgency. The gods will guide, he thought to himself.

Chapter 9

S ai awoke alone. Her garments had been hung neatly upon a rack. Nobuoki's valet stood attentively, impassively nearby. "I shall take you back," he said.

"*Arigato*", she answered gently.

Sai was led out of the chamber in a different manner than she entered. The valet silently escorted her through a convoluted confusion of corridors; fortunately though, artifacts displayed in the halls assisted Sai in being able to recollect the manner of her departure. One thing she noticed was that the floors did not squeak. She descended a wide staircase, in contrast to the other staircases which were very narrow, indeed. This one was a formal staircase. It led to a massive hall, and beyond the elaborately decorated entrance were heavy but beautifully ornate iron gates. Outside, a magnificent rock garden graced a pond and waterfall. The garden was full with flowering bushes, banzai trees, and elegantly situated rocks; the pond was teeming with golden Koi. Sai had never seen a garden so handsome. She realized she was being escorted though Oda Nobuoki's private quarters. So, this is how and

where he lives, she thought to herself. The valet continued
through the garden along a stone path which was bordered
by even more carefully arranged rocks, small watercourses,
and trees. The path eventually spilled out onto a large stone
terrace and then spread to an impressive staircase thirty
or forty feet long and at twenty feet wide, descending to a
walled compound.

Standing at the edge of the palisade Sai looked down
upon countless numbers of samurai and soldiers in the large
walled enclosure. Thousands of men in red and black war re-
galia were assembled, preparing to depart. Oda Nobunaga's
dreaded *mokkou* insignia emblazoned the court yard banners.

Oda Nobuoki, ceremoniously dressed, stood upon a platform erected half-way down the stone gray steps. Below,
facing him mounted on horseback, armed for battle, were
the generals from the night before. Sai could not hear what
Nobuoki was saying to them, but she could tell by their obvious restlessness that they were more anxious to begin their
journey than to listen to his uninspiring oratory.

When he finally concluded, Taiko war drums sounded:
slowly at first, and as the martial beat progressed, rhythmically and purposefully, increasing in volume and intensity,
the horses, accustomed to the percussive prelude, began to
neigh and shake their manes; some reared in the anticipation of a sudden release from the confines of the yard into
the expanse beyond the castle. They were ready to run. The
pounding ceased abruptly and a terrifying war cry issued
from the thousands below, inducing a spasm of anxiety into
the very depths of Sai's chi.

The gates of the walled enclosure groaned open, and the

ranks of men divided, forming a wide corridor; whereupon, the generals on horseback turned and galloped through the mass of black and red clad, cheering soldiers. As soon as their commanders crossed the threshold of the palace gates the horde followed, issuing unholy grunts and hollers.

Without waiting for the compound to clear, Oda Nobuoki turned and ascended the stone steps. Sai turned to the valet and whispered, "Why did you bring me here?

"My lord wished it so."

"Why?"

"I do not know. Ask him yourself."

As Lord Nobuoki climbed, he lifted his head and saw Sai. "Ah, you are here. I was hoping you would be. Did you see? Three hundred samurai, three thousand warriors from allying provinces, as well as two thousand of my own men. Off to Kyoto to face the traitors in the north. Impressive! No?"

"Yes."

"May they continue to victory and may the enemies of my illustrious brother understand that opposition to the unification of Japan is fruitless. Japan will be one nation under one sword. It is fate. Too long has Nippon suffered and wasted its people with warring clans pitted against one another, senselessly fighting for honor, pride ... control over a small parcel of land. For hundreds of years, war has divided and weakened us, daimyo opposing daimyo. One clan eventually ascends only to be tormented with when and how their dominion will be usurped; how long will they possess what has cost them so dearly to achieve?

Deceit, subterfuge, treachery are necessary essentials for survival in this land: son against father, brother versus brother, nephew killing uncle. Is this how we were meant to live? And what is the cost of this iniquity? Countless lives lost to war; towns and villages destroyed. Once Japan is unified by one imperial ruler, relentless and senseless slaughter will cease. Order shall be established. Peace will become reality.

And now to add more to our concerns, the world is at our doorstep. The Portuguese priests tell us how countries beyond our isolated island are developing, powerfully. If Japan does not change, it will be lost. The English and Dutch are already upon our shores, not many now, but more will come. If we are not unified and strong, together, thousands of years of heritage will disappear. We will be swallowed by the Western world. If we do not unify and if we remain divided we will succumb to forces stronger and more sophisticated than us; however, unified we may endure.

The world is changing. My brother sees this; unfortunately, his enemies do not. They hold onto the past. They are short sighted in trying to keep their pathetic little provinces. A new world is before us. Ah, but I see you do not fully understand what it is I am saying. I am sorry to have troubled you with my diatribe. I did not mean to. I meant to give you this."

He held out a small parchment "It is my seal. I wish for you to return in a few days, at a more opportune time. Present this to my guards at the castle gates. They will summon an escort to have you brought directly to me. I wish to hear you sing and see you dance again."

Sai was silent. After a long awkward moment, sweetly lying she answered: "I would be honored."

"Now, you must go. My attendant will take you to your friends. They are waiting for you."

Sai bowed, and he continued alone across the terrace and into the palace gardens. Sai sensed a melancholy and sadness in him as he disappeared behind the bushes and the trees. She wondered if he really believed what he was telling her. Sai believed he sought peace, but she wasn't sure if he truly believed that his brother's warring ways were the means to ensuring Japan's future. Unfortunately, he was impotent, too fond of comfort to protest. For a brief moment she felt sorry for him, but she quickly reminded herself that he is the demon's brother, a collaborator, an accomplice to the violence which has ravaged the land. His fortress must be destroyed; he must die.

Coldly, without sentiment, Sai was satisfied. She knew how many men left to join Oda Nobunaga in Kyoto and she knew that the defenses of the castle were now compromised. As she followed the valet down the massive steps into the courtyard, she impassively surveyed the walls making note of the ramparts running along the top. She noted that archers positioned there could easily fend off an invasion of the grounds, and that unfortunately the ornate iron gates could protect the inner palace. Further, the confusing halls and corridors would give Nobuoki and his entourage enough time to escape through any number of secret passages out of the castle. She reasoned that a small invasion force was necessary: first to dispose of the regent, and then for a full out assault on the remaining forces to eliminate Ogie as a defensive bastion against Kyoto.

Nobuoki's valet did not escort Sai across the compound as she thought he would; instead, he turned right at the bottom of the steps and led her to the west wall. He reached a barricade of solid stone and magically opened a small hidden portal. It was entirely invisible; no one could have noticed this gateway from the courtyard.

The opening led to a small stand of coniferous tress. Though there was not a path clear through, one could make a way under the limbs. After battling a few branches, they emerged onto a path that she and her companions were on the previous day. She was taken to the captain of a gate and he was instructed to lead Sai to the performers waiting outside the castle's south wall. The valet bowed politely, smiled and promptly vanished into the complex.

—————◦《◉》◦—————

Seeing that Sai was safe, Saburo and the others were ready to depart. As Yoshi helped her little cousin into the carriage she looked into her eyes and asked, "Everything alright?"

"Hai," said Sai. "I will tell you everything," and she stepped into the coach.

By the Hour of the Snake, Sai had told Yoshi and Saburo all that she knew. They were making headway along the road, anxious to return to home. Raiden, on post for any signs of trouble, looked behind him and saw a slight cloud of dust in the distance. Horses he noted, racing horses. "Saburo-san," he shouted. "We are being pursed."

Saburo turned to where he could see. "Five, six horses riding quickly," he said. "They must be from the castle. Arm yourselves." Everyone withdrew a weapon from the secret compartment in the trunk filled with props: knives, short swords, bows and arrows.

The cloud of dust disappeared around a bend and the sound of galloping hooves became entirely too distinct. Shortly, the riders were visible in the distance. They approached quickly, shouting harsh commands: "Halt!"

Saburo stopped and waited for the horsed men to reach them. The leader dismounted … along with four others. One remained astride his horse. He was holding the reins of an extra steed. Saburo immediately understood why.

"Where are you going?" The leader, a samurai, shouted in a gruff, belligerent manner. "Where are you going?"

"Home," Saburo answered obsequiously, so as not to offend the officious, angry warrior.

"The girl, Sai, is to come with us."

Saburo made a mistake and answered, "But, we are on our way home."

The samurai exploded and withdrew his sword. "Lord Nobuoki commands she return with us. It is done. Seize her," he pointed the blade towards the carriage. The four samurai ran to the *jinrikisha* and flung open the door. Sai and Yoshi were firmly pulled from the coach.

Sai looked at Saburo and by the look in his eyes she knew what she must do, as did everyone else.

Yoshi shuffled to Sai and hugged her and giggled, "Oh Sai, the gods have blessed you. You have been chosen." She coyly turned to the samurai and asked, "Is there room for one more? I am sure I can make the Lord equally happy."

"We have only one horse."

"I can ride with her," she begged.

"No! Only her."

Yoshi gambled and approached the samurai. Demurely, she asked, "What about you? Are you not in need of comfort? I would be very good to you. I have taught her everything she knows."

Sheathing his sword, he said, "No!"

Yoshi persisted and pressed herself against him. She placed her hands upon his chest and began to massage. She found his ribs and using her thumbs she rubbed firmly. His mistake was to accept the attention for a moment. It was long enough. With her right hand she reached into her sleeve and grabbed the handle of a long, very sharp, thin blade concealed there. Finding the spot over his heart, she plunged it into his chest, between the ribs. He issued a soft, "Ugh!" stood motionless for a moment and fell on top of Yoshi pinning her to the ground.

The others laughed thinking the samurai was going to have his way with this accommodating courtesan - right there, right now. They turned, blocking Saburo and the others preventing them from interfering. While their backs were turned Yoshi rolled the dead captain onto his back and straddled him pretending she was a willing participant. She hoisted her kimono and continued. The four guarding the group were distracted, turning their heads watching the samurai.

One of them shouted, "Captain, maybe we should bring her back with us. We could all enjoy her." An ugly laugh followed. They all looked at each other with smug, fatuous grins on their faces.

Sai ran to the guard, still upon his horse, placed her hands upon his thigh and suggested he dismount. He acquiesced, and got down.

Yoshi was putting on a captivating performance. The men were now fully engaged with the samurai and his pleasure. That was the moment Saburo was waiting for. With their heads turned, he reached for his short sword and swiftly swung it up from his hip across the throat of the brute closest to him. Crimson splatter sprayed the face of a nearby warrior. Angrily, he turned to protest the intrusion without realizing it was the blood of his comrade. A flurry of violent movement ended their preoccupation with the show. Kenta initiated his move as soon as he saw Saburo reaching for his sword and was upon his man in an instant. A short blade passed through the back of his neck. Raiden was too far from his man to strike with a knife or a sword so a shuriken between the shoulder blades was sufficient. Two remained, outnumbered, they sought to flee. Sai stood in the way of the horseman and his horse. He laughed at the diminutive figure standing between him and his escape. She raised the blowpipe and puffed a lethal dart into his forehead. He fell to his knees and then Saburo was upon him. The remaining warrior not wishing to succumb to a similar fate dropped to his knees and begged for his life. Raiden struck him in the neck; he buckled and fell to the ground.

Saburo immediately began to slash the dead bodies. Kenta watched as he stood and studied each dead man then methodically cut at the arm, or the face. "Saburo -san, they are dead! Kenta said in a subdued, quiet voice. Saburo replied equally as calm, "When they do not return with Sai within a reasonable amount of time, others will be sent to look for them. We must make it seem as if they were attacked by thieves. Take their weapons!" He ordered. "Put them in the trunk. There are enough horses for us all. We ride until we reach the village."

The seven rode furiously through the night. The horses aggressively pounded a path home. Saburo, driving the wagon, skillfully kept up, coming, several times, close to careening over a ledge in the dark.

The dawn was a troubled gray when Sai and company drove into the compound. Tomoki roused by the commotion was standing on the porch anxiously. He knew something unexpected had happened.

Sai dismounted and approached her father while the others led the horses to the stable. Konnyo-sama looked deeply into the eyes of his daughter. She respectfully bowed and stoically proceeded inside. Tomoki followed.

She recounted the mission. He was pleased with the intelligence, but somewhat troubled by the samurai encounter. It would place the castle on alert. They may not know what happened, but they will know that something is amiss, and they will be on guard. It would only make their next mission more complicated.

Naki waited impatiently, outside. When Sai emerged, she stopped and smiled at him. "You were successful?" she said.

He studied her carefully. Was she changed? She seemed the same. She didn't seem different.

"Yes," Naki said. "And you?"

"Yes," and she left it at that.

Naki didn't press. He wanted to know the details, but he knew his place.

"Come," she said, "let us go see the new horses. They are beautiful."

Naki followed full of questions, but he dared not ask, even one. She will tell me when the time is right, maybe, he thought.

The horses whinnied and neighed when she entered the stable. She greeted each one with a loving stroke of the nose and each one responded … with a neigh, a flicker of the mane or a swish of the tail. The horses sensed her spirit immediately and accepted their new surroundings. They knew their home was good. They would be cared for.

"Choose one," she said, "It will be yours."

Surprised, Naki gratefully inspected the animals. He chose a medium sized, well muscled horse with a prominent white stripe on its back. "I shall name it *Jun*, swift steed, as it looks strong and quick. I believe it has a strong heart.

Sai agreed, "I also would have chosen that one."

Naki led the warhorse to a stall near his quarters. "I shall take good care of you," he said, "and, I know you will take care of me." *Jun* snorted and bobbed its head as in agreement.

Sai laughed. "You have a friend."

"I have two, Naki said seriously, looking directly at Sai.

"Yes, you do Naki-san," she replied with a smile. "Do not worry, all is well," as if she were able to read Naki's thoughts. "I must go," and she left.

Naki struggled with his thoughts of Sai. She is fine he told himself. Do not trouble yourself, he thought. He let go of his preoccupation and proceeded to the little shrine for meditation.

Chapter 10

Hisao found Naki at the sanctuary seated upon the plain wooden bench.

"Nakamura-san, Konnyo-sama wishes to speak with you. Please come."

Naki found the *Chunin*, sitting alone. Eventually he spoke, "Nakamura-san, the Abbot is ill. There is weighty concern. He suffers bouts of delirium. His disorder came upon him very suddenly ... too suddenly. There is something amiss. The monastery is in turmoil, much dissention, I am afraid. Apparently, it was the Abbot's will for Zatoichi to marshal the monks for the attack on Ogie, but he is recklessly endangering lives. What he is planning will lead to the senseless death of thousands. The elders do not condone his methods, but he claims he had the confidence of the Abbot, and now that the Abbot is indisposed he has assumed authority over the planning and strategy of the attack, as well as ministering to the Abbot's recovery. No one gets to see the Abbot but him. Somehow, he has commandeered control over the monastery and the Abbot. Opposition is difficult; the elders are powerless as Zatoichi has support among many of the younger, vociferous and volatile monks. While many see his actions as an unadulterated usurping of control, they find themselves incapable to reverse what the Abbot has seemingly decreed. The Abbot is rarely lucid and is sequestered by Zatoichi. You are to go to Mt Hiei. Speak with the Abbot if you can…if he can. The Abbot loves you; you are a son to him. Find out what is to be done.

You can gain access to the Abbot's room via the north wall, no one will see you. It is sheer and high, but I know you can climb it. The Abbot is unattended at night.

After you meet with him, if he has anything to say, you are to tell the monk, Sora, to send me a message. By morning, the elders will receive a response. It will tell them what they are to do; the Abbot's official seal upon it will dispel any doubt as to its authenticity. We must displace this Zatoichi. Return immediately.

Go! Take your horse. Sai said you chose a good one. Hisao-san will guide you to a road with which you will be familiar. Ride quickly."

"I leave immediately."

The sun at its zenith burned powerfully. Occasionally, small clouds provided intermittent shade as Naki furiously charged down the mountain road. Jun was everything one could expect of a horse: strong, swift and full of life. Naki was entirely occupied with his horse, with his riding, with his own horsemanship. He felt empowered, full of himself, oblivious to everything including the intuitions that hinted he was in danger. He ignored the subtle warnings and continued to ride, recklessly.

However, Jun sensed danger, coming to a sudden stop, sending Naki tumbling wildly and painfully onto the stony path. His loud indignant howl of profanity was drowned out by an overridingly fierce sound: a roar. The monster panther stood on the road in front of him, snarling, hostile. Agitated, it skulked back and forth from one side of the road to the other repeatedly growling and bearing its massive, white fangs. Naki lay on his back paralyzed with pain and fear. Jun whinnied sharply, reared onto its hind legs, and beat the air with its hooves. It did not turn or run, but stood its ground. The panther continued its side to side swagger, bellowing horrifying yowls and growls. Naki heard himself punctuating the cacophony with expletives as Jun continued whining shrieks of panic. The hellish clamor could have terrified Tengu, the mountain demon himself. Then the panther stopped. It stood still a moment, gazed into Naki's eyes and then vanished, as suddenly as it appeared. Jun quit pounding the air with its hooves.

Bewildered and bleeding Naki rose; he looked around to ensure that he was safe. Securing Jun's reins, he whispered, "Thank you Jun for your courage. You saved me. I knew you would take care of me. Your warrior spirit frightened the beast, and we are both safe."

He inspected his abrasions and determined them to be superficial. Nothing was broken. He was intact. Mounting his horse, he looked into the woods for any more signs of danger. It was quiet; the horse was still. With a hand upon Jun's chest, Naki could, feel the beating of his heart: slow, rhythmic, strong. He looked up and saw a hawk perched upon a rocky outcrop high up the mountain. He could see its large yellow eyes sternly looking down upon him, its hooked beak open, its tongue protruding. He heard it squawking, chastising. Its wings half open, vigorously flapping, obviously distressed, yet not ready to fly. He looked to the tops of the trees. In the pines, he saw a dragon fly struggling with a sticky spider's web. A patient predator was waiting on the edge of the web for its victim to cease struggling and for it to begin its digestion. Naki sniffed the air and the scent of death assaulted his nose. He mounted Jun and departed quickly, but not recklessly. His former exhilaration had sobered and Naki was now attentive – to everything.

The road down the mountain led to a level clearing and a cluster of buildings. Slowly, he proceeded through the maze of dwellings that comprised the cloister of Mt. Hiei, down through narrow roads which connected thousands of buildings, homes, shrines, and temples; thirty thousand people found sanctuary in the complex, and they owed their lives, their safety to one man: Abbot Kosa, and he was ill. Why?

As he wound his way towards the main temple, people stirred with excitement. They were aware that he had returned. Naki was astounded. The closer he came to his own barrack the greater the commotion. No one approached him but the smiles and chatter were clear. He tied his horse to the post outside his quarters. A large crowd followed him. Not a moment more after he dismounted, Ryun came storming out the door and enveloped Naki in a joyous embrace. He lifted him up, spun him around shouting expletives of happiness and admonition. "Where the hell have you been? You bastard! Oh it is so good to see you. You are safe. I was worried. No one knew where you were. Where have you been? Let me look at you. Ugh! You are scraped and bloody! What happened? Rogues, bastards! I will kill them. Who did this to you? Tell me! I will destroy them!"

"I fell off my horse."

"You fell off your horse? A roar of laughter boomed from the burly beast, and he grabbed Naki and squeezed him again till Naki thought his eyes would pop.

"Stop!" he managed to scream. "You are killing me."

Ryu let him go. Gasping for air, Naki bent trying to recover from the overwhelming welcome only to be greeted with a stupendous slap to the back nearly knocking him flat to the ground.

Ryu grabbed him by the back of his shirt and lifted him up onto his feet. "Where have you been? I have missed you my friend."

"I have missed you too, my friend." Naki looked around at the amused crowd, "But we cannot speak here." Shortly thereafter, the crowd dispersed. The two friends watched as the crowd disappeared and then proceeded inside for privacy.

"So, where have you been? How could you just leave without telling me where you were going and what you were doing?"

"Abbot Kosa sent me for more training," Naki answered trying to be as forthright as possible but without revealing too much.

"Where could you get better training than here with me," Ryu cracked, his infectious smile spreading across his face.

"Nowhere," Naki replied.

"Correct!" Ryu resounded.

"Ryu? What of the Abbot? He is ill."

"Sadly, yes. Suddenly, he became sick. No one seems to know why. It came upon him very quickly. We see very little of him."

"Does no one find this strange?"

"Yes, everyone, but we are preoccupied with our preparations against Nobunaga. Zatoichi has told us he has the physicians monitoring the Abbot's affliction and that we are to concern ourselves with the upcoming battle."

"How does that go?"

"Not well, Zatoichi is a harsh and ruthless master. He is training the monks for open field battle. They are not familiar with this style of war and they are not adjusting well. He is imposing traditional methods of open warfare: ranks, flanks, marching. We are monks. We ambush, we surprise, we strike when the enemy does not expect. We are not rank and file warriors. We are too independent. We fight, overwhelming the enemy with spirit not with strategy, nor with battle field tactics, but with the ferocity, numbers and stealth. He refuses to accept this and tries to mold us into what we are not. When we do not execute as he commands he berates and punishes. The morale is very low. Many believe that he is preparing us for doom. However, he has a faction of monks who are with him and support him with fanatic devotion. It is beyond my comprehension as to why."

"I must speak with the Abbot."

"That will be difficult. He sees no one. Zatoichi ensures that he is not disturbed."

"I must see him, where is he?"

"He is sequestered in his chambers where he has been for three weeks."

"Sequestered?"

"Only Zatoichi's doctors are allowed to see him and sometimes Daiske-sama, but he tells us that Abbot Kosa is never coherent when he sees him."

"There is something wrong, Ryu."

"I do believe so, but what can we do? Zatoichi tells us that the Abbot in times of occasional clarity tells him what to do and that we are to obey."

"Daiske-sama is powerless. The monks are disheartened. They will not fight well.

"I will see him. Please Ryu-san, inform the elders and have them meet me in at the temple."

———— ≈《O》≈ ————

Naki stepped out into the courtyard where Zatoichi was stroking his horse. "Ah, so you have finally returned. I thought you had been killed or perhaps had fled. Is this your horse? Where did you get it?"

"It was a gift."

"A very special gift. Do you know what kind of horse this is?"

"No."

"It is a Kiso. A rare breed. A fine horse. Much too fine

for you. You must have been very successful in your mission to have been given such a horse. Good then, come you must tell me everything you have learned."

"I will see the Abbot."

"No!" he thundered. The Abbot is ill. I am in charge. You will tell me everything and you will tell me now. Come!" Ten men that Naki did not recognize appeared around him, threatening. Naki understood the samurai mentality. If angered by someone they consider to be beneath them they lop off a head. Naki knew that Zatoichi was intoxicated with power, and that if he chose to kill him right then, he would do so with little remorse, so choosing to comply and follow was an easy decision.

Zatoichi led him to the Lotus Hall. Once seated in the Abbot's seat, Zatoichi commanded, "What have you discovered about Castle Ogi? How many warriors?

Naki lied. "Fifteen to twenty thousand men are stationed." He did not want Zatoichi to know that Ogie was guarded by only a skeleton crew of men; he did not want Zatoichi to change his plan; he did not want Zatoichi easily taking Ogie and gaining power and prestige. Zatoichi needed to be removed.

"Well armed, well trained."

"Ah, is that so?"

"Yes." He replied and remained silent.

"Is that all you have to report?"

"*Hai*, the castle is infested with samurai. We were not able to discover anything other than it was heavily fortified with many men."

"Nothing more?"

"No."

"You useless piece of shit. Is that all you bring back? Is all you have to report? I could have surmised that much myself and without wasting precious time. I do not know what the Abbot sees in you or why he sent you and that silly girl to get information. So, who gave you the gift!? And, why? And, what of the girl? What did she discover?"

"Nothing. She did not go. She fell sick."

"Sick, eh?"

"Yes. She did not go. Just me and a few others."

"You and a few others?

"Yes."

"I see … .You are to return to your barracks!. Tomorrow you will train with the monks."

"I must see the Abbot."

"No one sees the Abbot!"

Rather than challenge him and grateful that he didn't press any further about his horse, Naki bowed obsequiously and left.

Ryu dependable as ever gathered the elder monks and was waiting for Naki at the temple. Daiske-sama was seated in front of rows of wise and wizened men. He motioned for Naki to take a seat beside him. Naki was stunned at the honor. He sat and waited for the elder to speak. Ryu was sitting at the back of the room. Just being allowed to be in the presence of this esteemed group was an honor for him. He sat, beaming,

Daiske-sama spoke. "We must conduct this business quickly. Zatoichi has spies. If we are discovered collaborating and plotting he has enough influence to have us put to death. What says the honorable Tomoki-sama?" He turned to Naki.

Naki flustered that he was to advise this eminent group of men coughed and cleared his throat before he spoke. "Tomoki-sama agrees. The open attack upon castle Ogi is not the way. Ogie can be taken more efficiently in a different manner. The Tomoki clan and the warrior monks of Ikko-Ikki are prepared to join with the Tendai to incur at night."

"Very good! It is as I had hoped. If Tomoki-sama believes a night incursion will succeed, that is what we shall do. We have many loyal, shrewd monks who can temporize, play the fools, and pretend incompetence to retard his plans.

"How is the Abbot sick?"

"We do not know for sure but we suspect he is being poisoned. Zatoichi is in charge of his well being. He feeds him and doctors him, with the intention of eventually killing him."

"Then he must be stopped, immediately."

"*Hai!* However, he has followers, young and foolish. They protect him. Any displacement of his newly acquired power would result in bloodshed. Abbot Kosa erred in placing too much trust in this man. He seeks revenge upon the Oda clan, but he wants to do it his way, gloriously. He wishes to restore his respect and to be elevated to his former position of power and prominence, and he sees the warrior monks fighting in a conventional battle as a means to do so. He wishes to rule: the monastery, this province, maybe many provinces; maybe he wants to replace Oda Nobunaga as the unifier of Japan, who knows. He is obsessed, drunk with power."

"I must see the Abbot before I send the message."

"It is impossible. He is well guarded."

"Is the monk Sora here with us?"

"*Hai,*" a voice responded.

"Good, then meet me in my quarters at the Hour of the Tiger. We will send a message after I meet with the Abbott."

With that the clandestine meeting concluded. Everyone disappeared into the recess of the temple. Naki and Ryu sat alone. Ryu spoke. "What do you intend to do?"

"See the Abbot."

"How?"

"Come with me." The barracks were empty and Naki unrolled his travelling pack to reveal the claw like apparatus for climbing walls. "They are *shuko* and *ashiko*. I will use them to climb the wall to the Abbot's window.

"Nakamura-san, the walls are stone and the window is high. How can you do this?"

"Easily, my friend."

Ryu shook his head in disbelief, but did not argue.

"When do you plan to do this?" Ryu asked.

"At the hour of the Rat. The moon is dark and I will not be seen. I will have enough time to speak to the Abbot and return to meet the elders. You will wait for me at the base of the wall. If anyone comes by distract them from the window."

"Hai, I will do so. If anyone passes they will forever regret they ever ventured out on a moonless night."

"Good, so then we wait."

"Tea?" Ryu inquired and began poking the embers of a nearly dead fire looking for a spark of life.

The sun set and clouds further darkened the sky. Rumblings of thunder were heard in the distant mountains. Ryu slapped his sword. "I am ready." he said.

"So am I," said Naki as he emerged from behind a bush He was dressed in black cotton from head to foot. A hood covered his head and a mask his face. His hands and feet clad in metal claws.

"You are terrifying," Ryu whispered. "You look like a black cat."

Under the mask Naki smiled. "Cats can't do this," and he proceeded to scale the stones leading to the window forty feet above the ground.

"I will catch you if you fall," Ryu whispered.

"I won't fall".

Ryu marveled at the quickness of his ascent. When he disappeared up the wall, Ryu squatted and waited.

Naki was up the wall and to the window ledge faster than even he himself expected. He peered through the wooden slats of the shutters. The room was dark except for the flicker of one solitary candle. The weak flame threw enough light for Naki to see the Abbot's form lying on the cot. He was alone. Naki entered. He perched himself on the window's ledge and removed his claws. Padding softly across the wood floor he approached the Abbot. Removing his head dress so as not to startle the weakened monk, in the delicate light of the candle, he saw a much smaller man than he remembered. The illness was profound. The Abbotts's eyes were sunken, and dark purple patches underscored them. His face was yellow, and he had lost much weight since Naki had seen him last. His face was tense; his lips were dry and cracked, and his breathing was labored.

Naki looked for water and found a vessel close by on the floor. Gently, he cradled the revered monk's head in his arms and dripped a little water. His lips moved slightly licking the drops. Opening his eyes, "Nakamura-san!" he wheezed.

"Do not speak, Abbott Kosa-sama. Drink!"

The Abbot opened his mouth and drank. With the little strength he had in his arms he pulled Naki's head close to his mouth. He spoke with great difficulty, hoarsely, quietly, punctuated with long pauses. "Nakamura- san, I have made a mistake .... I trusted Zatoichi ... I do not know how I could have been so foolish. He now controls everything: the elders ... the monastery ... my house ... and me. I am in his care and he is poisoning me.

"Venerable Abbot Kosa-sama, I will kill him ... you will be free of him and his treachery."

"Nakamura - san, ...we cannot hazard so many lives. He has many supporters ... some who believe his authority comes from me ... others who just follow him for whatever reason. I gave him license to train the monks and plan against Nobunaga. In my illness, he has assumed complete control ... unfortunately, my loyal monks follow his directives, re-gardless how foolish or misguided they may be. Many may die, either at Ogie or in rebellion against him. I cannot re-scind my edict without division and loss of life; I am declared delirious, incompetent, my authority is no longer sacrosanct; no one can see me; he has me on my death bed. Should I die, he could take the monestary."

"Abbot Kosa-sama, I will send a message to Konnyo –sama. He will issue a document which will correct the mat-ter; the document will be official with your seal. The monks must then believe you have relieved Zatoichi of his authority and must listen to the honorable Daiske-sama instead."

"No, Nakamura-san, this will not work. Zatoichi will not relinquish authority without a fight. We must remove all doubt. Only my physical presence, my spoken words, can restore my mandate."

"Then we will storm the residence and free you."

"No! Men will die. My blunder will diminish confidence in me as spiritual leader and physical protector. We must conduct this differently, so my supremacy is unequivocally restored.

"How do we do this?"

"I must seem to die and then return from the dead to restore order."

Naki, dumbfounded, listened with mouth agape.

"Daiske-sama is to gather a mushroom from the forest's edge. It grows in the dark moist parts of the woods. It is all white with a rounded top and a thick ring around the stem. He can recognize it, and he will make sure it is fed to me. It will place me in a coma with all the appearances of being dead.

The mushroom Zatoichi uses acts slowly; this one acts more quickly. Zatoichi will think he succeeded with me finally dead. Tradition dictates I am buried with the dignity of my position, and I will be prepared for burial by the elders. Once my body is out of the hands of Zatoichi and in the hands of my own trusted people, it is then that Daiske-sama will administer seeds from the milk thistle which will counteract the poisons I have been fed, and I will revive. Keri tea will cleanse my body and I quickly will be free from all toxins. After having recovered, within a matter of days, I can appear … and resume charge. Zatoichi will never know that he has been thwarted; he will only think that it was unfortunate fate that his plan did not succeed. No blood will have been shed and the monastery will still be in my control."

Naki was astounded by the plan. "Abbot Kosa-sama, this sounds too dangerous."

"No, it must be done." Once I have recovered then we shall attack Ogie castle in the most prudent manner, at night, a surprise attack. We have men to accomplish this."

"Abbot Kosa-sama, the castle is lightly guarded. Most of the samurai left to fight Asakura, to the north."

"Even better!. Good then, I have renewed hope. Naki-san you have done well. Now go and deliver this plan to Daiske-sama. Take this as proof that you spoke to me. Daiske-sama gave it to me the last time I saw him. He will know what you say comes from me and is my wish."

Abbot Kosa gave Naki a string of beads. "Now go before you are discovered. I will see you soon."

Naki took the beads, placed the Abbot's head gently on his pillow and left.

Ryu was still waiting at the base of the wall and heard Naki descending. Once on the ground, Naki removed his iron claws and brusquely said, "Come we must go."

Ryu followed as Naki raced ahead. At the steps of the temple, where they sat and waited for the elders to arrive, Ryu, struggling to catch his breath, said, "So, my young friend, you leave a man and return a spider? Where did you learn this trick?"

"Ryu, my trusted friend, I cannot tell you."

"I understand Naki-san. Secrets, here, are a way of life."

Both sat in silence in the dark waiting to enter the temple. Behind them they heard the large wooden doors creak, and they slipped through the opening made for them.

The elders, already assembled, were waiting for Naki. Again, Ryu took his place at the rear of the assembly. He assumed he was a defense should there be an unexpected intrusion.

Naki once more sat in the place of honor and esteem. Ryu was proud of his young friend who had risen to such heights of respect.

Naki spoke. "I have seen the Abbot." Murmurs of surprise purled through the small assembly. "He gave me these to assure you that what I say is his will." Naki handed the beads to Daiske-sama.

"These beads I gave to the Abbot the last time I spoke with him. Naki-san has seen Abbot Kosa-sama. What did he tell you?"

The dangerous plan was revealed and the monks were silent. At last, Daiske-sama spoke. "The Abbot is familiar with poisons and antidotes. The plan is perilous, but possible. I can see how this will solve our dilemma. We will begin immediately."

Naki reminded them that a carrier pigeon is to be sent to Tomoki Konnyo. Sora was dispatched to do so. Daiske-sama said we will send another when the Abbot is revived and resumes control. In the meantime, we will continue training to battle the castle according to Zatoichi's plan. If all goes well, the Abbot should be well in a matter of days.

Chapter 11

Naki said farewell to Ryu this time."*Doumo*, goodbye, my friend." Ryu stood stolidly, like a stump. "*Dewa mata*, see you later."

Digging his heels into Jun's flanks, Nakamura cantered into the night.

Unfortunately, Ryu's intuitive senses were not as acute as Naki's and he did not sense that he was being watched from the shadows. He returned to the barracks where his fellow monks were sleeping after a day of rigorous training. Zatoichi's minions worked them daily for long hours never giving them any time to rest nor recover from injuries. They were a disgruntled lot, abused and berated: however, they endured Zatoichi's training as he was the Abbot's General and in complete command of the preparations.

Ryu smiled to himself when he thought how grateful they will all be when the Abbot returns. He fell asleep, a dark, fitful sleep.

Naki rode cautiously along the mountain's path. The night's pitch sobered him; he did not ride recklessly. Jun apparently was accustomed to riding at night and confidently negotiated the perils of the narrow black road. This time Naki's senses were on alert. He had a foreboding feeling. Other than the normal nocturnal issuances from the woods and Jun's rhythmic clopping, nothing seemed out of the ordinary. No matter how hard he peered ahead and around him he could not see anything: nevertheless, he was disquieted.

Just before dawn displaced the night, Naki arrived at the mountain compound. Quietly, he led Jun to the stable. He rubbed him down, fed him hay, and gathered water from the bubbling brook. Now, it was time for him to rest. His quarters had been tended to. His cot clean, neat and tight, it awaited his tired body. He lay down and quickly fell asleep.

This time his dream was different. Instead of pounding hooves, clamorous hollering, and screeching shrieks fouling the air it was whispering: nervous, agitated, chaotic whispering. He saw shadowy men huddled tightly together hissing to each other in a frenetic mania. Amidst the clamor, central to the pandemonium, sat a stumpy bearded man, with massive shoulders, no neck to speak of and a face dominated by a bumpy nose. As the din rose in intensity the ugly man's grotesque head transformed into a bird's with small cold eyes and a hooked beak. The creature man lifted his arms and they turned into large wings which lifted him above the bedlam. His feet had changed into large claws with prodigious talons. He beat the air and the men beneath him with his large wings and lifted himself/itself above the crowd of cowering men and took to the air.

"Naki?" Sai's gentle voice floated into his consciousness. He opened his eyes and examined a creature of delicate beauty smiling dazzlingly upon him. "Are you well?"

"Yes," Naki responded.

"Your face was contorted. You were tossing restlessly. Did you have another of your dreams?"

"I did, but this one was unlike the others."

"How so?"

"A hideous man was among many men angrily whispering about something. Then this man turned into an ugly bird and flew into the sky."

"Tengu!."

"What?"

"Tengu, the demon of war. You saw a spirit, a demon. He foreshadows war. Religious clerics, who live in the mountains, who follow the teachings of Old Shinto, Buddhism, most specifically, *Shugendo*, which means the path of training and testing strive for enlightenment through the study of how man and nature bind with one another. The enlightened ones claim the demon of war is part bird and part man. That is what you saw. Your meditations are progressing very quickly. Devoted men have spent years trying to achieve an understanding between man and beast, trying to bring them together in the spirit of harmonious coexistence. You, however, within two meditations, envisage your own animal spirit, and now you have seen *Tengu*. You are a blessed being."

"The cat! I saw him again," Naki exclaimed. He blocked

EDMUND KOLBUSZ

my path on the way to the monastery. I was thrown from my horse and he growled at me ferociously, snarling, blocking my way. I thought he would tear me apart, but he did not attack. He just disappeared into the trees."

"The cat is your protector. He was protecting you."

"How?"

"He was warning you."

"About what?"

"I am not sure. How did this occur?"

"I told you, on the way to the monastery, on the road. I was the wind. Jun and I were one with the road. I had never felt so exhilarated. It was magnificent. There was nothing but me and my horse."

"And the cat?"

It blocked the road; I was thrown to the ground; Jun stayed to protect me rearing and striking out with its front hooves. The cat paced back and forth across the road as if it were angry, as if it was chastising me for something. And then it vanished."

"Perhaps, it wanted to tell you something."

"Such as what?"

"Not to be so preoccupied with one thing that you block important signs.

"What was I preoccupied with?"

"Your enjoyment in riding like the wind, perhaps; you were inattentive to your surroundings. You were on a dangerous road. You needed your wits about you. Maybe, it was telling you to keep all your senses alert. The cat hears, sees, and smells to survive. Apparently, you had forgotten yourself and were in danger."

Naki, listened. He knew she was right. He had learned this lesson even before Sai made it clear to him now, since on the way back, he was mindful of everything.

"Sai, I think I understood somewhere deep within my spirit what the cat was telling me, for on the way back, I was more attentive. There was no threat; however, I felt anxious … and now you tell me I can see … demons? Was the demon after me?"

"I don't know, *Tengu* is the spirit of chaos and war, but, sometimes it is seen as a protector; it is dangerous, yet strangely helpful. I do not know what the significance of the dream was. We must be most careful in everything we do; there is danger everywhere."

———

Ryu was deep asleep when he felt the first whack of the bamboo stick across his arm and then his legs. The pain numbed his appendages. He received several more as he rose up to challenge whoever was beating him, but was struck harder and more viciously, and then he was violently hoisted out his cot. Many hands dragged him from the barracks. By the time feeling returned to his limbs he was tightly bound and on the floor of an abandoned ramshackle hut. He was surrounded by many men. The circle of bodies parted and a stout set of legs stood before him. They belonged to Zatoichi. The samurai towered over him and sneered. "Ito Nakamura, where has he gone? He rode north into the mountains late at night. Where did he go?"

Ryu rolled onto his back and looked at his inquisitor. Defiantly he growled, "Untie me now and I promise not to rip off your arms." Zatoichi nodded to one of the encircling party and Ryu was struck several more times.

"I will not ask again. Where did he go?"

"I do not know. He did not tell me."

"There is nothing north of here. No towns, no villages, nothing. Where did he go?"

"I tell you, I do not know."

"What do you know?"

Ryu decided it was not wise to further infuriate the samurai, so he chose to play the fawning fool. Obsequiously, he replied, "I know you are the most honorable commander in charge. I know that the venerable Abbot Kosa to whom we all owe allegiance and servitude has entrusted you to lead us to victory. I know this."

"Do you know the Abbot is dead? Do you know that I am in charge? Do you know I perceive that you and that insipid little friend of yours to be traitors? Now, where did he go?"

He nodded again and Ryu received an unholy series of strikes. A lesser man would have lost consciousness, but Ryu was solid and withstood the assault.

"He is ninja. So is that stupid female. Where did they go? Where are they located?"

Again Ryu truthfully replied, "I do not know."

"Why was he here? He had information. To whom did he pass this information? Conceivably, it was that incompetent, Daiske. I shall deal with him after the funeral."

He nodded to his men. "Maybe the fragments of bamboo

driven deep under his nails will loosen his tongue. I will come back later to see if the iron man bends any." Zatoichi left the hut as did another, but in a different direction.

—————————

"Were you in danger?" Naki tendered to ask.

"Twice," Sai replied. "On the way to castle Ogie a desperate group of bandits attempted to rob us. Their leader was a ronin samurai who had seen better days. Unfortunately, his company was not terribly competent. They were successful enough to bully defenseless travelers, which they thought us to be, but Saburo was too much for them."

"So, you were not harmed in any way?"

"No, but a hideous little man made the mistake of peering into the *jinrikisha* where I hid. I dispatched him with a dart."

"Your first?"

"Yes, he was my first. First of many I fear. The next time we encountered trouble was on our return. Samurai from the castle chased us down on the road and demanded I return to Ogie. This time it was my cousin Yoshi who distracted them. I used the blowpipe again … on a samurai. Afterwards, Saburo tried to make it seem as if it were robbers who attacked them, as unlikely as it seems. I am afraid the castle will be on high alert."

Naki was quiet for a moment then he said, "I have fought many times, but I have never killed a man."

"It happens so quickly, you don't have time to feel, or

think even, only react. Upon reflection, even though each death was necessary it disturbs me to kill a man. The repulsive creature I undid will mark my memory forever. His expressions of surprise, pain and eventually the frozen grimace, which he will wear into the next life, will never leave me. I do not regret killing him, but to see the light of life pass out of his eyes is profound. I was so close. I had him by the throat; I looked into his little face, and I watched as he shed tears of blood and finally die. How unceremoniously the breath of life quells. In an instant, everything the eyes can express, pain, pleasure, hate, love, is gone. Empty, all connection to this earth vanishes. All that remains are two orbs as full of life as dull gray stones. I am afraid our destiny prescribes much more killing. Death is our stock in trade."

Sai shook her head in regret. "I am so foolish to be so tender, yet I am my mother's daughter. She loved deeply. She loved my father and me very much. She was exquisite ... her face ... her beautiful heart - full of life. She was gifted: singing, dancing, composing poetry. She could arrange a single flower in the most elegant fashion. All men loved her, including Nobunaga, as she was a favorite court concubine, but she only loved my father. She loved him so much she sacrificed her life for him. When injudiciously warning my father to abandon a futile mission, Nobunaga discovered her deceit and had her killed. She died ... my father lived.

She dropped her head and remained quiet for a moment. Naki watched a tear drop onto her lap. She hid her face in shame. With head bowed, she continued. "Where does love fit in this life of ours? Everyone is a merchant of death: the daimyo, struggling for power, kill all who oppose them; they in turn die when they are overthrown or betrayed. Samurai kill indiscriminately, anyone they chose, with impunity, on the pretext of social superiority or allegiance to their master. Destruction and death oppress our lives daily. Those who cherish peace are under constant attack from those who wish war."

She paused again before continuing. "It is strange. I long for simplicity, yet I live in complexity. I pray to find the strength to be useful; I train to deceive, lie and kill; I battle the gentleness with which I was born, the peace for which I yearn ... it is getting hard. Yet, I am resolved to do what I must ...for the greater good. I am in the hands of the gods. They have given me gifts and I am obliged to use them even if it means I must deceive, lie, and kill.

At that moment, it was plainly clear to Naki that he loved Sai. He panicked. He didn't know what to do ... or say...clumsily he mumbled, "I do not look forward to the moment when I must take a life."

Sai looked at him with kind and gentle eyes and said, "You will have no choice. You must do what must be done. It will be you or him. Better it be him. If you believe your actions are righteous then killing will come easily. Perhaps, you will be spared. Perhaps, you will be so relieved that you lived that any stain upon your mind will be blotted out.

"I am not sure. I recall the death of my parents, my uncle, and my dearest sister, Keiko. The memories haunt me incessantly."

"Come," Sai said. "Let us go to the shrine and I will instruct you in the cut of the *Sah*, the healing of one's self and others."

"Naki having recovered from his momentary awkwardness took hold of her arm and looked deeply into her eyes. "I too wish for peace and tranquility." Sai understood that he meant more than personal peace, and that she was part of his world of simplicity and happiness.

She demurely dropped her eyes and took him by the hand to the little sanctuary.

Chapter 12

Tomoki Konnyo was sitting in the Lotus position meditating when Saburo appeared in the doorway requesting permission to enter.

"Konnyo-sama, we have received word from Mt. Hiei. The most honorable Abbot Kossa has revived. He is free of his delirium and his strength is returning quickly."

Tomoki Konnyo smiled. He was confident that the Abbot would transcend this minor dilemma and resume control of the monastery.

"What does he say?"

Saburo replied, "The next bird which arrives will signal the assault. Many birds with the same message may arrive as the Abbot is concerned the enemy's falcons could disrupt communications."

"We will wait."

"The communication also confirmed that the monks of Ikko-Ikki will deploy hundreds of men. We are to dispatch fifty men two days after the arrival of the message. We are to remove the tower guards and open the castle gates to allow the monks to enter. They will assault the barracks where the majority of the remaining forces will most likely be sleeping. While they are engaged with the barracks we are to infiltrate the palace and send Nobuoki and all who attend him to the next world."

"We will be ready. Thank you Saburo-san."

Saburo bowed and left.

Tomoki Konnyo resumed his meditating.

------=◆=------

Daiske was tending to the Abbot, sitting upright, with some Keri tea. His vigor returning, he issued directives for a bloodless resumption of control.

The news was that the Abbot was dead, so Zatoichi wasted no time in proclaiming his ascendancy. The Abbot would receive perfunctory funereal rites and immediately, thereafter, the attack on castle Ogie would commence. Strangely, the upstart samurai had assembled a dedicated mass of followers, men of lower status, who believed Zatoichi would improve their lot in this life faster than what the Abbot offered. Whatever incentives he promised them, most likely spoils from the castle, worked for they were ardent in executing his commands . They would surely be disappointed in hearing the Abbot was alive and that the ransacking of Nobuoki's castle was not in their destiny.

However, the Abbot knew that thousands of warriors in the monastery were loyal to his reverence, but he did not wish to lose even one man from either camp in a senseless internal battle. It was hoped that the preternatural reappearance of the

Abbot would astound every warrior to the degree that he would accept the Abbot Kosa's supreme authority without question. Their allegiance would return and their faith in him would be reaffirmed and strengthened. Since the people of Japan are exceedingly superstitious this plan with its aura of mysticism was not without merit. The plan was to avoid any kind of coup and bloodshed. Zatoichi, of course, would have to die along with the staunchest of his followers, but this could be done secretly and quietly and the monks could quickly resume preparing for the smaller surreptitious invasion of the castle.

The revelation that the Abbot lived was to be wondrously announced at the funeral which was scheduled as the sun rose at the Hour of the Hare. The effect would be profound, but first Zatoichi needed to be apprehended, and the monk Ryu needed to be rescued.

—————◦《◎》◦—————

Ryu's left arm was stretched out to the side and lashed to a low bench. His hand was secured at the wrist and metal spikes nailed into the wood spread his fingers apart. Blood surrounded a maimed hand. Three fingers on his left hand had protruding slivers of bamboo. The splinters, deeply embedded under the nail and into the soft tissue, caused Ryu to wriggle and writhe like a pinned slug. His moaning only ceased when he passed out.

Zatoichi would leave to tend to some affair and then return to see if his captive's degree of compliance had improved any. If it did not, another finger was brutalized.

"You have ten fingers. Let's see how many it will take before you tell me what I want to know," he said with a degree of sadistic pleasure in his voice.

Hours passed between each inquisition. The pain was so excruciating that Ryu regularly lost consciousness. Yet, he did not say a word. It had been two hours since the last infliction and Ryu was not sure how much longer he could hold on. He just wanted to die.

From the rukus outside, Ryu assumed it was time for more torture. The door burst open and men with lanterns entered the dark hut. His guards, three vulgar ruffians, jumped up startled by the intrusion.

"Release him, now," a gruff voice demanded. The three buffoons stunned stood stupidly still. Hardwood bo sticks struck each one of them to the ground. The men with the light untied Ryu's hands and skillfully extracted the wood from his fingers. The acute stabbing of sharp, nerve twitching misery thankfully ceased and was replaced by a duller slightly more tolerable throbbing. He was lifted off the ground by each arm and led out of the hut into the night.

"You are going to be tended to," one of them said. Ryu's stout legs could not carry the rest of his exhausted body and his liberators dragged him to a small temple where help was waiting.

———◆———

"I can't see a thing," one complained.
"Nor can I," another whined.

"Shut up!", the one in command hissed. "Look for a light, a fire anything."

"Why does Lord Zatoichi believe that we will find something in these mountains?"

"I don't know. He told us to find the hidden village."

"There is nothing in these mountains."

"Shut up; keep moving!"

Fortunately, these dull scouts were heading in the wrong direction. If by some regrettable chance they had stumbled across the compound, the intrepid eyes in the woods, watching them, would have had to kill them, and their deaths would only confirm to Zatoichi his suspicions of a secret compound somewhere in the mountains was correct. If one were not actively searching for a forest hideaway, it could never be detected; however, if one were, then with time and skill, it might be uncovered. However, time was not on Zatoichi's side, nor was skill. The eyes that kept watch knew that if the intruders discovered nothing Zatoichi would give up the search. He didn't have the luxury at the moment of prying further. The men in the woods were imbeciles, simpletons. They had neither desire nor skill for the job. They would soon return with the report they tirelessly scoured the area and found nothing.

⸎

Not all of Zatoichi's agents, however, were incompetents.

"He's alive?! How is that possible? I saw him dead. The doctors confirmed it."

"I do not know, Lord Zatoichi. He is to appear at his own funeral," the quivering messenger replied as calmly as he could. The frightened man was aware that the Samurai's volatile disposition may explode upon him at any moment, the bearer of ill tidings.

Zatoichi paused for a moment and reflected upon the beauty of the Abbot's artifice. It was not beyond him to appreciate the elegance of it. To appear before the monks, alive, when they were expecting an internment, would, indeed, have a profound impact. To the simple minded he would be viewed as immortal, to the less superstitious he would appear ingenious, which Zatoichi conceded, he was. Whatever the perception, Zatoichi realized his temporary control over the monastery had ended and he had to flee. A large vein appeared upon his forehead pulsating and bulging with angry blood. Zatoichi dismissed the fawning messenger, and the messenger was relieved that he was allowed to leave before the samurai exploded; but instead of a volcanic eruption the samurai demonstrated self-control. Alone in the temple, he concocted his plan for survival. He could not remain. He would have to leave, immediately. But where to go? He would decide that when he had opportunity, but at the moment he needed to leave.

As he was bridling his horse, his mind's eye saw Naki. He was not sure exactly how, but he knew the upstart had something to do with the unraveling of his plans. He had been so close assuming complete control of the monastery. The Tendai monks, under his authority, would have elevated him to his rightful station. With these monks he could have destroyed Kyoto and Nobunaga. He would have acquired

the loyalty of dozens of lords, dominion over countless provinces and thousands of samurai. He would have obliterated
Nobunaga's dream of one land under one sword, and become
a formidable daimyo.

Zatoichi was accustomed, under the young Lord
Kitabateke, to the power and glory of position; he had been
a trusted advisor, a competent confidant and a prodigious
samurai. The young regent entrusted, to him, Zatoichi,
the command of the military and the economy within his
province. It was under Zatoichi's auspices that the province
flourished and dominated militarily. It was his brilliance
which raised the prefecture to prominence.

Unfortunately, his successes attracted the attention of
Oda Nobunaga. Nobunaga knew that if he controlled the
powerful Kitabateke territories his dream of a unified Japan
would be greatly enhanced. It was his Lord Kitabateke's
youthful exuberance and vain pride which foiled Zatoichi.
In battle, against Nobunaga, the conquest was initially his,
Zatoichi's. Kitabateke, stupidly, foolishly, countermanded
Zatoichi's order to press and chase to secure the victory; he
demanded the troops rest and they would easily demolish
the villain in the morning. Nobunaga, however, during their
time of rest, reversed his retreat and attacked the camp, thus
thwarting Zatoichi's victory. Kitabateke was beheaded.

He, Zatoichi was captured, but would not submit to
Nobunaga's entreaties to join him as an ally; nor did he wish
to kill himself. He had been given some time to consider his
options. He reasoned he had not dishonored his position;
he was poised to win. Kitabatake was the culprit for the defeat, and he met his appropriate end; therefore, Zatoichi, in

unwonted samurai fashion refused to accept blame for the
folly and die with his Lord.

He remembered the narrowness of his escape. Dozens
of Nobunaga's guards died by his guile and he was able
to escape into the darkness. His fate was not to die there.
Since the Tendai monks were most instrumental in many
of Kitabateke's previous victories, it was only reasonable to
seek shelter at Mt. Hiei. The Abbot was most receptive. The
Abbot realized that he, Zatoichi, was Nobunaga's equal in
military acumen and insidious intrigue. The Abbot believed
that he, Zatoichi, could stop the demon; little did the Abbot
understand the depth of Zatoichi's treachery.

But he, Zatoichi, underestimated the shrewd Abbot. The
Abbot somehow eluded his treachery and lived despite an ingenious plan. Now, he would not martial the monks to glory
against Oda Nobunaga; now he was ronin again, masterless
and powerless. He promised himself he would, one day, achieve
his rightful destiny. How, he did not know, but he would, and
the young shinobi that ruined his plans would die by his hand.

His horse ready, he rode off into the night.

＊＊＊

Three thousand monks dressed in white stood before
Enryakuji temple. Villagers stood where ever they could. The
funeral pyre was prepared, meticulously, and all waited quietly
for the Abbot's body to proceed from the temple to fiery in-
terment. When the heavy wood doors of the Temple opened,
instead of somber monks bearing the body of the revered

Abbot, an assemblage of sage men walked unencumbered, carrying nothing towards the throng. A murmer of confusion rippled through the crowd. The procession stopped at the lowest level of the ceremonial steps and faced the mourners. When the sounds of disquiet finally ceased, the rows of monks parted to reveal the Abbot Kosa standing amidst them, humbly quite alive. His appearance elicited a shocked collective gasp. His wearing a *kesa*, a patchwork of fine silk brocade over his black robe, was not lost upon the audience: the meaning of the garment's variety of geometric patterns were symbols of harmony in the universe. When the Abbot stepped forward to speak the sea of monks yielded and fell to the ground. After a moment of profound silence, the Abbot spoke.

"I humbly apologize for the most dramatic manner with which I conduct this affair. Given the circumstances it is imperative that I eliminate any confusion about the state of my being and any division among us. I, through the will of the gods, did not pass into The Pure Land. I live, just like you do, so let there be no doubt, or division among us; I want everyone to see me; I want to oppose the tyrant in complete solidarity. The Evil One is powerful, and we must be united, strong, to eliminate him and his minions from this world. The gods determined that my time to leave this realm and burn upon the funeral pyre is not yet at hand. My destiny is to preserve the sanctity of this monastery, to preserve the lives of its people and to help free Japan from the clutches of the Demon. We must be singular in our quest. In consultation with the elder monks, a new plan has been devised, one in which fewer lives are put at risk and one in which the chances of success are enhanced. Now, please disassemble the funereal pyre and return to your lodgings. We, once again, are united."

A joyous cheer resounded. The confusion cleared and hope and purpose coalesced. With vigor hundreds stormed the pile of wood; within minutes it was gone. The great news spread throughout the thirty thousand who lived on Mt. Hiei. In a matter of hours, the fog of malcontent and dissension clouding the monastery dissipated; the Abbot's dominion was restored.

―――⟫⟪⟪⟫――

All the dispatched pigeons arrived safely, and Tomoki Konnyo was relieved the Abbot had recovered. Now, he was deep in thought about the assault. Fifty of his men and a thousand warrior monks from Mt Hiei and the neighboring Ikko-Ikki monastery were to gather in the foothills outside the town of castle Ogie. The Hour of the Tiger would signal the preliminary incursion. The clan members were to eliminate the sentries on the towers and the gates. Then the gates would be thrown open and the thousand monks would besiege the barracks and since the samurai numbers were small they should be easily overtaken by the monks. Tomoki was pleased: his casualties should be low; Oda Nobuoki will be dead; the castle will be razed and Kyoto's eastern flank will be vulnerable.

―――⟫⟪⟪⟫――

In the central yard of the compound, the shinobi assembled. Sai, the only female, sat stoically upon her steed and waited, Naki by her side. Tommoki Konnyo, the *Chunin*, stepped out and gazed upon his daughter and his men; without a word, he simply nodded, and the assembly moved.

Passing through the mountain's hidden canyon, the shinobi were extremely clandestine. Once upon the main road, the fifty unleashed their horses into an unrestrained gallop. They needed to arrive before the monks did. Naki rode behind Sai, but she did not speak to him. The riders were silently focused, and only the pounding of the horse's hooves upon the muffling edge of the road disturbed the mountain's tranquility.

High upon a ridge, overlooking the rows of riders a set of amber eyes watched. Its form was indiscernible midst the shadows. As the mounted ninjas rode below, a muted growl was carried upwards resonating against the rocks and cliffs.

Chapter 13

Intrusively, the giant gingko tree's massive roots spread into the road. The venerable deciduous stood like a sentinel along the byway overseeing the thoroughfare to and from Castle Ogie, almost protecting it. The giant tree separated the hilly forest's edge form the town's gently rolling hills and fields of wheat, barley, potatoes, rice, fruits and vegetables.

From its lofty branches, one could see the castle perched upon the mountain rock: towering, imposing itself upon the landscape as a defensive bastion between the East and Kyoto castle. However, today, the tree served as an assembly point, a conspirator, almost.

Sai, Hisao-san, Naki and company arrived first. South of the great tree a large ravine provided adequate cover and space for the entire contingent of invaders. The family ninja set about quietly industriously setting up camp, organizing weapons, and reviewing strategy. Guards were posted along the road to wait for the monks. By mid morning of the next day during the hour of the Snake, an alarm signaled …

movement along the road. Warriors snatched weapons and disappeared among ferns and trees.

Hundreds of slovenly, rough-cut men trudged, sloppily out of file along the road carrying bo sticks and long handled scythes. Swords hung from the hips of some and others bore bow and arrows. What the monks of Ikko-Ikki lacked in order and discipline they more than compensated for in roguish vigor and ferocity.

A predetermined signal sounded, and the company of scruffy monks halted. Hisao-san dispatched messengers who ushered the four hundred quickly and quietly down into the ravine. Now, they waited for the monks of Mt. Hiei to arrive, and before the hour of the Horse, the assembly was complete. One thousand men waited patiently for the sun to set.

The sky colored monstrously crimson and night's darkness besieged the castle and town. Twinkling inn lights eventually expired; the town was sleep. Only the flicker from sentry sconces stood sentinal as the thousand advanced.

The intrepid fifty raced ahead on horseback, determined to prepare the way. Just outside of the town proper, they sequestered their horses and proceeded on foot to the castle gates, silently, invisibly to the fortress walls.

The torches delineated the entire complex, making it easy to choose a dark location from which to hurl *shoge* atop the castle outer works. Scrambling up was simple for everyone, as the walls were not designed to thwart ninja ingenuity. Once up each small mob waited for their signal to assault the battlements.

Sai and Naki were in a gang who weren't to wait for a signal, but to scale the walls straight away and race to Nobuoki's chambers. As Sai was determining the path leading to the unique stone wall when she heard the attack cue faintly in the distance. It was a natural sound, a nighttime sound which would not draw any unwanted attention or suspicion. With any luck, the palace guards would be dispatched without alarm, and the gates of the castle will be flung open for the monks to enter; however, she would not worry about that, for she needed to locate the path which led to the door in the stone wall. Recollecting correctly, she found it. Hurling her *shoge*, she clambered up and over the courtyard wall. Inside the ceremonial court, she triggered the mechanism and sprang open the door. They entered.

Before them, lay the massive steps, leading to Nobuoki's inner sanctuary. Softly padding up the stone stairs to the outer garden gate, they found it, incredibly, not locked, but it did emitt an alarming screech as it was opened. Sai cursed herself for not noticing that it made noise; quickly they dispersed into the garden. Hidden by foliage, they watched a guard descend the stairs to investigate. Naki surmised that he was the sentry posted to guard the entrance to the inner rooms. It would be good to take care of him here in the garden. He had an unsteady walk as he approached. He was either drunk or he had been dozing. At the gate, he torpidly investigated, but discovered nothing. Sai's blow dart stung him in the neck, and Naki's short sword sliced his throat. Not a sound was issued. He collapsed. Naki stood horrified for a moment. Holding the dead man upright, he realized he had just engaged in his first kill. Stunned, Naki held onto the guard and looked at Sai. She nodded approvingly, and motioned that he place him off to the side in the bushes, away from discovery. Naki composed himself and quickly tucked the man away. Regrouping, they proceeded up the staircase.

Naki had surmised correctly; there was not a guard at the top of the stairs, and the door to the inner apartments was open. Now, it was up to Sai to lead them through the confusion of corridors to reach Nobuoki's private chamber. Distinctive artifacts guided her to the exact door; her memory did not fail her, but who was behind it and how many were there?

Kichiro signaled for everyone to move away back down the hall. Quietly, he whispered that he had seen an ancient formal kimono on display. Sai should don it and knock upon the door and inform the guard she has returned as requested. When it opens we surprise whoever is inside. Raiden ran down the corridor and retrieved the ceremonial garb. Sai pulled it on over her clothes, and bundled up her hair, pinning it with one of her poison darts. Her guise was not perfect, but it would suffice as an initial distraction. In the palms of her hands, she cupped two *metsubushi* eggs. The others pressed themselves flat against the wall in order not to be seen, ready to enter. After rapping gently upon the royal chamber door, Sai slid her hands, which were holding the smoke bombs, into the wide sleeves of the kimono and began to giggle, as if she were drunk. The wooden door slid open and an intimidating samurai peered out.

Upon seeing her and her seemingly intoxicated condition, he chastised her for disturbing Lord Nobuoki at such an hour. Sai giggled again and said that she was Sai and his lordship commanded her to return. Confused, he told her to wait. Several moments passed before the door opened again, and the samurai, much more obsequious, asked her to enter. The door opened wide and Sai stepped inside. As soon as she was in, she looked about the antechamber and saw two more samurai on guard. She drunkenly wobbled towards them. They politely bowed and gestured that she enter Nobuoki's chamber. Seizing the opportunity, Sai yelled, "Three!" and launched the egg bombs. Black smoke and irritants immediately overpowered them. The guard who opened the door unsheathed his sword and rushed towards Sai, but he was too late. Kichiro's blade struck him down, and he crumpled into a heap. Naki, rushed the blinded guards and quickly put an end to their misery, two more dead.

Nobuoki's valet slid the bedroom's latticed door and stood agape at his master's bloody and vanquished guardians. Young and faint of heart, he collapsed.

Appearing at the threshold of his bedchamber, Nobuoki stared at Sai. He looked at his dead guards and at his fallen valet, and in a drunken stupor, he slurred, "But you said you were not going to kill me."

"Yes", she replied, "I lied."

Sai's regret was the young valet; he was innocent. However, he could not have lived. Grief stricken, he roused himself and fell upon his master's lifeless body and that is, unfortunately, where he died.

As silently as they entered, they left. Descending the stairs, they heard the pandemonium of the pursuing guards.

Instinctively, everyone reached for their poisoned balled barbs. Scattering them over the patio landing, they ensured themselves an end to the chase or at least a retarded pursuit. In any case, they would have time to traverse the enclosure and reach the gates to allow the monks entry into the grounds. Across the common, painful yelps were heard. The pursuit ceased. Opening the compound's gates, they fled into the dark. Monks would shortly pour through and tend to the palace properly.

Once outside the castle walls, secure and safe, they looked back. Flames were licking various levels of the palace. Hellish sounds rose up: screaming, wailing, whooping, and howling. Metal clashed, timber tumbled, sparks flew and smoke swirled. Outside the castle walls, dim shadows fled; afraid the conflagration would engulf them. The sounds of chaos and suffering were mixed with roars of triumph.

Naki closed his eyes. His senses heightened, the squall of the battle engulfed him. It was as if he were in the castle fighting along with the monks of Mt. Hiei and the Ikko-Ikki. Swords rang, men grunted in exertion and pain. Wooden beams groaned and collapsed. Bo sticks thudded, muffled against muscle, cracking against bone. The distinct smell of burning flesh reached him, violating his nostrils. He envisioned the anguished terror on the faces of the sufferers as they tried to escape the horror of the holocaust; he shuddered.

Sai touched his arm and said, "We must go." His sensibilities directly returned to normal, and they hurried to their horses. Astride Jun, deep in thought, he galloped through the black moonless night. His thoughts were of the men gripped in their savage struggle for life and of those who succumbed to the villainy of death. However, he was safe; Sai was safe, and those with him safe. He had struck his first blow against the Wretch. The brother was dead; his fortification, Castle Ogie was no longer a buffer between him and his eastern enemies. Now, Nobunaga had to occupy himself with threats from the North and the East. How could he prevail? He wouldn't. He couldn't. His quest was doomed. Naki felt a smattering of satisfaction; although, vengeance did not taste as expected. The sweetness of victory was adulterated by bitter pangs of mortality.

The undulating rhythm of Jun's gallop lulled Naki into a stupefied state, and he did not think any more of what had transpired that night. He just rode, Sai beside him, silent and centered on returning home. They just rode and rode.

By midday, they road into familiar mountain terrain, and when they entered the compound, delighted family members surrounded them with overwhelming jubilation, cheering and singing over their safe return. They were the first to arrive, and questions about relatives proliferated, but neither Sai, nor the others, could answer. All that could be said was that the mission was successful, beyond that they would have to wait to see.

Konnyo-sama stood patiently on his porch waiting for his daughter's report. His stony chiseled features betrayed a modicum of pride; his face cracked a subtle hint of a smile.

Once free of the crowd, Sai headed home to her normally reserved father who embraced her warmly.

"I thank the gods for your safe return," he whispered in her ear.

"I thank the gods for my return as well, and I pray for the souls of those who were not so fortunate."

"Come inside."

Naki and the others were ushered into the house and sat before the Chunin to recount what they could.

A meal was hastily prepared and the group ate, and related. Sai told what she knew. Konnyo-sama listened. After they finished, he said a carrier bird had arrived with news of the enterprise: the castle had been razed, the troops had been destroyed, and losses were minimal. In every aspect the attack was successful.

"Now, go get rest. We will greet the others tomorrow."

All bowed and left. On the way across the compound Sai spoke to Naki. "You performed well, Naki-san."

"Thank you Sai-chan. You have taught me well."

"You were born to be a shinobi, Naki. It is in your blood."

Naki nodded, but had his doubts. The horrific casualties were still vivid in his mind.

Chapter 14

News of the destruction of Ogie and the inglorious death of his brother violently incensed Oda Nobunaga. A dark reddish flush inflamed his tawny face, his black brows knitted angrily; a scowl distorted his lips revealing large teeth bitterly grinding in vexation.

He brusquely dismissed the messenger and stared at his disquieted generals assembled before him. The standards bearing his feared *mokkou* symbol flapped viciously in the wind; the large *mokkou* banners behind the dais billowed and strained against their posts, as if a sudden fierce flurry of wind rose to palpably give expression to his rage. After a considerable silence, he finally spoke:

"wormy thatch molders rotting
brotherly tulip
mushrooms revel"

His generals, squatting before him were confused. Only Tokugawa Ieyasu, his one time rival but now loyal ally, understood. He knew, Nobunaga, in times of dire stress, would resort to haiku, song or dance, or something dramatic to gain control over a complex situation, even if it were only poetic. Offering the predicament to the muse and creating an artistic expression, he believed, would lead to temperance and a pragmatic resolution to a thorny problem.

Ieyasu paused and asked. "Nobuoki-sama?"

"Hai, dead, and left for worms."

"Ogie castle?"

"Ash."

"*Kuso!*"

"Hai, *Kuso!* Monks … ninja, they have destroyed Ogie, so they can assault Kyoto, I assume; but they are ridiculous; Kyoto is invulnerable; they cannot infiltrate my castle; they are no match for my men. *Kuso!* If it were not for my traitorous brother-in law, I would not be here fighting the Asakura, and my brother would be alive. However, once I end the Asai – Asakura resistance, I will take care of the monks and the ninja. They have reminded me, yet again, how much I have no use for them. They are a plague upon the land: their willfulness, their lawlessness and lack of loyalty. I have only maimed them before, but now, I will eradicate them!

However, it is time for Asai Nagamasa and Asakura Yoshikage to understand they can not prevail against my will … they are "under my sky." He smiled smugly and viciously spewed, "The pompous Asakura! They believe that I should still be fawning under them ... how ludicrous! He thundered, "They are under my sky!"

The host of generals cheered and laughed derisively in agreement at the deprecation, but abruptly ceased when they realized that this moment may not be the time for jocularity, all quieted and bowed deeply in deference to their lord's loss.

"I thank you, but you need not concern yourself on my account. My brother was my people, but he was an imbecile. It was only a matter of time before his destiny overwhelmed him. How he sprang from my father's loins I do not know. He possessed nothing of the Oda spirit. He was weak and naïve and doomed to failure. I regret only the loss of my castle; however, it shall be restored, and it shall be greater than before."

The generals all murmured in agreement.

"Now, let us continue."

Tokugawa Ieyasu spoke. "My lord… the arquebus …we have five hundred, but only fifty of our men are competent in using them - or willing. The Europeans show us how to use the weapon, but our men resist, refusing to learn. General Takenaka Shigeharu nobly attempts instruction, but our samurai balk at discharging musket balls, nails and sundry metallic debris upon the enemy. They find no glory in the fight. Most believe antiquity will not recognize nor respect their warrior skills, but rather credit the Portuguese mechanisms for the victory.

"It is not important what they believe. Eliminating Asai Nagasama is important; punishing his treachery is important; securing the Northern reaches of our territory is important! Honor has its place so does tradition; agreed, they are the foundations of Japanese culture, and without them there would be chaos. But a greater chaos is Japan's destiny if it does not embrace the outsider's weaponry. Japan needs their weapons. If we do not learn to use them, they will be used against us. They will destroy us. Arrows against guns? Stone walls against cannon balls? We will vanish and then what of our illustrious history and tradition? Our very existence depends upon modern weaponry. If we do not adapt we will be trod upon by the vanquisher like an autumn leaf upon the path. Too bad the future is not clear to these fools; nevertheless, we will use what guns we have. Once the honorable samurai see how useful they are, they will eventually accept them."

"*Hai,*" my Lord. Ieyasu paused and said, "Then, we are ready to move against Odani Castle."

"Good! We attack in the morning." A drum banged; the generals were dismissed.

————)«(0)»(————

General Endo Naotsune stood atop Odani Castle's palisade surveying the river Ane meandering lazily, carelessly towards Lake Biwa Bay. The morning sun burned the mist from the lake, and the sky was bright clear, the air dead still. For the most part, it was a glorious day to be alive. Breathing deeply through his nose, he absorbed the magnificence of the majesty before him. However, he was not here to celebrate pastoral surroundings. Scouts had informed him that Nobunaga's camp was showing signs of deployment and that this day may be the day of the attack.

He squinted through the glass. A marvelous device, he contended. How fitting, he thought, that he should be using it now against this degenerate. It was a gift from the despot to his lord, Asai Nagamasa: a wedding gift. Portuguese priests first presented it to Nobunaga four years ago as a token of gratitude for being allowed to preach Christianity to the people of the provinces. It was only one of the favors Nobunaga gave to his lord when he married Oichi, Nobunaga's sister. The marriage was a cunning contrivance to destroy the alliance between the Asakura and the Asai. Without the Asai, the Asakura posed no credible threat to Nobunaga's campaign, but thankfully Lord Nagasama came to his senses and rejected the devil and his nefarious plans, and returned to the age old allegiance between his clan and the Asakura.

Naotsune's reflections were interrupted by movement within the forest. To the naked eye, the positioning of men and horses would have been invisible, but with the glass he was able to see through the trees to commotion in the woods. He scanned the tree line following the river south to the lake. Another set of shadows were forming further down river. Ah, he thought to himself, assaulting two sides of the castle. The enemy is not sure where our weakness lay, so he attacks on two sides. Well, we have a surprise for him.

General Endo Naotsune was ready; he gave the signal to move. Taiko drums boomed. Iron castle gates opened and horses bearing a thousand samurai charged out of the castle grounds. Behind the samurai and lancers moved archers and foot soldiers. To him, the idea of siege warfare was reprehensible. It would display weakness. Meet the opposition on the field. Fight the villain in the open. Use our high ground to advantage. His horse, padded, protected, waited for him in the courtyard.

Lord Asakura Yoshikage waited for General Endo Naotsune on the crest of a berm. Presently, the General and his cortège arrived. Both marshals silently surveyed the arrangement below. Ten thousand Asakura lancers, archers and ground troops stood to the right of eight thousand Asai troops, each clan hosting one thousand seasoned samurai. The spectacle was stunning.

General Endo simply nodded to Asakura Yoshikage and the drums sounded again sending the Asakura thousands one mile down river. It would appropriately be the Asakura would face Tokugawa to the south. the Asai would face Nobunaga.

The drums stopped ... deathly silence. Seven hundred Asai archers formed a line facing the river and the trees. The wind was idle. The sun hung unattended in the sky; not a cloud for company. A few black carrion crows circled above curious about the assembly below. The Asai standards dangled limply from the shafts of the lancers who waited to begin. Eight thousand men stood atop a ridge motionless, staring down at a narrow valley of land severed by a lazy river; beyond, up a slight rise, was a line of proud fir and cypress trees.

Out of the forest, a black and white *mokkou* flag appeared, first one, then ten, then one hundred. Out from the trees filed archers. They dashed to the banks of the river positioning themselves just beyond the range of Asai arrows. It was not yet time to fight. It was time for posturing. They spread out left and right along the river's edge. From an opening in the trees, Nobunaga's horsed lancers emerged but stopped their steeds just in front of the trees, and not directly behind the archers. General Endo looked upon two ranks of long thin lines; between them lay two hundred feet of open ground. The General puzzled by the unconventional placement of troops, realized his advantage had been annulled, that of firing down from the ridge into thick throngs of closely clustered men. He changed his plans. His lancers would begin the battle instead. Unconventional agreed, but he was dealing with Oda Nobunaga. Traditional conventions no longer applied. Attacking the thinly spread archers with horse and spear would surely counter this curious strategy. But, where were the rest of Nobunaga's forces? Hidden within the trees, he imagined. Why? He would wait to use the archers.

The adversaries stood silently opposite one another for a brief moment and then a Nobunaga drum pounded. His archers raced forward into the shallow water and sent forth a clumsy, ineffective, scattered spray of arrows at their enemy. The shafts fell ridiculously short.

General Endo and his troops let out a loud raucous jeer at the pathetic salvo. Lancers, at the ready, hurtled down the slight hill; charging, they spread out ready to skewer the long thin line of archers. Pandemonium erupted among the black and white archers as the red and white riders tore down upon them. The charge sent every archer toward the trees. Nobunaga's mounted-lancers inexplicably sat inert upon their horses watching as the Asai lancers descended. The Asai rode eager for slaughter. As they neared their quarry, from within the shadows of the forest, fifty muzzles flashed fire, belched smoke and spit musket ball and nails. Anguished sounds of wounded horses and surprised men punctuated the moment. Horse and rider fell.

Nobunaga's lancers struggled to control their mounts as their horses frightened by the gunfire reared and whinnied,. A command to reload and fire was given, but ... the inexperienced men, clumsy and slow were unable to discharge the second volley quickly. Lord Tokugawa Ieyasu's concern regarding the incompetence of the gunners was realized. Hurriedly, in order not to lose advantage over the Asai disarray, another command was given. An attack drum rolled and the retreating archers wheeled about and charged upon the vulnerable horse-men. Arrows at such range could easily pierce armor. A lancer slaughter was imminent.

Horrified but not dismayed, General Endo immediately ordered his archers to race down the embankment to deliver a storm of arrows at the catastrophe on the other side, to give his men cover and time to escape. Luckily, for the Asai lancers, the gun blasts discharged a cloud of smoke, a grayish–white blanket, which hung, dead still in the air, obscuring everything. The Asai, under the blurry fog of smaze, were able to scramble a retreat to the river. Some, nonetheless, were felled by their own archer's incompetent friendly fire as they fled for safety. Uninjured, but terrified horses followed under the hundreds of arrows flying overhead. Preoccupied with shooting at the fleeing Asai, Nobunaga's archers were surprised by the aerial counter attack and were struck by deadly bolts that rained down upon them through the cloud of gunpowder.

Endo's archers crossed the river; unassailed, they advanced confidently and fired at the tree line where Nobunaga's riders still sat upon their horses. Barrage upon barrage of streaming arrows forced them to retreat into the woods.

Unrestrained shouts of joy exploded from the Asai. Drums signaled reformation. The archers assembled along the enemy's side of the river poised to strike at any show of Nobunaga's forces from the woods. The lancers re-formed behind them in the shallow water and foot soldiers on the shore behind them. The thousands waited.

Hundreds of men lay on the flat of the western shore. Not everyone was dead; many lay bleeding, writhing in pain waiting for death to free them from their agony. The musket balls and bolts easily pierced the lancer's light armor. Scarlet pools of blood created grotesque patterns in the sandy soil. Arrows protruded from bodies, colorful feathered shafts stuck out in every direction, twisting and dancing in concert to the sounds of writhing anguish. Horses in their death throes labored, trying to rise, eventually succumbing to their injuries. Men's moans and horse's neighing were mixed with the scavenging caws of carrion birds flying overhead, anxious to feast upon the banquet below.

However odious the sights and sounds they were ignored by the warriors on both sides; they waited to continue the carnage.

The Asai watched as the branches of the trees began to bend and move unnaturally; it was as if the cypress trees had the charm of motion. General Endo peered through his telescope. He saw men positioning themselves on boughs, high and low, hidden by leaves. They bore bow and arrow. Some wielded guns. Immediately, he realized they were establishing an elevated and covered position from which to fire. The elevation from the trees would give their archers and gunners an advantage of distance. Did Nobunaga think we would charge the tree line and he could cut us down with impunity?

"No, my friend, you are coming to me," he heard himself speak aloud. He ordered his archers to prepare to fire flaming arrows onto the grass and into the thickets beneath the trees. The fire would flush the audacious knave out into the open for conventional warfare.

His problem, the fire arrows were heavy. They could not be launched very far, or accurately. He needed to get his men close to the trees; accuracy didn't matter; he just needed to set the bushes afire. However, given the enemy's elevation and cover the charge would be risky. A barrage of musket balls and arrows would be devastating.

Noise! He would rely on noise, screaming arrows fitted with hollow bamboo tubes; an angled hole at one end of a tube allowed air to pass through; they whistled. Five hundred screaming arrows were not accurate, nor were they deadly, but they created an ungodly racket. They would not need to advance as closely, since these lighter arrows flew further than the flaming arrows. The shrill clamor would cause confusion among the gunners and archers, hopefully spoiling their fire. This pandemonium would at least give his men a chance to draw near and set the brush afire. The flaming arrows with the tips wrapped with rags, dipped in pitch, would create an unspeakable fire storm and force the villain out of hiding.

General Endo decided he would give Nobunaga the illusion that he was going to brazenly march upon the forest. Drums thundered giving the sign to advance. Everyone moved up the slope. The archers formed into three groups. The first wave, armed with conventional arrows to spray the trees; the second wave would move forward and let fly with the screaming bolts giving the last wave time to light their weapons, advance and fire upon the woods.

The rhythmic beat of the Asai drums conveyed a confident advance. Defensively, arrows flew from the trees and guns smoked spewing their lethal loads. Men fell. Immediately, reciprocating arrows flew back toward the trees. The whistling archers charged and sent up a profoundly deafening ruckus. There was only sporadic retaliatory fire. The third wave ran to within sixty yards of the tree line and lit their rags. The regular archers continued to shower the trees with pointy reckonings. The plan was working. The awkward task of lighting the arrows was not hampered and when they were lit they were launched. As expected, they did not fly very far, but far enough to set the brush at the base of the trees afire. Then the Asai taiko drum pounded for a retreat to the river.

Patiently, General Endo waited for the vermin to abandon the forest and meet them in the open. They did not wait long. Out from the inferno, the archers and gunners, lancers, samurai and foot soldiers emerged overpowered by flame and smoke.

Thousands of Nobunaga men streamed out of the forest and formed conventionally and safely away from the inferno. General Endo raised his red and white banner, finally, traditional warfare.

The fighting ceased. The clans formed, assembled under their respective flags, the fire raging in the background, almost encouraging the ensuing onslaught. Through the looking glass, Lord General Endo Naotsune spied Nobunaga. The demon sat astride his horse appearing every bit the devil he was. His steed, the color of night, a blood red harness girdled its mahogany head, body covered with leather armor. The demagogue sat atop his fearsome mount dressed in a black helmet crowned with curved horns; thick black flaps draped his neck and shoulders. He was tall, upon his horse, lean and muscular, his armor, black, glistening, reflecting hues of red and orange from the fire. The wings of his vest gave him an added aura of power and ferocity. Chain mail covered a steel breast plate and his samurai swords hung by his side. Powerful arms and long legs were covered with leather and steel. His face was taught, and his eyes were hot coals of vengeance.

Lord and General Endo Naotsune understood that Oda Nobunaga had been generous to his master, Asai Nagasama, so Nobunaga expected loyalty from his allies, especially relatives; however, he received treachery, and now he sat upon his horse craving revenge.

The General turned. In the distance, he saw his Lord, Asai Nagamasa and Lord Asakura, upon a high ridge, observing. His Lord, fecklessly, would not enter the fray, but would watch well away from the chaos. Endo Naotsune wondered if Nobunaga would enter the fight. He was dressed for battle, but would he? He doubted it. Nobunaga was just posturing for his men. The opening skirmishes did not go well, and now, he needed to conjure some of his magic for which he was so famous; he needed to inspire them. Once the battle began he would undoubtedly retreat to his camp and leave the killing to others.

The Oda drums began to beat; men roared and charged. The battle continued. Foot soldiers followed mounted lancers and samurai. The river, naturally placid, roiled with turbulence. Lances leveled, chargers lunged; swords drawn, men fiercely, vehemently pitted themselves against one another. Warriors spilled from their steeds onto the river bed. Crystalline water turned muddy vermilion. Steel struck steel ringing choruses of discordant sounds ... sharp ... reverberating ... death knells. The devil on horseback watched.

Oda Nobunaga, indeed, did not fight but retreated to a place of safety to conduct the battle from a distance.

For a mile in and along the water tens of thousands of men struggled. Some fell quickly. Others fought until their strength ebbed and they succumbed to a fatal mistake; nevertheless, the Asai fought well. Their resolve was deeper than the tenacity exhibited by the Oda forces, and they pushed their enemies out of the river, towards the burning trees.

General Endo Naotsune sensing victory rushed through the river to the front of the line. He wanted his men to see their that their Chief was valiantly leading them, the vanguard of their glory, not like the coward Oda Nobunaga. He swirled his venerable sword slashing, slaughtering weak and confused men, but the noble blade now was pitted and dulled. It no longer cleanly severed shoulders nor sliced necks, but rather bludgeoned bodies and broke bones. Despite the vigor of imminent victory, the General suddenly felt his energy wane. He wasn't a young man anymore, and the toll of the battle enervated him. His head swam; his breath was heavy, his arms were leaden; for a moment, a lethal moment, he ceased his whirling storm of deadly strikes to rest. That was all that a nearby foot soldier needed. Seeing the General flag, he rushed the enemy Lord and lanced him with a yari. The blow struck armor plating but toppled the General who fell heavily upon rocky ground; the air he so desperately needed was viciously expelled. Writhing in pain, winded and vulnerable, General Endo struggled to thwart his attacker; however, it was in vain. His arms and legs would not move. The peasant warrior straddled him; yari poised. A brutal stab sprayed his noble blood onto rocky ground. Momentarily, he looked into the face of his vanquisher who wore an ugly, smug victorious smirk ... General Endo Naotsune's final image.

Stunned, the Asai warriors reeled in horror. Their General had been killed. The taiko drums signaled retreat. Tradition dictates when a commanding warrior falls, fighting stops. Chaotically, the Asai scrambled to reassemble on the far bank. Nobunaga's troops thankful for the momentary lull also retreated. Both sides scrambled to collect themselves on their respective sides of the bloody river. Panic polluted the confidence of the Asai, and they retreated in disarray.

Meanwhile down river, the formidable Tokugawa clan had decisively routed the Asakura, and the chaos presently gripping the Asai was mild compared to the confusion of the racing, Asakura. Racing to rejoin the forces of General Endo Naotsune in hopes of reforming an offence, but they discovered only a muddled moil of bedlam. General Endo was dead, and Lord Asai Nagasama along with Lord Asakura had departed the field of battle earlier, seeking the safety of Odani Castle.

Leaderless, the merged clans of samurai, lancers and remaining foot soldiers faced a rejuvenated Nobunaga force as well as a murderous Tokugawa onslaught bearing down upon them. Without receiving a formal directive, an astute Asai drummer, perched atop an embankment, beat the rhythm of retreat, and all Asai, and Asakura unquestioningly fled for the gates of the castle.

However, Nobunaga and Tokugawa did not follow, but were happily content to watch their enemy's shameful retreat. The victory was theirs; Nobunaga had exercised his dominance. As he coldly surveyed the battlefield, and saw tens of thousands of men lying dead mingled with blood, mud and feces his thoughts were that they would fight another day and most assuredly the victory would be his, again. Wisely displaying some compassion, in deference to his exhausted troops, he withdrew.

The carrion birds which had been circling overhead during the entire battle now descended and began their feast. Instinctively, they knew it would be hours before their gorging would be disrupted by men clearing the site. For now, they, surely, were the victors.

Chapter 15

It was not long before news of the loss at Anegawa reached the Abbott. However, he was tending to Ryu's wounded hand personally when the message arrived, and the messenger was instructed to leave the rolled parchment upon the small table in the sanctuary. The Abbott would get to the disappointing message later; for now, he needed to remove the cotton bandages from Ryu's fingers and inspect how the healing had progressed. Ryu sat grinning as Abbott Kosa unwrapped his hand. For certain, the squat powerful monk was not used to attention and most definitely not attention from someone such as the Abbott. Ryu reasoned that the attentive care he was receiving was due to his association with Naki. He was pleased. The pain was gone and the fingers nearly healed. The Abbot used a Chinese medicine called myrrh to treat the wound and relive the painful swelling. During sessions with the Abbot, Ryu learned that the ointment originally came from a far land beyond China, and had been used there for the past one thousand years. He didn't really care though; he was just happy that his hand was better. He was grateful to the Abbott, and promised him loyal and eternal service.

The Abbot smiled and said, "Thank you. We shall need many committed monks in the days ahead". Ryu bowed obsequiously and promptly left. The holy man made him uncomfortable. There was so much knowledge and depth to the man that made Ryu nervous. He didn't know what to say to him; he always felt the fool in his presence. He was glad his hand was better and that he would not have to experience his company anymore.

After a quiet moment, the Abbott turned his attention to the parchment. He read it with concern. So, the demon has once again managed to extract victory from defeat. Putting the scroll down, he sat upon a tatami mat, lit some incense, and became very still.

"Inspiration shall come to me if I am patient," he meditated.

<hr/>

In the Tomoki compound, the jubilation over their recent victory at Ogie turned to despair over the defeat at Anegawa. Fortunately, the Asai and the Asakura were not entirely decimated. Thousands of warriors survived. Nobunaga cowardly withdrew his forces and returned to Kyoto. Konnyo-sama believed that Nobunaga withdrew because he felt he had succeeded in punishing and humiliating Asai Nagasama for his treachery and that he needed time to regroup, so he was not so strong. Little did Nobunaga know the extent he was to be tormented by them now, and that the Asai and Asukara would regroup to fight another day. Nobunaga's time of reckoning was coming.

The elders of the Tomoki clan were summoned to council. Of course, Sai and Naki were invited to attend. Sitting within the modest wooden structure sequestered in the secret forest, the assembly plotted.

Konnyo-sama, as always, somber and composed spoke: "I shall be brief. Nobunaga collected three thousand heads, but the victory truly goes to Tokugawa; he is Nobunaga's strength, so we must weaken him. Apparently, the loss of a brother and Castle Ogie did not discourage him as much as we anticipated. We ultimately defeat Oda Nobunaga by defeating Tokugawa. We must punish him: disrupt his sanctuary, his supply of arms, money, and food. We must hinder, terrorize, and demoralize ... both him and Nobunaga. Thunderclap from a clear sky."

All heads nodded in agreement, everyone understood, not a word was spoken. Konnyo-sama finished with a nod. Gravely, the assembly dismissed. Naki and Sai were left alone with the taciturn *Chunin* brooding over his plans. He did not acknowledge that they were still sitting before him. Naki studied his face, severe, harsh and rigid. The ebony eyes were unsparingly deep. Sai understood that her father had hoped the attack upon Ogie castle and a victory at Anegawa would have ended Oda Nobunaga's quest upon the neighboring provinces. She knew her father was now being forced to initiate more raids which would endanger many lives, the lives of the innocent and not so innocent. She knew he was now being forced to undertake brutal and desperate measures; she also understood that no matter how justifiable the intentions when one sows strife one reaps strife. Life in the ensuing months would be difficult for the Tomoki clan, for everyone.

Naki's acute attention to the sensei's demeanor was distracted by a slight rumbling in the distance. Just like a cat, he was aware of changes in the air and he knew when it would rain. A storm was coming, a fierce one. He reached for Sai and gently touched her hand. She shifted her head slightly to look at him, and he signaled that they should leave. She agreed. They both bowed and quietly left, leaving the *Chunin* alone with his designs. .

Crossing the compound, Sai said, quietly and sadly, "He worries for me and for the clan." Her tone was soft and caring. Her eyes, her father's eyes, black, beautiful and now shiny with unrestrained emotion fixated upon his. They conveyed an intense longing and tenderness he had only hoped for but never expected, for she was concerned about him.

"When you have the opportunity, tell your father not to fear for his daughter. I will take care of her, whatever the peril." A reserved smile spread over Sai's full round lips.

The wind stirred and suddenly it began to rain, hard. Oblivious to the onslaught, Naki and Sai stood silently in the downpour staring at one another, drinking in their subtle professions.

Sai broke the moment first and grabbed Naki's hand and began to run. They were saturated by the time they reached Naki's stable. He lit a lantern and a warm orange glow illuminated the little cubicle. Reaching for a *shirayuki fukin*, a snow towel, he offered it to Sai. As she toweled herself off,

Naki could not help but notice how her cotton jacket clung to the form of her body. Her white culottes pressed against her thighs revealing patches of skin. Naki recalled how soft she was. Many times during training, he touched her: her hand, her hair, her shoulder, her waist. He was amazed at how feminine yet so manly deadly!

Blood, blackness, death! Warfare! Conflict! Violently these images manifestd thenselves before him bringing Naki back to the difficulty of the moment. He snapped out of his reverie, consternation disrupting euphoria.

Sai intrigued with his whimsy didn't say anything to discourage his obvious desire. She enjoyed the passion flooding across his face, but when she saw his sudden look of distress she knew it was fruitless to harbor hope. She also abandoned her own daydream and came back to earth from her fanciful flight of imagination. They stood across from each other, silent and wet from the late summer rain, longing for each other, yet neither had the courage to speak.

Finally, Sai said, "We meet early tomorrow. Father will have devised plans; he will summon us."

"Yes," said Naki.

"So, goodbye."

"Goodbye."

"I will come for you in the morning."

"Very well."

Sai left, and Naki reeled from the tension. He closed his eyes and breathed deeply.

"I must be strong," he reminded himself as he began to pace about. Eventually, he left the stable and went for a run in the rain.

———◦◉◦———

Naki had finished his morning meditations, constitutional exercises by the time Sai came for him, a vision of freshness and beauty.

"Father wishes to see us now."

"I am ready."

"Let us go.

They strolled towards the *Chunin's* quarters.

Yoshi, Saburo, Hisao-san, Naki and Sai sat surrounding a low table, Konnyo-sama amidst them, speaking quietly:

"Initially I believed we would conduct injurious retributions, "Thunderclap from a clear sky". However, our wise Jonin has other thoughts. At a time, as yet undetermined, the tenacious monks of Ikko-Ikki will foray against Tokugawa, and the Tendai monks will attack Nobunaga, and they will do so with vindictive redress. However, Nobunaga and Tokugawa will be expecting reprisals; they will be anticipating attacks; thus, they will be prepared, on alert. So, we must fool them; we must seem to be ineffectual. and that we are incompetent, disorganized, nothing more than rabble rousing lunatics that have nothing better to do than to harass him and his dream of a unified Japan; we must make him and Tokugawa believe that we are not a serious concern, that we cannot harm them, and that they are indeed invulnerable, and assured of safely amassing arms and resources.

Therefore, raids will be conducted, and they will fail; we will lure the enemy into a sense of complacency. Over time, Nobunaga and Tokugawa will come to feel indomitable, that we are a minor but tolerable annoyance and that is when they will make collosal mistakes.

When the time is right, we will conduct devastating maneuvers that will cripple them, destroy their morale, undermine their spirit. Unfortunately, these failed assaults will exact a toll; many monks will die. Even though they profess not to fear death, my heart is heavy for them, but what must be done must be done.

Konnyo-sama nodded to end the council. Hisao puzzled by the Chunin's unwonted sentimentality paused to say something, but then thought better of it and left, along with everyone else.

"Sai, please remain," the *Chunin* requested.

"My dearest daughter, you know you are the world to me. I am torn. I lost your mother whom I loved dearly when she took on a dangerous mission. I could not bear to lose you as well. In my soul, I wish to keep you close so you will not be harmed, but fate dictates otherwise. Do you see?"

"Father, you have no choice. Do not worry, I am prepared. I will return safely, but promise me that any mission that I am assigned will include Naki, for he will protect me. The two of us will look out for one another, for we are one."

Konnyo- raised an eyebrow. Sai returned his concerned look with an assertive almost defiant expression. She would no longer deny her feelings for Naki. She was acutely aware of the risk associated with romantic liaisons, but she also believed she was trained and disciplined well enough by her own father to avoid the inherent pitfalls. She stood still and silent awaiting her father's reaction. None came. Tomoki Konnyo simply said, "Fine," and then dismissed her.

Sai found Naki practicing. He had fashioned a straw dummy and was peppering it with arrows from a short bow, a difficult weapon to master. He stopped when he saw her. She smiled at him, and he brightened at her attention.

"Look," he said proudly, "I can hit the neck from thirty paces." He took her by the hand and counted off thirty steps; positioning her beside him, he raised the bow.

Relaxed and focused, he let loose. The reed flew across the barn into the makeshift straw man exactly at the throat.

"Well done, Naki-san. Rarely have I seen such power and accuracy."

"Sixteen times out of twenty it hit the neck."

"Consistency is the key to confidence. How do your meditations go?"

"Well."

"Good. You are an excellent student. I just wish that it was my teaching which helped you progress so quickly, but I believe that you were just born with natural abilites, and I was merely a passageway."

"Sai, I am greatly indebted to you.

"Your gratitude is expressed through your mastery of what I have shown you."

They both became silent but spoke through their eyes. Each, unfortunately, understood that their feelings for each other were secondary to their obligations. They knew they may not join as lovers until … they did not know when. Sai's eyes began to glisten. She once again began to regret the life she inherited.

Everything had been simple and uncomplicated in the past when she could focus on her duties without distraction; now, there was Naki and her wish to be a woman in the fullest sense.

Naki sensing her conflict comfortingly reached out to touch her face, but she drew back.

"I must go ... Naki-*kun*."

Naki was stunned by her intimate address, *"kun"*; he was elated; she verbalized her affection, and for Naki the subtlely of the expression did not diminish its significance. His eyes smiled. Without a word, she turned and left.

He stood dumbfounded for a moment. Then a flush of blood reddened his face. He thought how his life has been complicated because of one man, how his dreams of the future were compromised, how his childhood had been fouled. His fury intensified. Again, he felt rage beyond his control. He seized his sword, whirled it at the dummy lopping off its head. He attacked the arms, left and right, leaving them bundles of nondescript straw on the floor, and then with one accurately aimed blow severed the effigy of Oda Nobunaga in half. It fell to the ground in two pieces, a pile of stock suitable for bedding or fodder. He sheathed his blade; then walking out the small back door of the barn, he knelt by the small stream and began to meditate. His diaphragm pumped violently as he struggled to regain his composure. Eventually, his breath returned and he sought the peace of the first level of the nine cuts of Kuji-In, the cut of Rin, strength of body and mind.

Carrier pigeons circling about, flapping down, perching upon their posts, waitied to be relieved of their messages. The handlers rushed to deliver the latest message from the *Jonin*. It was the *Jonin* who directed every Tommoki mission. The *Jonin* is sagacious in every regard and the *Chunin* obeys every directive; even if it means risking his life or his daughter's. Such was Tommoki Konnyo's spirit of Confucianism; it was unwavering.

The *Chunin* read the message from his sensei. Happily, this directive was relatively easy: conduct reconnaissance ... continue for several months.

The *Chunin's* worries for the safety of his people, especially his daughter, were now temporarily eased. He wondered why after a lifetime of living the life of a ninja *Chunin*, after coping with the death of his wife, after dealing with the loss of many of his clan over the many years his fears now were so powerful. Never had he suffered as much anxiety as he was suffering currently. He could not understand why. Why did he feel such overwhelming foreboding? Perhaps the gods were telling him something and he just did not understand. He saw darkness on the horizon and it frightened him for the first time in his life.

Chapter 16

The Nakasendo Road, running between the eastern coastal city of Edo and Kyoto, was an important highway for Oda Nobunaga. Precious gold, silver, and copper coins were regularly transported along the route. Portuguese guns and ammunition were hauled, albeit, with great difficulty; but most importantly taxes ... taxes from the provinces: rice, packed in sacks was moved through the mountains, along the winding treacherous high-way. Patrols struggled to keep the road free from bandits, but the seven hundred and forty four *ri*, the three hundred and ten miles, were difficult to protect effectively, so every caravan on the Nakasendo road was well armed.

Abbot Kossa issued an attack upon a shipment of rice; thirty warriors, they were to bungle the raid; the demons must think the Tendai are incompetent, nothing more than ticks plaguing a dog.

Ryu was one of the twenty cowl headed *sohei* who waited in the thick mountain forests, who waited hidden by trees and ferns for the wagons of rice sacks to pass. Takumi, spotted ten samurai on horses preceding several wagons laden with straw bags. Large oxen lumbered along under the loads. Twenty foot soldiers armed with spears were positioned behind the animals which were clearly exhausted from their laborious task of hauling this rice up and down steep hills.

A signal was given: rear assault followed by a frontal offensive. The skirmish was to be brief; everyone was to escape unscathed. With uncharacteristic noise and clumsiness, twenty monks appeared on the road behind the rear guard. They made enough of a commotion to alert the foot soldiers to ready themselves for attack. Issuing frightening sounds the monks charged the soldiers who leveled their spears. Whirling and swinging their *naginatas*, pole weapons with a curved blade on the end, the highly competent warrior monks plunged forward parrying jabs and hacking at the defender's pathetic efforts to repulse their onslaught.

Five samurai bolted to the rear to assist their beleaguered spearmen. Five samurai, with katanas drawn, remained where they were. Ryu and the rest swarmed in upon them, and it soon became clear as to why these five guarded the front. From their horses they easily repulsed the ten scythed blades coming at them from all directions. They effectively charged, whirled upon their steeds and slashed, defending themselves and their cargo, against the marauding monks who were restrained enough not to take any chances against such skilled warriors. The oxen frightened by the commotion panicked, toppling their loads onto the road. The monks at the rear saw that their efforts had caused enough destruction extracted themselves from the fight and fled into the woods. The rear guard believing they repulsed the attack cheered their flight.

The ebullient shout halted the skirmish in front. The ten *sohei* took a defensive stance surrounding the horsed samurai, their long poles pointing upwards; the samurai gave no hint of taking the offensive; each group indicating that they were finished. Ryu looked closely at his opponents and saw a familiar face among them, Zatoichi! However, Takumi at that moment issued a signal and the cowl headed monks needed to flee.

High upon a rocky outcrop, a monk released a bird with a blue band attached to its leg, signaling success.

Over the ensuing months many more such raids occurred, each harassing Nobunaga and Tokugawa; interrupting food supplies, the delivery of taxes and shipments of guns and ammunition. Some attacks actually did manage to usurp some goods, but none of the raids really inflicted any real damage to either Lord other than being just annoying and a slight drain upon the resources required for defense; however, sadly, good men died. The first stage ended, and the next phase was simply a termination of the attacks. It was hoped Nobunaga would believe that the monks had had just given up the harassment and would leave him be.

Tomoki Konnyo reported that indeed tension in Kyoto had dissipated. The enemy had become complacent, fortress security eased and things returned to normal: daimyo regularly visited Oda Nobunaga; samurai casually strolled through their residential sections; theatre and entertainment spectacles resumed; all aspects of business continued especially in the pleasure district.

The Shimabara quarter was the district that Sai's cousin, Yoshi, had been assigned several months earlier. Since she was beautiful and highly skilled; she quickly became a favorite of the most powerful samurai and even daimyo. They visited her often. Her myriad of charms won her an outstanding reputation, and during countless nights of pillowing with drunken customers she discovered secrets which were most useful, which if it had been discovered that they were revealed to her would have meant immediate death to the divulgers; fortunately, she was perceived as a trusted confidant and she continued gathering information.

On occasion she was even invited to the citadel, but only as far as the *ni-no- maru*, the second circle, where the Lord's business was luckily still conducted by members of the inner court. It was on one such invitation that she met General Takenaka Shigeharu. He was a samurai who had risen through the ranks via his guile and strategic brilliance. He was discovered by Toyotomi Hideyoshi, one of Oda Nobunaga's most distinguished generals who himself had risen from peasant origins. Shigeharu selflessly contributed to Hideyoshi's ascendance by assisting him with the administration of the firearms factory, where production of arms had increased dramatically; furthermore, his reputation with Oda Nobunaga, as being an excellent strategist, was recently elevated in the Battle of Anegawa on Lake Biwa. He was on the rise.

He first saw her at a banquet in one of the formal reception rooms of a compound tower, a secondary building apart from the inner citadel. She was stunning, and she had mesmerized the entire chamber with her charm.

General Takenaka Shigeharu was smitten. He made inquiries and discovered that her services were highly demanded. Nevertheless, he asked for her the next evening, and despite her being promised to another, he exerted enough influence to procure her for himself.

His quarters were in a notable area of the samurai district. They certainly did not compare to the lavishness of the gilded palace where the Emperor resided, nor where Oda Nobunaga maintained residence in the donjon, nor was it as rich as the residences of the second tower, but it was a dwelling of comfort and distinction.

As a consort, she visited him frequently, consequently establishing routines. After their evening meal, they would take a walk before retiring. He would talk about his successes; namely, improving the quality of the guns being manufactured; he believed they were superior to the ones delivered by the Portuguese. He boasted about how quickly they could be produced and he told her of his techniques in training the other samurai to use them, even though they often objected to having to resort to this kind of a weapon, as it was inglorious. He instructed the common soldiers and found that they were more accepting of the weapon and they excelled in its use.

Yoshi always listened attentively and spoke to him in the most flattering manner and performed for him in the most satisfying fashion. Regularly, she did not accept payment, and he took this as a sign that he might cultivate a more personal, permanent arrangement. He entertained the thought that she could become his courtesan. Whenever he mentioned it, she smiled coyly, and said nothing.

Never once did he suspect that everything he said was conveyed via couriers to the Tomoki compound.

Messages arrived, carrying instructions for the assassination. General Takenaka Shigeharu, as shrewd and disciplined as he was, forsook all precautions when he spent time with Yoshi. He walked alone with her. He did not wish to share her with anyone. Many times his guards vehemently protested his evening strolls with her. They advised him it was ill conceived. He dismissed them as being reactionary. He placated them with the concession that he would not dress overtly and wear only the simplest of kimono so as not to distinguish himself as anything other than any ordinary samurai strolling with a mistress.

They always walked the same path. General Takenaka Shigeharu thought the route charming. The street outside his home was paved with flagstone. The other homes along the street were handsomely lit with orange lanterns and bordered by shrubs and flowering plants. Beyond his street, the road narrowed to a stone path which led to a shining, lacquered wooden bridge spanning a pond which was part of the moat system protecting the castle. It was on this bridge the couple lingered throwing morsels of rice to the red, blue and yellow Koi which were in the habit of surfacing to feast on the generosity of those who traversed it.

Beyond the bridge was a shrine, handsome in wooden splendor. The gate, or *torii*, marked the entrance to sacred grounds. It was a large architectural form with two stone posts surmounted by a double lintel. Just past the gate was another bridge leading to the shrine itself. They strolled to its crest only; they never passed completely over as the shrine was sacrosanct and only priests were allowed. They lingered leisurely upon it, for it offered a pacific view of the canal and lights which danced, glistening and shimmering upon its surface. A few moments were spent in silence; the place was hallowed and required appropriate decorum. A tender embrace precipitated a return to the house where the communal ritual continued. Ironically, it was on the sacred second bridge where Naki was to strike.

They would pass onto the bridge shortly after the Hour of the Dog, and Naki would know they were approaching because the time keeper would tinkle bells and clang a gong and shout the hour. Yoshi after their habitual moment of silence and gentle embrace would feign dropping her fan leaving General Takenaka Shigeharu open and vulnerable.

Dressed as samurai, Nakamura rode Jun almost recklessly towards Kyoto. Cognizant of his last wild ride he checked himself and ensured he took no unnecessary risks. Jun performed admirably, swiftly blazing ground along the Nakasendo road. There were relatively few post stations at this time and his papers and his dress would allow him unimpeded access all the way to Kyoto. He would raise no suspicion.

He was instructed to leave his horse with a farmer on the outskirts of town and change into the clothes of an artisan which would ensure begrudging but unhindered entrance past the castle gates. Once inside he was to take shelter with Yoshi who would be found in the pleasure district. She would hide him until it was time for her rendezvous with her … lover.

When the sun set Naki disappeared into the night. He employed all of the skills he had acquired. His gait was balanced, quick and quiet; his awareness of everything around him was astute - to a degree which he himself was surprised. He heard everything. He saw everything. He smelt everything.

He was invisible. The passages leading to the samurai district were convoluted, yet he knew how to get to the shrine bridge. Yoshi had meticulously delineated them, and he committed them to memory, as if he had lived in Kyoto his entire life.

Under the cover of darkness, from a tree he saw the bridge; everything was quiet. Few visited, especially at night. Ambient lights allowed enough visibility to see someone crossing the bridge. Yoshi had informed him of what he might be wearing and what she would be wearing so as to make sure he had the correct target.

Tinkle! Clang! Clang! "It is the Hour of the Dog! The Hour of the Dog!" Tinkle! Clang, Clang! Naki jumped from the tree and slid into the canal. Using his blowpipe tube, he maneuvered beneath the water hoping that the ripples would not give him away. The probability of anyone seeing him was slim, as the bridge was empty, the water dark.

He found a sloping shore which enabled him to stand. Balancing himself, feet planted firmly on the muddy canal bottom, pipe, clenched firmly in his mouth, leaving his hands free to conduct the execution, he had an excellent view of the bridge. A black mask cloaked his head hiding him well in the canal. He was undetectable.

Waiting, he wondered how Yoshi would escape. Certainly, it would not take much to consider her a suspect. He then reflected that they … she … had surely conceived an escape plan. He then reasoned that he was not to worry about her that she was clever enough to have devised an elegant getaway. He would see her at home, in the mountain sanctuary.

He focused his mind upon the mission. Two figures appeared upon the bridge: one, a middle-aged male, dressed in a simple black kimono, swords at his hip, no armor, no guards in sight, and the other a svelte beauty, Yoshi.

They paused in the middle of the bridge, leaning against the rail closest to Naki. They stood still, momentarily drinking in the charm of the night. After a few moments, he turned to her and held her in his arms. When she was released, free, Yoshi dropped her fan and bent down leaving Naki a clear shot.

He rose, aimed the blow pipe, took a deep breath, and with a breathy explosion propelled the poisoned missile.

General Takenaka Shigeharu slapped his chest at the sting, eyes widening with disbelief. The toxin did not take long. Within seconds the General was stumbling about; then he fell, convulsing three or four times before he died. Yoshi calmly removed the dart and tossed it over the rail. It floated leisurely under the bridge into obscurity. All that remained as evidence on the body was a pin prick of a wound, not even much blood. It would take some time before anyone would understand what really happened. It would give her plenty of time to escape. `

Naki, on the other hand, swam away quickly, once he realized the dart had struck the mark. He reached the shore, disrobed and donned the garb of samurai which he hid along the bank in preparation for his escape. Calmly, he proceeded to the farmer, to his horse; he galloped home, mission accomplished.

Yoshi, in the meantime, struggled with the General, lifting him over the rail, dumping him into the canal. With serene composure, she left and made her way to a tailor's shop; there, she was given a set of clothes, rags, those of an undesirable *eta*; and in the middle of the night made her way out to the same farmer who gave Naki shelter for his horse. Scant moments after Naki, Yoshi was on her way. The General, floating under the bridge, was wedged against some rocks, enwrapped in lilly pads.

⇒·⟨◉⟩·⇐

Sai was exhilarated over Naki's safe return. When he arrived, she threw her arms around him and openly embraced him in full view of the entire village much to the amusement and pleasure of all.

By the time Yoshi arrived safely at the compound, the General's body had been discovered along the bank. It was the hour of the Snake and an alarm was sounded, to no avail.

Initially, there was confusion over how he had died; eventually the puncture wound was found; the cause of death was determined: ninja!!!

Panic spread throughout Kyoto. The ninja mystique was terrifying. Shinobi possess supernatural powers. They appear out of air; they disappear into air; they are invincible. Superstition, supposition and speculation were rampant: Kyoto was in danger. Frightened folk superstitiously believed their fate was imminent and that they would be the victims of future furtive machinations of the infamous ninja. Less than stalwart men nervously feared that death would strike out of the dark; only the staunchest of men were not afraid.

Reports of the consternation pleased Tomoki Konnyo.

Chapter 17

Weeks passed; there were no further incidents and paranoia faded. Kyoto, quickly recovered from its ninja anxiety and supplanted its hysteria with preoccupation for the summer festival. Celebrations would last for days, visitors would inundate the town and the streets would fill with revelers. Elaborately costumed religious promenades, beseeching the kami to protect the harvest from harm, would parade along the main avenues. Feasting and drinking would occupy the collective consiousness. The festivities would consume everyone's attention: the Emperor, the regents, the samurai, the priests, the villagers…everyone …making an attack very easy.

——————— ⫸•⫷ ———————

The irony did not escape Tomoki Konnyo. Rather than good fortune showering Kyoto at the time of celebration, it would rain fear and terror. It saddened him that the festivities would be spoiled; nonetheless, it could not be avoided: it was war. The town's people were just as culpable for Oda's atrocities as he was; they supported his warriors with the production of food and the manufacture of weapons.

The activites at the secret compound paralleled the preparations at Kyoto city. The clan was unwittingly consigned by the Kyoto council to entertain during the festival. The family enthusiastically rehearsed their Kabuki and Bunraku presentations. The acrobats and magicians worked their flips and polished their tricks. Medicine men packed cases with herbs and salves. Surreptitiously, secret compartments were filled with more sinister items: black head gear, loose fitting jackets, trousers with numerous pockets; an arsenal of weapons was concealed in false bottom trunks: shuriken, tanto, shoge, metsubushi, yumi and ya, short bow and arrow, the *manrikgusari*, a chain with weighted ends, designed to crack and crush bone. Never was there a more engaging group of lethal entertainers assembled.

———

In spite of the fact they departed for Kyoto in staggered convoys, their departures did not go entirely unnoticed. A set of curious eyes watched from a mountain ledge as the various parties travelled along the secret mountain road.

Naki and Sai travelled together. On this occasion, they were to be actors. She was to perform in a "Woman Play", an entertainment about elegant, courtly women, and he was to be the protagonist in a "Warrior Play" from the *Tale of Heike*:

heroes who fought in the *Gempei War* four centuries ago. The design was for the summer celebrations to continue festively, uninterrupted, for two days; however, whenever possible the logistics for attacking the citadel were to be reviewed and refined. Habits of powerful samurai were to be scrutinized and weaknesses in the defenses were to be noted.

As expected, not one suspicion was raised about the arrival of these foreign entertainers. It was as if the memory of the recent murder of General Takenaka Shigeharu and the gripping fear of ninja assassinations had been obliterated by the excitement of the ensuing merriment.

Several small inns along a delightfully decorated street were procured where the entire clan could remain in close proximity to one another. The accommodations were cheerful and hospitable. Narrow stairways led up several stories to a variety of small yet well appointed rooms of which the most interesting feature was a carved balcony railing that overlooked the street below. Floral designs cut into the wooden rails cast delicate morning shadows onto the lacquered wooden floor for the enchantment of its occupants. The food was satisfying; the futons were comfortable; everything boded well.

Awkwardly, things went too well, for when the troupes took to the streets, their entertainments were so popular, and in such demand that crowds followed them about, interfering with their ability to carry out surveillance. Only through exemplarity focus and concentration could they conduct their reconnaissance. Gathering accurate information was paramount to orchestrating a perfect assault upon the citizens of Kyoto, demoralizing them, turning them into a quivering mass of fear fraught folks, filled with trepidation. The aura of Nobunaga's invincibility must be destroyed; he must be viewed as a pariah; he must lose face.

When the charade of entertaining crowds finished late in the afternoon, the industry of espionage began. Kyoto's twilight activities revolved around drinking and eating. The narrow town lanes packed celebrants together; the inns and tea houses brimmed with people; music, laughter and cheer proliferated. Perilously, drunken samurai wandered, boisterously looking for amusements; thus, when the troupe ramified and impersonated revelers, gleaning precious details for the ensuing assault, they were cognitive of the dangers posed by intoxicated samurai. They could be extremely belligerent and problematic. Fortunately, nothing happened.

Naki and Sai strolled together when they had the opportunity; they roamed the castle walls. It did not escape their notice that the drinking was not only enjoyed by the people in the avenue but also by the guards on the towers as well. Sentries were drinking openly. Sai coyly looked at Naki and smiled; he understood. Intoxicated guards were easy prey.

Concluding the days of celebration was a prime evening festivity in the castle courtyard where the grandest chapter and the final event of the summer event would take place. The courtyard would be transformed. Rich gold and red imperial banners would be hanging everywhere upon the stone walls circumscribing a myriad of chrysanthemums white, yellow, and pink carefully arranged throughout the yard, changing the massive square into a splendid botanical paradise. Thousands of lanterns would illuminate entrances and paths. The ceremonial halls similarily decorated, would be awaiting the company of a myriad of honorable guests; the Emperor, his loyal regents, and most notable samurai all dressed in splendorous formal garb.

Women, in an attempt to emulate the beautiful flora that surrounded them, would meticulously powder their faces white, and elegantly accentuate a red dot below a rouged lower lip. They would fasten their hair noir with gold and pearl combs; and with shaved eyebrows, carefully redrawn, and blackened teeth they would affect a complete and aristocratic elegance suitable for the summer occasion, and then they would waft like flowers in a gentle breeze waiting to be plucked.

It was common practice that following the traditional rites, dances and performances, the evening would devolve into a mass of drunken festivity: drunken emperor, drunken lords, regents, samurai, everyone would be drunk; it was a time for celebration; it was a time for storming the castle.

———◆———

Scores of high ranking officials, administrators and well armed samurai were to attend. Hundreds guarded the battlement walls; thousands were billeted within the barracks on alert should they be required; yet despite the fact that most would be drunk, the raid was dangerous. Ninety shinobi against hundreds ... thousands was an undertaking only for the ingenious and intrepid, yet they were ready.

The first incursion would be against the sentinels upon the rampart walls, the inebriated guards the first to go. The clan would then drop into the castle and disperse. Twenty assassins costumed in ceremonial garb would slip into the inner palace and spread out among the guests. But, before any attack upon the honorable guests would take place, the barracks were to be set ablaze ... killing the thousands inside.

The commotion and the alarms should panic the revelers, and then the extermination of the royals would begin. Notable individuals had been targeted. The challenge, however, was to locate them in the stricken throng. If finding them was not possible random slayings of those nearby would suffice. The Emperor Ahikaga Yoshiaki was not to be harmed. Oda Nobunaga would more than likely be surrounded by his samurai and his assassination was remote as the least sign of trouble would send him scurrying into the sanctuary of his residence; but if the opportunity materialized his death would be the ultimate gift.

The storm was to be quick and short. A prolonged assault would spell the end for the attackers. In – kill - out, that was the way it was to be. Nobunaga's invincibility and invulnerability were to be compromised. Seeds of fear and doubt were to be sown. Nobunaga's haughty aura of invincibility and magical charm was to be undone.

The morning of the assault, Naki sensed an increased tension in the humor of the family. The prevailing mood was sober. Former jocularity and playfulness was supplanted with focus and concentration. The day's entertainments were cut short by two performances, excused by pleas of exhaustion much to the disappointment of the audience. Everyone pulled back to the inns to rest and prepare for the night's grave business.

————※(◉)※————

The sunset was spectacular: a rose and blue horizon heralded an evening of glorious festivity. Dusk descended into night, and the sound of the celebrations from the palace drifted far beyond the castle walls.

————※(◉)※————

Meanwhile, four score and ten intrepid men and women prepared for a terrifying strike upon unsuspecting merrymakers. Instruments of death were readied to smash slash, pierce and burn. Mechanisms were checked and re-checked for their integrity to insure an unscathed escape.

As Sai dressed for the deadly occasion in a magnificent silk *uchiki* robe, skirt trousers, and a white floral *kosode*, an owl descended from the black of the night and alighted upon her balcony railing. Its wings flapped wildly to steady itself before long lethal talons grasped the banister for balance.

Large, very large round eyes, pupils black as pitch encircled by a startlingly contrasting golden irises stared at her disconcertingly. Its head and neck bobbed up and down three times before it resumed a still repose. Sai stared at the intruder. It stared back. Several fierce heart beats pounded within Sai's chest before the bird spread its magnificent wings and flew off into the night.

Flustered, she wondered. What did this portend? Owls had many meanings. Which was this? Was it an omen of her death, a promise of transcendence from this difficult life to another world, free from suffering and conflict? Did it forecast her successfully using her exceptional skills in this time of danger? Was it a sign others would die … Naki? What did it mean? What did it mean?

She rationalized this curious incident would distract her ability to function effectively, so she put it out of mind. She conceded that whatever the gods decree, will be. If she is to die then that is her destiny; she will die. If she survives, then that too is what will be. Stoically, with awful effort, she dismissed the omen and continued preparing.

In the mirror, she studied her costume. Her black hair, piled upon her head, was fastened with an exquisite white pearl comb; one which would make any royal concubine or palace wife jealous; her robe, lavishly decorated with a dramatic diamond and floral motif of deep ebony contrasted elegantly against the whiteness of her gown; she concluded she was a magnificent effect. Within the secret pockets of her *kosode* she placed her blowpipe and darts; the billows of the costume completely concealed her arsenal, her guise ingenious.

———·«(◦)»·———

Meanwhile, in the courtyard, the religious rites having concluded, the throng turned its attention to fireworks whistling above the palace, bursting thunderously, spectacularly:blue gold and green displays, lighting the night, spraying splendor across the sky, reverberating rocking and stupefying the crowd below.

Taking advantage of the pyrotechnics to breach the walls, the hooded invaders silently disposed of the guards fortifying the castle, and then made their way towards their next target, the barracks.

Sai, Naki, and company managed to slip inconspicuously amongst the royal party, mingling with the crowd. As stunning as Sai was, not one person realized she just suddenly appeared. The intoxicating effect of the festive ambiance dulled the minds of even the most attentive and wary. The imperials of Kyoto were, at the moment, exceedingly vulnerable.

———·«(◦)»·———

Hisao-san led his black-clad brethren to the garrison where thousands of men reveled. Contrary to orders, they were drunk. The few guards posted outside the doors of the long, narrow quarters were equally inebriated. Their senses impaired, they fell quickly. Now the empty avenue between the rows of barracks was uncontrolled, open to the machinations of the intruders, bent upon setting fire to the structures and sealing the fate of the luckless inside.

Without a whisper, without a word the raiders barricaded doors and placed straw about the structure. Striking flints they ignited the stalks and their arrows. Thud upon thud pounded the building as flaming arrows struck. The deadly shafts with their licking fiery tongues quickly engulfed the dry wood into a conflagration of hellish containment. Orange light lit the dark avenue illuminating the shadows of death scuttling about ensuring not a soul escaped his fiery fate.

Sounds of alarm sprang from within. The barricaded doors were tested by violent pounding from inside, but the pounding ceased rather quickly, for the fire now raging prevented any break out from the flaming wooden fortification. Makeshift rams pummeling the doors from inside only succeeded in infuriating the inferno into blazing hotter, deadlier.

The sounds of terror turned to sounds of suffering as clothing ignited and flesh burned. Screams of insufferable agony supplemented the chaos encumbering further efforts of escape. Flaming bodies fell, some on top of one another, piling up, creating an even more gruesome barrier within. Eventually, Hisao-san deemed the trapped good as dead and ordered everyone to withdraw to a safer distance, as the heat became too intense. They retreated and formed a phalanx; armed with bow and arrow in case anyone did break through the dam of flame into the avenue, they were prepared to fire. No one escaped. The troops were living Hell.

Satisfied with their success, the shadows withdrew, scuttling off letting the blazing holocaust burn itself to its fiery conclusion.

The flames reached the roof rafters illuminating the western sky with an orange glow. One mile away, the drunken celebrants of the courtyard began to express concern over the new curious light display, a mild panic stirring.

Shouts of pandemonium from beyond the court walls turned angst into fear, unrest into hysteria. The confusion over the tangerine sky, the agitated squall of the commoners outside the courtyard walls generated terror amongst the guests and negated any rational recuperative response from the feckless within. Screams punctuated the night air. Abject fear fogged reason, even among the seasoned samurai. Confounded, no one knew exactly what was happening or what to do; dissension ensued; the mayhem outside the walls paled to the craven bedlam within. Shouts and shrieks rang uncontrollably. The collective thought was to retreat to safety, the castle proper: a fatal mistake, Royals, ranking officials and women fled for the palace stairs. Samurai clustered in a circle at the foot of the steps, confused, looking for the enemy.

Having ramified effectively and positioned well amid the horde, the bold seized their moment. They began their slaughter. Sai commenced. Feigning fear, she recoiled from the blithering bewildered General, who moments earlier had been trying to seduce her, and withdrew her blowpipe. In an instant, she punctured his jugular vein. Thunderstruck, he slapped at the prick in his neck. General Go Yozio fell ingloriously. Sai viperously moved on to her next victim, a terrified senior councilor stumbling towards the stairs.

With proficiency, the shinobi encircled the samurai and loosed a rain of arrows upon the bickering lot. The quibbling ceased. Gasps and groans replaced the confused babble. Someone managed to usher a cry of, "Ninja!" The retreating royals, already terrified, elevated their panic, stumbling up the stair case, in clumps, trampling one another. Arrows and shuriken flew unmercifully and indiscriminately.

Oda Nobunaga, as expected, encircled by his men, having ushered the Emperor to sanctuary, stood atop the stairs before the palace, and stared furiously upon the mayhem below, his hatred for ninja reaching new levels of antipathy.

His livid fury rendered him still as stone, tall upon the palace staircase. Naki, at the base of the steps, dispensing arrow upon arrow into the anonymous mass notched another one and raised his eyes in surprise to see the Devil, recognizable by his hard eyes, stony features, and ebony ceremonial garb, fuming with madness above him. Instinctively, without thought for he had not a moment to lose, quivering with nervousness, he raised the bow and fired. The missile flew straight and true but struck a guard at the last instant. He fell. Nobunaga dislodged from his delirium by the near miss, looked to the direction of the shot and locked eyes with Naki. The loathsome, riveting, hateful stare paralyzed him; such was its dark authority. It lasted mere moments but for Naki it was an eon of time. The world around him collapsed, blackness enveloped him, an absence of sound and light, save for two red spiteful eyes piercing his, and that of a horrific hiss filling his mind and ears issuing from a mouth vilely twisted and curled. It was only when Nobunaga raised his head to the sky and let loose a maddened howl did the bedevilment cease.

The villain disappeared into the castle, out of harm's way

from the turmoil in the courtyard. By now scores lay dead or dying: samurai at the base of the stairs, nobles on the steps, and guards at the top of the stairs. The damage was done. It was time for the assailants to depart.

Shedding their masquerading attire, the courtyard marauders let their raiment fall where they stood. Beneath their costume they wore orthodox ninja cottons in order to invisibly escape into the night.

The clan fled. The samurai, transcending the shock of the incursion, although much too late, rallied in pursuit. The lanterns hung so gloriously to festively illuminate the courtyard had been torn down by Hisao-san and his men after torching the barracks. Now the ninja ran, darkness their ally. Ropes and chains were lowered to allow their kin to retreat over the walls. Smoke bombs and barbed balls were thrown down to impede the chase. It worked. Already shocked and stunned, wounded and drunk, the men of bushido were thwarted. The smoke confounded them and the pointy balled barbs efficiently ended their reprisal.

Naki reached the high wall and assisted his brethren by forming a human ramp and springboard to launch each one up and over. Others used ropes and chains to clamber up. Within minutes they were on the other side of the enclosure.

Hisao-san had horses ready, and they rode, thundering down castle roadways towards the town to the open fields. This was the most dangerous stage of the attack. They could not predict what they might encounter … nothing or everything. It was supposed that since the barracks entombed the troops there would not be much resistance against the ninety who rode furiously; they were correct.

Not one ninja casualty. Not one kin, dead, injured, so successful was their foray. The main gates were open as they had left them, and into the town they fled. Villagers, frightened by the fire, smoke and screams from the castle retreated indoors and the roads were clear. Galloping, as only samurai and ninja could, they left Kyoto behind disappearing into the hills.

━━━◦《◎》◦━━━

The fire was contained to the barracks and did not spread to the other very vulnerable buildings nearby; however, the quarters were leveled. The painful industry of rebuilding began immediately. The town's *eta* was ordered to carry out the gruesome task of disposing the melted, charred bodies. A large pit, dug on the Temple grounds served as a grave, and a prodigious stone marked the thousands interred. Fallen nobles, generals, administrators, some one hundred of them, were tended to by untouchable undertakers. For the outcasts, disposing of the noble dead was bewildering, unnerving. *Eta* were not to speak to or look upon nobles, and now the wretched were touching, arranging and preparing so many for their transmigration to the world after death.

Cynically, ironically, some thought, as they were lifting or hauling a body, "When you were alive, I could not venture to look upon you, and now that you are dead you look to me to prepare you for your last rites."

Standing alone atop the stairs where he almost met his own death, Nobunaga surveyed the removal of his generals and friends from the courtyard. Rage overrode grief.

Involuntary convulsions distorted his handsome face into a mask of spasmodic fury; his eyes burned revenge. He always hated the shinobi clans and now his rancor was volcanic. Again, he stood still as a mountain watching the indignity below. A warm wind stirred, rippling his black kimono, carrying the virulent, heavy smell of death. He swirled and retreated into the palace.

Chapter 18

"Lord Nobunaga, I thank you for indulging me during this time of extreme sadness. Your kindness and your wisdom will not go unrewarded," Zatoichi groveled. He was prostrate before the Lord Unifier of Japan, somber upon the dais. Nobunaga, flanked by surviving retainers, wore a severe expression, dark and angry; it was obvious that the slightest annoyance would transport him into a volatile rage and the perpetrator would pay dearly for the mistake. Zatoichi, aware of the danger, nevertheless chose to flatter himself before his Lord.

"Most honorable Lord, as you know I was away when the insurgency occurred. Had I been present, I assure you, my Lord, the vile dogs would not have escaped." Nobunaga, not in the mood for baseless assertions, waved him on to get to the point. Zatoichi, relieved that his gambit to elevate himself suffered no ill repercussions, said what he had to say.

"My lord, I, according to your judicious direction, was searching for the ninja village, and … my Lord … I found it … cleverly concealed in a mountain valley north of the Monastery.

Nobunaga's surly disposition promptly switched to guarded skepticism. "You had better be correct," he warned. I overlooked your offence when you refused my offer to join me; rather than submit to me or to your duty, honorable death, you chose to flee." He debased Zatoichi mercilessly before the attending regents, exacting revenge. "You soiled your honor."

The public humiliation was not one Zatoichi was expecting nor wanting; he stood mute. "Nonetheless', Nobunaga continued, surprisingly magnanimous, "I was impressed with how you avoided death; with how you managed to overpower some of my most excellent samurai to escape. And then, when you returned to me, begging for your life, knowing full well that it could have ended the moment you presented yourself, I again admired your courage. Your audacity is outrageous; it reminds me of my own, for I too have looked death in the face and survived. You have indeed proven that my benevolence in sparing you was not misguided. You are indeed a man worthy of a second chance …and now, propitiously, you bring me news of the ninja?"

"Yes, my lord." Zatoichi spoke softly. Not only that, my lord, but my agents have also informed me of a planned assault by the Ikki-Ikko against Lord Tokugawa."

This time Nobunaga's explosion was one of delight. His face broadened into a vengeful grimace. "If what you say is true, we will crush these creatures and destroy them forever. You have indeed lifted my foul mood, Zatoichi-san: you will be rewarded. We will talk further at another time."

He instructed Saito Dosan to give Zatoichi new quarters in the coveted second circle, and then dismissed him. Zatoichi could not have been more pleased. He knew his cleverness would restore him to his rightful position; it was just a matter of time.

———«((O))»———

For Nobunaga, retaliation too, was just a matter of time. Within days he met again with the regents. He disclosed his intentions menacingly; all sat gravely serious, listening.

"General Akechi Mitsuhide has promised to replenish our troops. He is sending replacements, three thousand men, and they will be here within thirteen days. It is imperative we redress the wrong inflicted upon us, immediately; so their imminent departure for Kyoto will be revealed to the Enryaku-ji and the Ikki-Ikko monks."

Mutterings of confusion rippled through the room.

Nobunaga continued, "Upon realizing replacements are moving in, these meddling monks will try to attack them."

The disconcerted voices grumbled in perplexed agreement.

"And we will let them."

The sounds of consternation intensified.

"But we will lay a trap."

And the clatter of confusion ceased.

"Zatoichi-san and his people will make sure the monks believe only one thousand five hundred men are marching for Kyoto, and that the troops can be easily overcome. Since the Ono Valley is a natural location for camp through the mountains, that is where and when the monks will plan to strike; but we will be ready for them."

Murmurs of approval rippled through the hall.

He continued. "Half of the three thousand will march a day before, secretly, during the night, ahead of the rest, and hide in the hills surrounding the Ono Valley and lay in wait. When the infernal monks attack, what they believe is the entire contingent of replacements, seemingly bedding down for the night, we will attack them, swarm down upon them and destroy them!" He paused, "Only thirteen days to reprisal my friends ... thirteen days to righteous redress!"

Voiced sounds of approval reverberated throught the hall. Oda Nobunaga's cunning plans have succeeded before, so the generals believed that this one would work too.

Eyes narrowed, black, cold, a frozen smirk fixed upon his face, Nobunaga was congratulating himself, but not over his clever plot, but rather upon his astuteness for utilizing Zatoichi. He has become very useful even though he is ambitious, arrogant, willful, devious, and utterly disloyal; and as soon as he is no longer valuable, he will die. Nobunaga had forgiven traitors in the past and turned them into loyal allies, but Zatoichi is different. He will never be loyal to anyone but himself, his ambition too strong, so eventually he will die.

"Within a fortnight our first retaliation against these dogs that plague us will begin," Nobunaga thundered, "we will wipe them from the face of the earth, monks and ninja!"

The roar from the attending generals was deep, guttural ... animalistic.

Naki had trouble sleeping again. The dreams had returned, but this time they were different. He no longer saw his little sister, Keiko, impaled, sliding down the shaft of a massive spear into the gory mud of her own bloody issue. He wasn't listening to the terrorized screams of villagers helpless against the black leather clad death which descended upon his village. He didn't feel the heat of the humble wooden structures aflame, blazing infernally. He didn't smell the death of those engulfed in the maelstrom of Nobunaga's malice. He saw faces he didn't recognize, strangers, men, women, all wearing the same agonized expression of pain and fear. He experienced their terror to where his heart beat with the same intensity as theirs. He looked into their eyes and saw confusion, torment and death. He felt them. They were strangers to him, yet they weren't.

Sai woke Naki. "Your dreams have returned," she said. "I could tell by your face while you slept."

"Yes, they have," Naki mumbled, not fully awake. "How long were you watching me sleep?" Naki inquired as he collected himself from his nightmare.

"Not long ... long enough to see you are troubled again."

"I am. I see unfamiliar people suffering and dying. I do not know why?"

"I do, "Sai said with conviction.

"Why?"

"You are an empath."

"A what?"

"An empath, you feel others, their suffering as well as their evil. You have the ability to sense people and how they feel or what they might do, predict the future so to speak. It is a spiritual gift, hereditary. I have it too. It is common among ninja. It gives us the ability to know how to react in difficult situations; it is our secret. It is what helps us survive. You have it more profoundly than most; unfortunately, you suffer as a result. That is why you dream so vividly and feel so deeply. It is what separates you from other people.

"How do you know this?" Naki asked.

"Ninja clans realized this long ago. That is why we do not accept anyone from outside. They don't possess this quality that is so important for everyone's survival."

"So, how do you cope? Feel so deeply and kill so dispassionately"

"Dispassionately? No … we regret the killing, but we have no choice. The fates have determined this is our destiny in this life. Japan has been a confused jumble of warring provinces, for hundreds of years. Daimyo against daimyo, brother against brother, father against son, for what? Power, glory, riches? We serve a purpose to bring in a just order of things. We do not indiscriminately embark upon a mission because someone has the purse to pay our fee, at least not our clan. We accept our assignments because we believe in our Jonin, who has the vision to comprehend what is correct and what is not. We submit to his understanding of the higher order of things, and we obey. Some clans yes, they do accept money for whatever reason, and they suffer the consequences." She continued, "We, however, have survived for generations because we are special and every one of us hopes one day what we do will no longer be needed." Pausing, she took a deep breath, "It is a hard life. Not a day passes when I wish that I were born a simple farmer's daughter, but I was born with talents and abilities which I must use to fulfill my destiny, whatever it may be. I have been able to keep my feelings under control without too much difficulty ... to do what I must - until you arrived. Now, I struggle more than I wish to. Now, I want to forgo this life, terribly, to live peacefully, quietly, raising children, free from the anxiety of the next mission and free from possibility of an early painful death."

Naki was astounded. He reached for Sai, but she pulled away. Tears welled in her eyes. She looked intensely at Naki. He reciprocated with intense compassion. Shyly, submissively, she pressed into his arms, seeking protection, comfort. He wrapped her up and held her gently for a long time. He could feel the cool wet of her tears upon his cheek; she trying to restrain her sobs. He nuzzled his face against her ear and whispered,

"*Daisuki desu*." He dared not whisper anything more, like," I love you," for those words had such import of meaning, and he understood they may cause her more misery than comfort.

She drew back and held his hands; dropping her head, looking at her feet, she said the same thing. They stood a moment in silence, still and fragile like porcelain statues.

Naki, moments ago troubled by dark foreboding, muddy grey agonized images painfully imprinted upon his soul, stood before a magnificent manifestation of bright white light: loving, tender, sensual and pure, healing.

He placed his hands upon her delicate shoulders and

drew her toward him. Together they sank onto the cot holding each other almost afraid to let go. The stable normally astir with the snorts and shakes of the horses was silent, all sounds faded but for the brook which burbled outside.

———◦◦◦———

Ono Valley is situated near the western foot of Mt. Hiei a half day's march northeast of Kyoto. A wide flat strip of land it was routinely used for bivouac when troops traversed through the mountains. Oda Nobunaga was correct in assuming the Tendai monks would strike here, for it was an easy descent down the mountain and a quick and relatively safe retreat to the monastery.

Nobunaga hadn't assaulted the monastery previously for numerous reasons: one of which was that it constituted some three thousand buildings and housed some thirty thousand people scattered over acres and acres of land. So, for years, he suffered the warrior monk insurgencies; he had too many other wars to wage, but now they had incited his wrath and commanded his attention. He would deal with them forthwith. This scheme would be his first of many ploys and assaults against the Enryaku-ji monastery. The ninja raid on his castle, the loss of so many good men, the monks infernal and incessant harassment impelled him to destroy the monks first, the ninja second.

One thousand five hundred men lay encamped in the valley, waiting. One thousand five hundred men hid among the trees on the southern hillside ... waiting. The question was how many monks would actually descend, his three thousand men against how many monks? Nobunaga, watching the camp below guessed one thousand men would attack. They believed the attack would be a surprise, so they would not need to use many men. The tactic works, after all, he surprised and defeated twenty five thousand men with three thousand.

Nobunaga, believing he had superiority in numbers, was still slightly apprehensive. These men were ferocious. They did not fear death. Their skill in battle rivaled his best samurai warriors. He hoped the troops Mitsuhide sent were seasoned. He waited.

The men in the valley were ready. Nobunaga convinced himself he would win. If they attacked they would be slaughtered; if they didn't attack then all his forces would reach Kyoto safely. He endured the wait. Waiting to fight was worse than fighting. He wished they would attack and that retribution could be extracted.

Zatoichi knew his life depended upon him having orchestrated everything skillfully and that they would attack. Nobunaga summoned him. Taller and heavier set than Nobunaga, Zatoichi positioned himself beside his lord. Patiently, he waited for him to speak. Nobunaga stared at the valley. He watched as camp fires were lit.

"You are assured of an attack this evening? "Nobunaga spoke without looking at his listener.

"My lord, my best men have assured me they will, this night. My men risk their lives. They believe in a future with you through me. I hope you will grant them favors worthy of their efforts." Again, Zatoichi's audacity, and arrogance surfaced.

Who does he think he is talking to, Nobunaga wondered? With his notorious charm and charisma Oda Nobunaga turned and smiled. "Most certainly, they will be welcomed and rewarded. Zatoichi's spirits soared. He knew as long as he could prove reliable and useful his future was promising. He believed in himself and he knew he would succeed by his wits and that he would indeed be rich and powerful as he once was.

Nobunaga, on the other hand, could not wait for him to fail, to become dispensable and thereby meet his due. As he turned his attention back to the encampment, wild almost feral cries rose from the forest edge and hundreds of long robed monks raced towards the tents. Some with cowled heads, some with helmets, some with nothing more than a straw hat. They were armed with bamboo bows, swords, *naginata*, bo sticks and little else.

Sardonically, Zatoichi smiled. What a motley crew he thought.

"So let the carnage begin," Nobunaga exclaimed, quietly to himself. He waited until the flood from the forest ebbed; He let the men on the valley floor fend for themselves, for awhile. Troops spilled from tents, ready to damn the flow from the mountain.

The fighting was magnificently furious. *Naginatas* swirled, glistening in the setting sun, slicing arms, abdomens, throats; bamboo arrows flew striking necks. Sturdy bo sticks walloped heads, broke arms, and exacted painful reprisals upon the less skilled; but eventually, by the power of sheer numbers the valley troops soon gained an upper hand. Sohei after sohei fell. It was then Nobunaga unleashed his forest forces, the defining blow. They emptied the hillside, cheering and yelling, overwhelmingly anxious to join the fray.

The monks had miscalculated. They sent seven hundred, hoping their surprise would be sufficient to overpower, to decimate the fifteen hundred in the camp. They had not counted upon fifteen hundred warriors prepared to retaliate, and they panicked when additional troops descended into the valley. Warriors rushed straight across the flat valley floor encircling them completely, assuring no escape for the monks.

Bones cracked, blood sprayed, men groaned, men died, mostly monks. Nobunaga looked at Zatoichi standing beside him and asked him what he was waiting for. Zatoichi, startled that his lord would demand he join the battle, knew better than to utter a word of resistance. He gathered his reins and rode into the valley. Nobunaga smiled and somewhat hoped he would survive, as he might still prove useful.

Indignant that Nobunaga ordered him to battle, Zatoichi rode with piqued fury. He charged across the valley, planning to cut off retreat. From his position on the periphery of the battle he saw monks fleeing for the woods. Believing he was safe, he thought he would have some fun. He reached for his bow and began a systematic shooting of men taking flight across the field. He unloaded his quiver of arrows at four seconds a shot. Nineteen arrows and fifteen kills, he smiled smugly to himself at how skilled he was with the weapon. He reached for his last shaft, notched it and let loose. It missed the target and the lucky monk disappeared into the trees. He sat upon his horse reveling in smug satisfaction; he didn't see the monk run up behind him. However, he sensed someone and turned to look. Staring, hatefully, at the arrogant samurai, was Ryu, his *naginata* poised, ready to strike. Zatoichi's eyes bugged; he held a bow with no arrows, his sword still within its sheath.

Ryu smiled and said, "This is for you," and swung. Zatoichi, recovered from the surprise, masterfully urged his horse forward to avoid the swinging blade. Ryu, managed to strike his back. ... Zatoichi tumbled, but grabbed a hold of his horse's neck and held on. He trotted forward clear of another blow, hanging upon his horse. Grabbing the horse's bridle, he tugged left. The horse, amazingly responsive, did what his master wanted, and Zatoichi circled round to face Ryu who was running at him with his blade raised ready to hit again. Regaining his saddle, he righted himself and cowardly bolted past the charging monk, not wishing to engage any further. He had been hit, hard. He wasn't bleeding but he suffered a stunning blow to the back of his ribs. His armor saved him, and Ryu watched him canter to safety. Unable to pursue, Ryu fled into the woods and disappeared.

—— ◦◉◦ ——

Thirty eight of the seven hundred monks survived, returning to the monastery, Ryu one of them. One hundred of the Mitsuhide men were dead, several hundred wounded. The victory satisfied Nobunaga for the moment. Riding into the valley, he reveled with the men surrounding him cheering their victory. Nobunaga raised his sword and roared, "It is just the beginning!" The elated warriors saluted his shout clamorously, vigorously pumping fists and swords into the air.

— 227 —

In a tent, among the Mitsuhide generals, Nobunaga ordered camp to be struck first thing in the morning and the march to Kyoto to resume. The Tendai monks were to be decapitated and their heads fixed upon poles facing the woods from where they came, a foreshadowing of what was to come. Their bodies were to be left for carrion birds to dine upon.

The harshness of the dictate alarmed the marshals. Their lord, Mitsuhide, was not this cruel, but they did as was bid.

Nobunaga and his minions raced ahead that night and covered the sixty *ri* by the Hour of the Rat. Arriving at his palace without thought of sleep, he summoned his advisors and generals, as well as Zatoichi.

Having administered some soothing balm to his wound, which amounted to a nasty bruising of his muscles and ribs, nothing more severe, but in pain, Zatoichi appeared wondering what Oda Nobunaga had to say.

Happily, Lord Nobunaga was in a jovial mood, eager to discuss plans for his next assault upon the monks of Mt. Hiei. Most of his address was directed at Zatoichi.

"Zatoichi-san, you have once again proved most useful."

Zatoichi bowed deeply at the compliment.

"I watched as you dispatched twenty arrows with fifteen kills, most impressive."

Zatoichi was astounded that Lord Nobunaga was watching him that closely. A spasm of anxiety gripped his chest, hurting his ribs. He was already resentful that Nobunaga ordered him into battle and now he was scrutinizing his warrior ways. Did he see him flee from the damned monk he should have killed? He knew he was not secure with his new lord and master, yet. However, his arrogance overpowered his insecurity and he convinced himself an assured place in time. He would succeed, he told himself. Composed, he thanked the lord for his kind words and promised further important contributions to his lord's plan of a unified Japan.

"Yes... yes, this is what I want to know. You know the monastery grounds?"

"Yes, my Lord."

"Good."

"You know where the ninja camp is located, correct?"

"Yes, my Lord."

"Good. You are dismissed, for now. I shall summon you after you have recovered from your wounds."

So, Nobunaga was aware of his encounter with the monk Ryu and how he fled rather than fell the squat mass of monk. Regardless, he thought, I am still valuable and will ascend to my rightful position in this world. He had no doubt. He rose to leave.

Nobunaga stopped him with, "Are you comfortable in your new quarters?

"Oh, yes, my Lord."

"Good." He turned to his regents and told them to make sure one of the finest women of pleasure comforts him and tends to his wounds.

With that Zatoichi again bowed deeply and left.

Pleased, yet disconcerted, he retired, believing that the fates would deliver his just due.

Naki awoke with Sai in his arms. Tenderly, he looked at her sweet face as she slept. The dawn was burgeoning, the sky clouded and overcast. He roused Sai . Demurely, she batted her eyes as she adjusted to her surroundings. A smile spread over her lips, Naki's face inches away from hers.

"I must go," she said.

"Yes," Naki murmured.

She rose, dressed, and with a loving glance left.

Naki felt her frustration. He felt the same. Anger welled within him. Life's lightness and joy faded, and darkened like the morning's sky, grey, black, ominous and overbearing. He closed his eyes and breathed deeply, forming his fingers into the cut of Kuji-In, Toh, harmony with the universe. He found it difficult to concentrate.

Chapter 19

Over the next few days, Naki's feelings of despondency deepened. Six hundred and sixty two heads transfixed upon six hundred and sixty two bamboo spikes; this manifested a chilling and haunting reminder to him of the vicious savagery Nobunaga was capable of dispensing. Revulsion overwhelmed Naki. He stirred restlessly, agitated. He couldn't sleep. He ate nothing. He avoided Sai, as he did not wish to burden her with his misery. His mind raced devising ways in which he could kill the monster; he still believed it was the only way to relieve his despair. He was constrained, however; he was not to do anything alone; the Abbott was very clear on that notion, but then again … would he? His thoughts of vengeance, black and vicious, were fierce. The meditative cuts no longer worked against his wretchedness. He needed to speak with his mentor, the Abbot.

EDMUND KOLBUSZ

Jun's confidence in negotiating the rocky terrain gave Naki assurance he was doing the right thing. The moonless sky, profoundly dark with heavy clouds, the drizzling rain, did not deter the horse or the rider from navigating the tricky mountain paths with urgency. Naki planned on meeting with Abbot Kosa at the break of dawn.

The head of the abbey rose dutifully at the Hour of the Hare, 5 a.m. and meditated before attending to the day's affairs. Naki wished to present himself before the honorable man became engaged in matters more pressing than his disquietude. So it was with great surprise that the Abbot received him warmly and accommodated his request to speak with him. He told Naki to go to the Lotus Hall. Naki felt relieved, grateful that the Abbot would give him time and attention.

He waited before the dais, trying to meditate upon the cut of the Rin, strength of mind, when the Abbot appeared in a simple brown robe carrying a sword in a scabbard.

"I am pleased you are here, Abbot Kosa said warmly, "I was to summon you."

"I was apprehensive that you would not have time for me considering Ono Valley."

"Yes, that was a disastrous miscalculation, and we were betrayed!"

"Betrayed! By whom?"

"By one whom I mistakenly trusted, even though I knew better that he was not entirely trustworthy. I wrongly assumed his hatred for Nobunaga was so profound that he would ally with us and lend his considerable talents to defeating our common enemy. We were betrayed by one whom

I believed that nothing would stop him from seeking the villain's destruction. Not, even after his treacherous attempt to usurp control of the monastery, did I suspect he would defect … prostrate himself before the Devil, but he did … another miscalculation. I am afraid I have made many mistakes, and I fear there may be more. I am getting old. I thought with age and wisdom foolish mistakes would fade and disappear, apparently not.

After a long silence, Naki snarled, "You speak of Zatoichi."

"Yes! Nobunaga has been has been cutting our supply routes with blockades. It has caused considerable difficulty for the mountain, for the monastery. In my cleverness, I believed if we could harass the demon we could free the routes, force him to deploy his forces against other more urgent affairs.

However, I did not recognize the measure of Zatoichi's treacherous ambition until it was too late. After he failed to seize control of the monastery, with unashamed duplicity, he fled to the enemy. Obviously, he has no concept of loyalty; this is where I made my mistake; I believed he had some constancy, some steadfastness in defeating the Oda clan, but he does not; he was only thinking about his own rightful glory. Lucky for him, Nobunaga overlooked his intransigence.

Naki seethed. Now, he has another nemesis. He recalled the blackness and the evil he felt when he fought against Zatoichi in the compound months ago; he remembered the dark and treacherous chi.

"Then there was Ryu."

"Ryu?"

"Yes, he tortured him with bamboo shoots, to force him

to disclose where you were. Ryu did not know, said nothing and suffered monstrously; fortunately, he survived, and happily his hands have healed.

Naki's head reeled with dizziness; his face flushed red with anger. He must die, he told himself.

"I will find him, and he will suffer," he growled beneath his breath.

"Nakamura, it is time you learned the truth about who you are."

"What is it you say? Who I am? ...who am I?"

"Do you recall I told you that you were special? The exception? Do you remember?"

"Yes master, it had a profound effect upon me. I followed your counsel and devoted myself to do what was impossible, as best as I understood to the best of my abilities. I trained with rigor ... but ashamedly, I was distracted, somewhat, by meeting the female ninja and her family. Yet, she taught me well. Now I am ready kill both Nobunaga and Zatoichi."

"Yes you are, and no, you are not. You are skilled enough; you have come far in a short amount of time, but again, I repeat, you cannot do this alone: you need Sai; you need the clan. Patience, your time will come."

Naki inhaled a heavy breath.

"What I am about to tell you unfortunately will not help you cope with your impatience, so, it is imperative you control yourself. What I am to tell you, however, will, clarify things for you, and give you even more motivation to become masterful to where you may eventually succeed in your quest, but more importantly it will determine your future."

Naki fixed his attention upon the Abbot and waited.

The Abbot began. "You told me your first recollection of me was when I was carrying you from the village. You were five. I was carrying you, the sole survivor of the massacre. Your village was destroyed ... because it was special.

Your father ... your family ... were special and that is why your village was destroyed. Oda Nobunaga hated ninja since his iniquitous beginning. Your family was a ninja clan that hindered Nobunaga as he attempted to usurp power from his uncle for Owari province. Your father, as Chunin, assisted Nobunaga's enemies many times; your family was a persistent irritant to Nobunaga – too many times. Nobunaga needed to extirpate them in order to continue, unimpeded, so he destroyed them. You alone survived. You believe your feelings of revenge stem simply from witnessing the destruction of your village... no, it goes beyond that; your heritage was annihilated. You have ninja blood. It is in your *seishin*, your spirit. You survived, and you alone are what remain of your lineage. I witnessed your father's skills and admired your mother's intuitive instincts. Your family was unique; you embody everything Nobunaga tried to kill, so you must live to continue your line. The Tomoki clan will help with that. They will protect you. However, I believe you will not be at peace until you wreak vengeance. I understand this, and that is why I have allowed you on various raids without entirely jeopardizing your existence. Hopefully, these reprisals mitigated some of your dangerous feelings. Have they?"

Naki's eyes scrutinized the floor. His mind whirled trying to assimilate everything he had just heard. He looked at the Abbot. "Why did you not tell me before?"

"You were not ready to hear this. It was better you lived in ignorance. You were too rash, too impetuous; you might have become more of a threat to yourself ... to others. However, in these past months, you have realized there is more to life than living for vengeance, death. You have met Sai. She is your salvation. Live for her. Do not jeopardize your life and the continuance of your line for the sake of reprisal."

"He torments me ... and Japan."

"Yes, he does, but he will be vanquished, so we must wait and endure. The gods will deal with Nobunaga. We must be far-sighted. You must protect yourself, your true destiny. This sword was your father's. Now, it is yours"

Shaking, Naki took the sword.

"It is of the *Dotanuki* Group. It is strong, durable, and sharp, like your father ... like you; it has superior cutting ability. I gave it to your father. When I rescued you, I found it in the rubble which was your home. It served him well, as it will for you."

Overwhelmed, all Naki could muster was, "Thank you, master."

He had to leave, for the demons within were rebelling.

Avoiding his mentor's eyes, he bowed and left.

◆◆◆

"Father, have you seen Naki?"

Tomoki Konnyo looked up at his daughter from his cot. He had been stricken with *byôki,* being ill, which had rendered him confined to bed. "No, my daughter, I have not."

"Jun is not in his stall. I have inquired and no one has seen Naki."

"I am sorry, my daughter, I know not what to say."

"You need not say anything, just rest and get well. I fear the strain of the last few days has somehow weakened your spirit."

"Ono Valley weighs deeply on my mind and my soul. It seems no matter what we do the demon strikes back."

"Rest, Father!"

"I shall try."

Dark circles circumscribed his eyes, creating a sickly contrast with the sallow pallor of his face. He had not eaten for three days. His usual calmness in the face of calamity had vanished. Lately, Sai had noticed a lessening of her father's inherent resistance to the reversals of fortune. He was not the same stoic stone she remembered. He was getting older, and the worry of protecting his clan, and the war against Nobunaga was diminishing his resistance. She had been noticing this for a long time, but chose not to dwell upon it. Now, she could not ignore it. Her father was sick: weak, enervated, dispirited; his head and body ached; he sweated profusely, even during the cool of the night. Massages, hot springs, meditations had no effect upon him. His sage wisdom and lucidity were noticeably moderated. He was no longer the man she knew, the stone which never cracked or … broke.

He, himself, wondered what had happened. Had he offended the spirits, neglected memorial ceremonies and lost their protection? Was this an omen of things to come? Why was he so sick? Something he ate? What? He was at a loss for an answer, and his progressively debilitating condition assured him that he may not find one. His daughter was his hope. She would tend to him now and take care of him now and in the after life, should that be the case. He believed for some reason he would not survive this sudden turn of circumstance.

"Do not worry about Naki. He can take care of himself."

"I do worry about him. He, like you, has not been the same. Now, he is gone."

"I understand your apprehension; unfortunately, I too see dark clouds upon the horizon. Difficult times are ahead. I know not if this premonition comes from my weak state or if I am indeed sensing correctly. Perhaps we have lost the divine protection of our ancestors. I do not know. Please leave me, for now I must rest, think."

Sai obeyed her father's wishes and left with a intense feeling of hopelessness: her father ill, Naki missing; she crossed the compound and entered the stable. Jun was gone and Naki's cot was empty. She stood and stared. Tears welled in her eyes.

The night was pitch, moonless. Jun ambled confidently, but cautiously along the road to Kyoto. Naki knew of the toll ahead. He dismounted and took Jun by the reigns and guided him through the trees to circumvent having to deal with the guards. It cost him an hour's worth of time, but he knew he would make Kyoto before the sun rose. Naki knew a tailor, a contact, who could be trusted.

As he rode on, his feelings about his exploit were mixed. Despite Jun's apperant confidence and sure footedness, Naki was apprehensive. He knew he should not have ventured out on his own. He had no sanction, nor support. He recalled the last venture to kill Nobunaga, pathetic. Was he a fool again, this time? He knew he was tempting fate, yet he could not help himself. The demons drove him onward. He was determined. Increasing his disquietude was that his innate senses, his early warning system, recognized something: something was watching him, following him, dangerous, powerful; yet, he remained resolute; he disregarded the sentience and focused on vengeance. Naki sensed Jun's disquietude too; however, the horse plodded onward, with big heart.

Naki reasoned that if he could not kill Nobunaga, he would kill Zatoichi. He tortured Ryu; he knows too much about the monastery; he betrayed the monastery; he must die.

————«(◉)»————

Daisuke, the tailor, was indeed surprised when Naki appeared at his door. *Big Help* recognized him and quickly ushered him inside. He ordered his wife to prepare tea and he sat down, bewildered, looking upon his early morning guest.

Naki spoke. "I have come on my own: to right a wrong. I need your help."

Daisuke was understandably cautious. "What do you wish me to do?"

"Nothing more than to hold my horse, feed him, give him water, and have him ready for me when I leave later this evening."

"My humble home is yours Naki - san. I shall take care of your horse."

"Thank you."

"After tea, you must rest, as it seems you have ridden all night."

"Yes."

———⊸⟪◉⟫⊸———

Naki slept until the Hour of the Cock. The sun would set in two hours. He would have time to stretch, prepare his weapons, ready his mind and body for ... whatever may happen.

When at last he was ready he checked his weapons again, aware of every one of his armaments, which pocket contained which device. He patted: checking every one, extracting them smoothly, dexterously: the *metsubishi*, blinding smoke bombs, nine of them, for good luck, his father's *Dotanuki* sword, sharp, durable, flexible, a rope for climbing, and lastly the *shuriken*, death stars without the poison. He checked for his water pipe. He was confident he was adequately armed, yet a nagging feeling tore at him.

At dusk, shadows lengthened and night crept upon the Kyoto. The streets bustled with activity until the Hour of the Boar then the traffic diminished significantly; only taverns and tea houses provided light enough along the alleyways. It gave Naki opportunity to weave his way unseen through the town, mentally rehearsing his escape route; he finally made his way to the castle wall. The moonless night helped camouflage his mount over the stone fortification, and then he proceeded to the coveted second circle where Zatoichi had been given quarters, according to Daisuke. In the shadows he lurked and waited, and when he moved it was with the grace of a panther.

Inside the castle grounds, his trespass into the second circle sanctuary went unnoticed. He chose to climb a steeply sloped wall with a narrow rocky base bordering a deep water moat. Only Naki would think to ascend a forty foot barrier in the dark, yet it was worth the risk; it afforded little chance of him being detected and once he was up and over his destination was just ahead.

He didn't use the metal hand and feet claws for they were too cumbersome to carry; the stones were large enough to grasp and gain hand and foot holds. The ascent was smooth: mystical, surreal, and blissfully serene: the night black, the town quiet, and his climb firm and sure. He was not even out of breath when he reached the top. It was an unremarkable ten foot drop to the street below, an easy jump. He padded quietly in the blackness following the inside wall till it curved around a bend. A stone building on the corner was his marker. He knew that at this spot the outer wall dropped forty feet straight, into deep moat water. This served very well as his escape route. He withdrew four iron spikes from the folds in his black garb and drove them into the masonry between the stones. The first one at a one foot level, the next one staggered to the left four feet and six feet high. He tested the spikes; they held his weight. He used these two spikes as hand and footholds to drive two more into the wall a little higher, so that clambering the ten foot wall would be easy, even if he was being chased. Once satisfied, he dropped back to the ground and crouched. He waited, listened, then he moved.

Sprinting to a gate, he slipped inside the samurai district. He climbed a nearby wall, and waited hidden in the black. It was not long before a party of revelers approached the gate and passed along to the comfortable quarters beyond. Zatoichi was not among them. Naki waited. Not long thereafter, another, party, smaller, two people, approached. It was Zatoichi with a concubine.

Visibly intoxicated, he was leaning upon his little mistress for support, she giggling demurely at his drunken foibles, he stumbling, and she catching him before he completely fell down; both laughed without care. Naki waited till they cleared the gate and headed down the road before he descended. He would soon discover where Zatoichi lived, and where he would die.

The samurai was too preoccupied with his little mistress, too inebriated to notice the shinobi, black head to foot, following him. Naki was becoming more and more confident; such a shame the villain was drunk. He would have preferred to kill him sober, on equal terms. His pride as a man was at stake ... or was it? Was he really that vain that he needed the glory of a fair fight to feed his self-esteem, or did he really just need the vermin dead, for he was a threat to the lives of those he loved? He determined he just needed him dead, drunk or not.

The couple led Naki to a long row of adjoining residences with a well appointed porch edging the front of the structure. Solid flagstone served as the road along the building. The stones would issue no sound of Naki's approach.

The pair unaware disappeared inside, entering the second residence at the top of the row. Zatoichi's elevated status afforded him the luxury of being close to the primary road to the main tower and the palace proper. This afforded a beneficial advantage for Naki: its location would make escape quicker and detection less likely.

The pair did not close the entry door when they stumbled through. Naki slipped in noiselessly and pressed himself against the vestibule wall. Now, he waited. Remembering the incident with the cat and with Hisao-san in the bath house, he focused upon listening. Slowly, his hearing became more acute: giggles from within the room. He envisioned a bed chamber. He heard the discarding of weapons and clothes. Did they cover the weapons when they fell? He couldn't tell. Finally, the heavy breaths subsided: silence, then female whispering, masculine agreement, soft rustling, bodies arranging themselves upon the futon, silence. Trained well, Naki waited, listened and imagined what was transpiring behind the double sided sliding shoji screen.

The silence was prolonged, but eventually he heard Zatoichi's deep voice direct the little one, to knead his back harder. So, he was lying on his front with her atop. He was vulnerable. Naki moved.

He slipped before the shoji screen. They were distinctly silhouetted against the rice paper, clearly visible by the candlelight within. Through the cherry tree blossom pattern on the door, Naki could see she was indeed atop him, servicing him. She naked, standing, gingerly stepping with her little feet, one foot here and one foot there, pressing with all her insubstantial weight over his knotted back; he relaxed, arms and legs splayed, wildly akimbo, deep in a euphoria courtesy of his expert masseuse, his mistress of pleasure.

Naki chose not to cut through the rice paper door; the cross pieces would make too much noise for a surprise attack, so he determined to slide the door open and race to the cot for the kill. Hopefully, he would not have to kill her too. He shifted his weight to propel the attack when the floor creaked, loudly.

Despite the drunken stupor and the pacific transport of the massage, Zatoichi reacted decisively. Rolling violently to his left, he threw the little concubine off his back; she, landing heavily on the floor, usherd a startled cry. He stretched his arm for the pile of clothes upon the floor. Naki slung open the screen and charged, *Dotanuki* sword in hand. Zatoichi did not need the fifteen feet to right himself for defense. By the time Naki reached him, he was at the ready with katana; Naki paused. The samurai had filled out substantially since the last time Naki faced him; his abdomen was larger, rounder; his shoulders and arms thicker, meatier, his legs heavy. Had the situation been less perilous, Zatoichi would have rendered a comic sight: corpulent, naked, sword in hand. Even though he seemed laughable, Naki knew he was dangerous. The element of surprise was gone, so that advantage was no longer in Naki's favor; however, his intoxicated state might slow his reflexes as well as his extra weight, but Naki knew better than to assume an easy victory and was wise to reject thoughts of a simple kill; overconfidence was the enemy of every warrior.

As he faced him the samurai growled, "Who are you? What do you want? Do you want to die?"

Naki was sure that if he responded, Zatoichi would recognize his voice, so he remained silent; instead he swung his sword, but the samurai easily deflected the blow. The metallic clash of the finely honed steel swords forced a cry from the naked little courtesan curled in a tiny ball. Naki realized he would have to be quick and skillful if he was to kill him and retreat unscathed. Hopefully, the fat man had slowed some since his last encounter. He hadn't. He was still fast, and Naki knew he was in for a fierce fight.

The blades sang, whistled and clanged as the engagement continued. Candles flickered with the disturbance of air as swords and bodies whirled. More than once the close shish of a sharp edge startled Naki, heightening his senses, forcing him to reevaluate his strategy. The man had not lost any of his prowesses, even fat and drunk.

The nymph, by this time had collected herself and bolted from the room, screaming, calling for help. "Ninja, ninja", she called.

The fight was over. Naki knew he must now run. Help would soon arrive, and he would be overpowered. He had to distance himself from his opponent and execute his escape.

Zatoichi emboldened by the cries of his little lover, rushed Naki, hoping to use his substantial mass to bowl over the smaller, leaner assassin. Deftly, Naki sidestepped the landslide of oily sweaty flesh and the mountain fell heavily onto the floor. He heard Zatoichi grunting and breathing heavily. Naki wished he could finish him there, but voices clamored in the distance. Without thought of ending it, he fled for the door, swiping at the fat burly back that was on its hands and knees attempting to rise. He did not wait to see what damage he had inflicted. He did not wait to see a thick gash open and fill with blood: he was on the run.

The doors were open … a quick departure; the stones made no sound and left no trace of the direction of his flight. Like a swiftly moving shadow, he flew to his landmark and found the spikes, ascending them, up and over. Perched atop the wall, he paused to assess where his pursuers were. They had not yet filled into the street. He used the rope with a loop on the end and fished for the pegs. He found them and plucked them from the wall, leaving no trace of the means of his escape. Then he jumped.

He struggled for balance, whirling his arms and legs in the air. He must cut the water cleanly, or the impact will crush him. Toes pointed, he sliced the surface and sank, the weapons dragging him down. Discarding the pegs, the rope and the *metsubushi* smoke eggs, he lightened his load; all he had left was his sword and the breathing pipe; he kicked … .

Breaking the surface, he peered up at the fortress wall to assess his situation. He looked and listened. No shadows atop the wall yet, but there were the sounds of agitated discussion on the other side. They discovered the place of his escape. They knew he was in the water, but they did not know where. Peeling off his head gear, he slipped the mask into a pocket and then pulled out the pipe. Exhaling, he sank beneath the surface, placing the reed into his mouth, and poking it out of the water just enough; he used what air he had to clear the pipe of water.

Kicking powerfully for the far shore, he traversed the pond and soon felt vegetation: lily pads and reeds. Letting his feet drop, he found a muddy bottom. Head poking up from between the pads, like a turtle, he surveyed the situation. The far shore was quiet, but he heard noises ... on his side of the bank. He submerged and waited.

The noises grew louder. They were near, but they would not see him, even with their lights. With torches brightening the water, they were scouring the shore. Twenty to thirty firebrands lit the water, clearly.

Watching from beneath the surface, he saw the brands illuminating everything. Clad in black, in water among large leafy pads, and only a tiny reed protruding from the water, Naki felt confident in his invisibility. Beneath the surface, he could hear the calamity of cries as they barked orders as to what to do.

"Slash the water, you idiots," Naki heard a familiar voice, Zatoichi. He was there with them. *Naginatas* hacked at the lavender *yuri* poking out of the water and at the large green pads covering the surface. A scythed blade swished just beside Naki, then another to his left. He did not move. The slashing and arguing continued and then moved on. After the lights finally receded he thought to surface, to poke his head up, to take a look, but an innate instinct told him not to. He remained submerged. Surely enough, his feelings were correct. A lone torch appeared, shining directly overhead. It hovered for a long time before it moved away, not far, just a few feet, and again it paused ... the bearer carefully scrutinizing the shore. Naki waited.

When it was once again completely dark, Naki surfaced, slowly, careful not to make a sound. He slithered through the pads and grabbed a hold of a stone on the rocky shore. Hauling himself out of the water, he flattened. To the left and to the right, it was quiet and dark. The search had disappeared into the distance. They would soon come to the end of the pond and double back. If he stayed, they might find him. Ahead of him was an open space, grassy ground cover, beyond a shadowy copse of trees.

The traverse across the open break took just a few seconds. Now, he was sheltered by the black of the grove. It was an old wood and some of the trees were large, giving him the occasion to climb and hide. Peering out from one of the branches atop the tallest tree in the thicket, he was able to see the dim castle wall, the black pond which still bore the vestiges of disturbance. In the distance, he saw lights refracting across the water, dancing on wave crests. They were indeed returning. He waited in the tree.

The still night air carried sound distinctly. The agitated discussions he heard earlier were now even more heated by the frustration of failing to find him. Zatoichi was entirely incensed. He berated his gang mercilessly. Naki could see them as they approached the bend in the shore; they were tired. Dispirited, they hacked at the water, but it was more token searching than earnest. This infuriated Zatoichi even more. Suddenly, he stopped, exactly where Naki had clambered from the water. He called for light. Men, eager to please, eager to escape the scathing abuse heaped upon them, fell over each other to provide light.

"There … there is where he escaped. The rocks are wet," the samurai thundered.

He turned and looked towards the grove. The grass and ground cover was wet with dew, the water trail gone. He looked at the trees. Naki felt he was looking right at him.

"You three go, check there. The rest follow me. He is probably in the town by now. We will find him … come!"

He turned to inspect the pond again, and by the light of the torches Naki could see a large red stain across his back, blood seeping through his white shirt.

They hurried off, and three remaining torches loomed listlessly closer. As they approached, Naki descended.

He found a low bough and spread across it. The three entered the woody copse lethargically looking for any signs of the shinobi. Any fear of finding the ninja had obviously vanished, for they were extremely sloppy in their method. A cursory swipe of torches convinced them the assassin was long gone and any more searching was useless. They assembled at the base of the tree where Naki lay and discussed their strategy.

"Let's wait a while and leave. There is nothing here. We've searched. He's gone. He probably flew away; the demons can fly; I've seen them."

"Ninja don't fly, fool" one of them shouted, "they are men … not demons … simply men … no magic … no special powers … nothing… they are just men!!"

"They appear, disappear … vanish in an instant. They descend like birds of prey, and then fly off into the night. They fly, I tell you."

"Superstitious idiot, shut up and remain quiet!"

The dissention was all that Naki needed. Two of them moved ahead leaving the harebrain brooding over his rebuff, beneath the tree. Dropping, indeed like a bird of prey, Naki knocked him down. He hit the ground face first with a loud thump, issuing a painful grunt. His torch fell to the ground; Naki kneeling atop of him, pinning him to the ground, picked up the firebrand and struck him at the base of his neck producing a sickening resounding crack. The man lay still.

Naki looked up. The other two whirled about to see a black clad figure dominatingly balanced upon their fallen companion. The flame from the brand illuminated Naki's face giving the illusion of some sort of demon, a shadowy face with deadly eyes. The braver of the two and the least gullible squared off; the other fled. The challenger was samurai, undaunted, unafraid; he charged.

Naki drew his weapon and faced the charge, without rising. Kneeling, balanced and strong he angled his sword down and to the left when the katana slashed down, from above. Naki sent the blade sliding down throwing the man a little off balance and from his kneeling position, he thrust the lit torch into the samurai's groin, pushing, twisting. The attacker stopped immediately, fixed in place from the pain, howling fiercely. A quick slash across the throat, curtailed the noise and sent a stupendous spray of blood airborne, raining red droplets upon Naki's head and face; toppling, the man fell. Had there been anyone to witness the scene it would have been horrifying. The torch, alight, casting dark shadows over Naki's intense face, illuminated black rivulets of blood flowing from his eyes, down his cheeks, conjuring a picture of demonic proportion: Naki, squatting atop the bloody bodies of two men was definitively reminiscent of a mythical evil entity ... Tengu.

Chapter 20

Zatocichi ignored the pain, and he disregarded the issue seeping from his wound. It wasn't important; instead, he focused on capturing the perpetrator who violated his cosmos: who arrogantly intruded upon his universe; who injured him. He reveled in vehemenant and malevolent machinations against the miscreant; he envisioned a satisfyingly gruesome penalty for this perpetrator, this architect of intrusion. Zatocichi seethed with malicious vengeance.

He suspected he knew the intruder ... that insipid little ninja from the monastery. What was his name? Nao? Naoki? Naki! Nakamura!!! He envisioned Nakamura dying a gloriously painful death. Relentlessly he abused, belittled and berated the men around him, unjustly taking his anger out upon them. They all, now, were regretting their obligation to his service, hoping fortuitously that he would bleed to death. His volatility increased with each passing moment, he fumed, and they hated him. Fortunately, they did not feel the full extent of his rancor, for it was mitigated by a plan.

Naki left the dead men to wash himself in the pond. He could not be seen in the village, covered with blood. Wet, his black cottons clinging to his body, darkly stained, he returned to the tailor's house, trying to rub red from his hands. It was near morning when he woke the good man from his bed, asking for clothes and his horse.

Dressed as a young low-ranking government official, Naki made the mistake of leaving as soon as the sun cleared the horizon

Zatoichi meanwhile had lost a lot of blood, but somehow between his determination to find the assassin and his indifference to injury the bleeding stopped. The encrusted coagulation formed a fragile, tender cover, assuring the pathogens a glorious infection, later.

Zatoichi knew which roads to watch, which road exited Kyoto, the *Ebisugawa-dori*; ah but when he would attempt this escape … that was the question … so he waited all night … he would wait all day, and the next day and the day after that.

The road was busy that morning: farmers with rice, fish and vegetables; vendors with a variety of luxury items; manufacturers with goods of every kind. Most of the traffic was into town and very little was going out, making it easier for

Zatoichi to recognize his quarry. The samurai had everyone leaving Kyoto stopped, roughly inspected, and when he was satisfied they were not whom he was looking for, with a nod of his head, he released them.

Naki spotted them conducting their searches from a distance. He couldn't turn around; it would be suspicious, so he chose to proceed as a prefectural tax collector going about his business. He trusted his acting skills and believed he could pass without incident, if he addressed the fool stopping him with a haughty, arrogant, and abrasive manner, intimidating him, confusing him, he should pass without incident.

He chose to steer to the right side of the road block in order to be interrogated by a less than clever looking guard. He saw Zatoichi on the left, standing upon a wooden crate, surveying everyone going out.

He almost entirely eluded Zaroichi's post, but at the last minute the oafish brute reached and grabbed Jun's reins. Startled, rearing, Jun almost threw Naki off. This gave Naki, the young tax collector, with the wide brimmed hat, righteous cause for a vehement verbal assault upon the fool that almost knocked him off his horse.

"My most humble apologies *Onī-san*. We are seeking a ninja who attempted to kill my master last night."

"Well, it is not I," Naki spewed caustically.

The man still held onto Jun's reins and Naki arrogantly yet nonchalantly, swatted the man's hands to release his hold upon his horse. Again, Jun reared, neighing and pawing his hooves in the air. The commotion attracted Zatoichi's attention. He saw the confused, panicked look upon his man's face. The guard did not know what to do, whether to listen to the officious official berrating him and let go of his horse or wait for the nod from his samurai master.

Zatoichi scrutinized the scenario closely and saw a young administrator, under a large floppy sun hat upon a Kiso horse. A Kiso horse!!! "Stop him!" he screamed.

It was too late. Naki's blade had already slashed the guard's neck, nearly decapitating him. He fell in a heap against Jun, and concurrently, with Naki's kick, the animal bolted for the open road. The horse was true to its breed, fast as the wind. By the time Zatoichi recovered and placed his corpulent mass upon a horse, Naki and Jun were just a dot in the distance.

Zatoichi watched Naki disappear; he knew he could not catch him, but he did not seem worried. Calmly, he turned around; instructing his men to take care of their dead friend, he rode back to the second circle, curiously calm.

———————

Naki rode Jun hard until they were deep into the mountains; dismounting, he led him off the road to a shallow stream for a drink; then, he clambered up a slope to see if he was being followed. From atop a rock, looking down upon the road, he saw no pursuit.

What he did see were birds, pigeons, three of them. They were soaring high above, following the mountain road he was riding, but a hawk interrupted and an aerial chase ensued. The pigeons scattered, hawk in pursuit. Unfortunately, for the white pigeon the hawk chose it, relentlessly trailing it to its end. The other two, the grey and black pigeons resumed their flight along the road through the mountains and passed overhead and out of sight.

Feeling secure that he hadn't been followed, Naki spent some time resting. When Naki mounted Jun, both rider and ride felt ready to continue.

The balance of the route was travelled at a more leisurely, relaxed pace, saving both much needed energy. The lull in anxiety and tension gave Naki an opportunity to ruminate upon what he had accomplished. Three men were dead, and he managed to warn Zatoichi that he needs to be vigilant about his safety. He came to the conclusion he achieved nothing. The whole venture, once again, was a loss. He failed. He did nothing other than kill men he did not know or wish to harm. Their deaths were Zatoichi's fault, Naki rationalized; he was to blame. Feeling guilty nevertheless, he rode listlessly over the road, through the mountains to the lair. The burden of guilt dulled his senses, diminished his chi.

The gnarled maple on the south slope was his marker to turn north to the hidden road leading to the compound. He was almost home when Jun suddenly stopped, refusing to continue. Confused, Naki urged him on, but he stood still. Leaning over, Naki patted his neck and whispered to keep going. The whistle of an arrow and its thud into a nearby tree shocked Naki out of his guilt ridden stupor and sent him into survival mode.

Kicking his flanks frantically, Naki urged Jun forward, but he refused to move. Sliding off, he sought cover behind a tree. He looked about for the archer, but couldn't see anyone. Jun remained immobile. Then he saw five monks appear from behind trees and advance upon him. Four wielded bo sticks and swords the fifth appeared with his bow armed ready to launch another missile. Naki slapped Jun on the hindquarters and this time the horse moved, leaving Naki alone to face this attackers.

The archer, Naki quickly determined, needed to be taken first. He rushed him, forcing him to shoot. The shot missed. The scruffy monk did not have time to notch a new bolt before Naki was upon him. Naki's sword swirled down upon him and his only defense was the bow which Naki slashed in two. With a forceful kick to the abdomen, Naki sent the archer tumbling into a small ravine. Turning to face the four bearing down on him with swords and sticks he spun about several times, blade extended. The action forced the attackers to cease their attack. Surrounded, Naki calculated his next move. The assailants stood balanced with bo sticks extended, ready to deflect a stike or strike a blow.

Naki was baffled. Why were these monks attacking him? "I am Ito Nakamura, from the monastery. Why do you fight?" he demanded.

They remained silent,

"I am Naki! I live at the monastery at Mt. Hiei. Stop what you are doing!" he screamed.

"We understand", said one of the ruffians, and then jabbed with his bo stick.

Naki parried the jab, and realized these men were not making a mistake. It was he they were after. So, it was settled; he would destroy them.

He had a sword, his father's, and they had bo sticks, longer than his sword and heavier, so he needed a bo stick. He scrutinized the four of them; the archer had not yet climbed out of the ravine. He chose the one who didn't make eye contact with him; he was the weakest. He attacked the man. Naki was correct; he was slow, unskilled. Naki was inside the man's strike zone before he realized it. The bo stick was ineffective and his hand was not upon his sword, but Naki's was upon his, and then it was across his neck. He dropped quickly. Naki snatched the heavy hardwood stick and waved it at the remaining three. They were taken aback at Naki's speed, but not intimidated. They attacked simultaneously; one swung high, at the head; one swung low at the legs, and one jabbed at his abdomen. Naki defended his legs and stomach, but not his head. It received a stunning crack which sent him crashing, stars swirling, pain. He fell on all fours. Three sticks descended to pummel his back, but he managed to evade them. Spinning about on his hands and knees he tripped one with the stick, slashed another with his blade, but he took a blow to his back. Weakened, but not vanquished he lashed at the hand swinging the stick, severing it from its host. The stick as well as the hand holding it fell onto the forest floor. The monk fell from the attack.

Only one monk remained and he was somewhat in tact; he was bruised about the ankle, but he was not truly injured. He looked at Naki who was crouched, looking lethal, like an animal; he saw his fellow conspirators, dead, maimed. Not wishing to suffer a similar fate, he vanished.

Naki dropped his head and heaved a sigh or relief. When he looked up he was staring into the eyes of the archer who had crawled out of the ravine, a bo stick raised, poised to crack his head.

Suddenly, a black blur swept the monk into the ravine again, ripping his throat; breaking his neck. Silence descended upon the glen, adulterated only by a low growl, and a rustling in the bushes.

Jun stood between two Kobushi Magnolia trees, patiently waiting for Naki to ride him back home. It took more vigor than Naki had ever had to expend to mount him. Beaten, sore, broken, exhausted, Naki pushed forward, only to fall off onto the rocky road a little further on. Jun stood by passively waiting for his master to muster the moil to rise and ride.

However, Naki just lay in the road bleeding, in and out of consciousness.

That is how Sai found him. When he came to, she was cradling his head wiping the blood oozing from the crack to his crown, applying herbs to dull the pain. Gratefully, with appreciative eyes, and without saying anything, Naki rose and climbed upon Jun; Sai helping. They rode to the compound in silence. The bleeding stopped; the pain, pounding, hadn't.

<hr>

Applying ointments to Naki's body, to relieve his discomfort and to improve the blood circulation, Sai stoically tended his injuries. Not a word was spoken, even though she was infuriated with him. She was thankful that his hurts were not grievous: deep muscle bruising, muscle strain, perhaps some bone cracked, a little, somewhere, nothing that would not wholly heal.

Naki's physical tribulations were minor compared to his

spiritual anguish. He knew what he had done was foolish. Nothing was accomplished and certainly detrimental consequences would ensue. He was thankful that Sai had not commented upon his stupidity and that she was lovingly taking care of him.

Not only did he punish himself mentaly for his impulsivity, but he also agonized emotionaly over why monks attacked him, and why there, at that point of the road, exactly at the path to the compound. He didn't tell Sai what he was worried about.

However, Sai had already thought about those unspoken concerns, and discussed them with her father. The hostile monks could be explained. They were rogue monks still loyal to Zatoichi, but the location of the attack? Was it coincidental that they attacked at such a crucially sensitive, secret junction, the hidden path to the complex? Or was the position deliberately chosen?

If it was deliberately chosen, the ninja community was in jeopardy. If it was deliberately chosen, someone who should not know about them is aware of their location. The concern added more worry to the *Chunin's* list of alarms. His health was not improving, and now the thought of having to abandon the mountain village distressed him even more. He decided he would increase the number of men assigned to watch the entry sites. Hopefully, it was just an unfortunate happenstance.

Naki realized he had threatened everyone's lives with his selfish, impulsive actions. He felt he let Sai down, Tomoki-san, the whole family. They had been secretly secure, safe before he arrived and now everyone was dangerously exposed. He felt lost, wretched over what he had done. He never thought his autonomous attack would compromise the secrecy and security of the compound. He was going to throw up.

Sai, despite her anger and concern, nursed Naki tenderly. Through tired eyes, Naki watched her as she ministered to his needs. Her voice, soft, comforting, loving; it never betrayed what she thought. She too was in a quandary. Naki, unwittingly betrayed them, innocently, unintentionally, but betrayed nonetheless. They were in dire circumstances. The family she had known all her life was feasibly in mortal peril, yet the person responsible for the hazardous situation she could not condemn, for she loved him.

Her innate senses told her this moment was a turning point in their lives. Exactly how, she did not know, but she was certain life would no longer be the same.

Naki dozed, ate, slept.

When he recovered and was completely cognizant, he humbly offered his apologies for his selfishness.

Sai, ever so calm and resigned shushed him quiet, and explained that the life they knew was going to change, and where that might lead depended on the whim of the gods.

Naki remained silent, over burdened with guilt. He struggled with trying to understand what had happened, and how could he mend this catastrophe? How could he return things to the way they were? Could he? He knew he couldn't do it alone. He needed help. He spoke to Sai about his worries. She again surprised him.

"Naki-san, what has happened, has happened. What is … is! There is nothing we can do. We must react to what we perceive to be the threat. If our location has been compromised, the first thing is to defend our territory. We have done that: we have more men guarding our perimeters; also, we have a new location should we need to move, and if we need to move ... we will ... quickly, efficiently, safely. We have survived this long, we will survive Oda Nobunaga; he will not hurt us ... we will survive."

Naki closed his eyes and wished everything Sai said to be true.

———————

The panther settled on a mountain rock, snarled annoyed by the sudden invasion of men, strangers to his terrain, disrupting his privacy, his peace, forcing him to hide, to change his habits, disrupting his subsistence; he couldn't kill them all, there were too many.

The men were stealthy, cautious, and numerous. They waited, never getting too close to the compound, never giving away their presence, shadows in the woods, watching.

Chapter 21

Yuuma, a Zen priest, a priest of emptiness, played his flute with single - minded concentration as Abbot Kosa, ceremoniously dressed, sat in an elaborate, pagoda shaped palanquin, carried by sixteen monks. It was the third and final circling of the temple at the top of the mountain.

The Bon *odori* festival on Mt Hiei was held in late summer to honor the spirits of the deceased, to welcome them back among the living, for a brief time in hopes of receiving blessings to shape future fortunes.

Thousands of devotees chanted Amida's name and sang traditional songs, while priests, skilled in complex ritual dances, performed to pay tribute to their honorable ancestors. Through music, chanting, song dance, all sought the path of enlightenment, the blessings of peace and eventual admission to Amida's paradise, the Pure Land, in their next life.

After prayer, celebrants distributed food to the citizens living in the towns upon the mountain making up the complex of Mt Hiei's Enryakuji monastery.

Not all of the thirty thousand residents of the mountain sought the metaphorical "other shore". Many were ordinary people who sought shelter within the fortified temples to protect them from the hostile world of Kyoto, Oda Nobunaga, samurai, and the ruthless hierarchical structure of Japanese society.

So, the sanctuary attracted the righteous and the ruthless, aristocrats and rogues. Some inhabitants were moral reprobates who were only just tolerated by the virtuous; they, by example, hoped that, in time, the unfortunate could be changed.

These souls still remained tied to the material urges of existence despite the exemplars of higher level truth among them; they were those who were still concerned with wealth, power, and reputation, friends, servants, loyalty, and disloyalty; they were those who did not understand that sudden misfortune could easily afflict them and render them helpless despite their most intense anxieties and precautions; yet they clung to the agitation allowing gnawing grief to trouble them repeatedly, never having peace or rest ... they were those who allied with Zatoichi.

For them, solace from pain was found in drinking, eating, fornicating, plotting against enemies and killing. Conversely, the honorable went to extreme lengths of self-discipline and restraint to attain clarification of the higher truths of life. An austere existence of self-denial and restraint cut through the capitulation and delusion of life's temporal temptations. Such were the practices of numerous monks on Mt. Hiei that hardened them in their present struggles and prepared them for the life thereafter.

And harden them it did. The Tendai monks of Mt. Hiei and the Ikko- Ikki of Nagashima developed disciplines which aided them with their earthly toils. Some practiced forms of asceticism to such a degree the practitioners were considered supernatural.

These feats were the basis for fear among Oda Nobunaga's and Tokugawa Ieyasu's *ashigaru*, foot soldiers and the *yarigumi*, spearmen. They were terrified of the monk's imperviousness to pain and their utter willingness to die in battle. For the common soldier they were terrifyingly formidable opponents.

Stories of them sitting or standing near river banks in the cold wind, or in an icy waterfall for hours, or meditating upon a hill or mountain top at noon, when the sun at its zenith, beat down fiercely upon their corporal essence, eschewing comfort, resisting discomfort; all this created a weakness in the knees of those faint hearted and feeble minded.

It was not only this effect on troops which concerned both Oda Nobunaga and Tokugawa Ieyasu, this courage debilitating influence, but also the formidable social, economic and political power the monks exerted over the people in their provinces. They were autonomous, influential, and uncontrollable; they impeded annexation of neighboring provinces and weakened dominion within conquered territory. They needed to be destroyed.

Monks had in the past faced assault ... by Tokugawa, burning the Ikko-Ikki temples to the ground, but he did not eradicate them, and they recovered. Nobunaga would not make the same mistake with the Tendai monks.

Life for the thirty thousand people who lived on Mt Hiei

was a panacea: food ...shelter ... self-development. Skills were learned ... perfected; weapons were produced: bows, arrows, *naginatas* , matchlock guns.

The production of weapons and using them effectively engaged thousands. Making strong bows from several types of wood was a source of pride for the craftsmen; coating hemp with wax, creating bowstrings of flexibility and durability was an art perfected; cutting the nock cut above a nod for shaft strength and adding three feathers, arranged perfectly, for accurate flight, and lethal deployment was skilled genius.

The manufacture of matchlocks was new, challenging but rewarding. Creating swords of quality made the monks believe that creating barrels of steel was entirely possible. Indeed, it was, and they made better creations than the Portuguese. Carefully copying theirs, they soon found ways to reproduce them quickly in quantity and to even improve upon the original: developing bigger calibers, thereby increasing their deadliness.

Nobunaga's samurai did not embrace guns the way monks did. The monks overcame initial problems of reliability, especially in bad weather, as well as the difficulty of using them at night. They increased the speed of loading and firing and developed a technique of sequential firing to ensure a steady rain of bullets. Farmers, commoners, and monks had no qualms about using the guns and they were ingenious with their innovations. They posed a serious concern for the Lord Unifier of Japan.

Even though the Tendai and the Ikki-Ikko became masters of the matchlock they did not abandon their practice of riding on horseback and shooting arrows at targets, holding the bow high to clear the horses head, the practice of *yabusame.*

Their drills with the *naginatas* continued and the monks were fiercely lethal.

However, not everyone at the monastery was of the warrior mentality. There were those who didn't fight, too old, lame, or feeble, who organized samurai armor in bins in the weapons building, those whose wives worked the rice fields and those whose sons helped fortify the monastery's temples with more rock walls.

There were those who produced the rice wine and the new red liquor cultivated from grapes which the Portuguese brought with them. Arrogantly, the monks extracted what they deemed useful from the Portuguese, and it certainly wasn't their religion, this Christianity, which was polluting so many minds and souls in Japan. Nobunaga, nevertheless, was intrigued by it, and gave it sanctuary, allowing the spread of it as he was not fond of Buddhism.

<hr />

Yuuma placed his flute into the folds of his robe, inside the pocket where it was safe until the next time he withdrew it to escape the clutter and the worries of the world, to seclude his soul in music. He shuffled along the mountain path to a cluster of buildings that for the time being provided him shelter. Nodding to farmers along the way who often gave him food, he smiled and bestowed appropriate Bon *odori* blessings upon them.

The farmers toiled happily in the rice field even through the heat of the day. They coped easily. The slope of the mountain helped their labor since they did not need to bend and strain as much to weed the plots. The men stripped, clad only in loin cloths, and the women bare to the waist, fought the heat effortlessly, cooling their heads with conical straw hats dipped in water to create a refreshing evaporative sensation.

He passed oxen trudging, pulling plows, cultivating fallow fields, preparing them for a vegetable crop the following spring. Despite the volcanic mountain soil the raising of rice, vegetables and grains sufficiently fed the inhabitants of Mt. Hiei.

Various industry busied the people of the villages - villages which dotted the sides of the mountain - fortifying temples against invasion, erecting shelters for the ever growing population, erecting new temples and shrines for the devoted, manufacturing basic necessities: tools, utensils, clothes, medicines, as the monastery was very self-reliant, producing weapons: swords, bows, naginatas, guns, and gun powder.

Few were idle. Most were industrious. The mountain was busy and generally happy. Everyone respected Abbot Kosa as their leader and mentor. It was his lineage over hundreds of years which created this growing haven of security and contentment. When not fighting Oda Nobunaga, Mt Hiei was as close to the Pure Land as anything could be on earth.

Ryu was practicing with his naginata when Naki called out to him. Spinning wildly, deadly blade extended, and then freezing at the sight his friend, Ryu took several moments to collect his wits before discarding the weapon to embrace Naki in a monstrous hug. Whirling Naki about like a hinged wooden doll, Ryu eventually released his young friend, but continued the welcome with slaps and pats and more hugs. Finally, calm, Ryu asked was Naki here to stay?

Sadly, Naki answered, "No." He was here to say goodbye. He couldn't explain to his good friend why he had felt the need to come to the mountain to bid farewell, but he was doing it. Ryu, saddened, somehow understood. He too had felt the winds of change blowing and that life would be different. So, he was not surprised.

Naki needed to express to his stout companion his gratitude for the garrulous, good natured friendship he extended to him during the past few years. He believed that he had never thanked him or expressed to him in any way appreciation for the tolerance and compassion demonstrated.

Ryu, taken aback, lost all joviality, became pensive and uncharacteristically serious. "I believe this indeed will be the last I see of you, Naki-dono for I myself feel that I am not long for this life; that I will be seeking the Pure Land soon. I don't know why this feeling comes, but it comes. Never before have I had such reflections, and so relentlessly; and so, do I give them credence or ignore them for it is just my imagination? I don't know, but if I never see you again, I too want you to know, my friend ... you have been a good friend ... you inspired me. I am not sure if you were aware of that, but you did, tremendously, and the benefice of your friendship humbled and gratified me, thank you, Nakamura Ito. If I never see you again, I wish the gods bestow you a blessed life. I know great things will come to you. You are a good friend, a great warrior and I feel privileged to have known you."

Naki was dumfounded. He never knew Ryu felt this way. Anyway, enough of this maudlin nonsense."

Naki believed he saw Ryu's eyes glisten for a moment, before he returned to his buoyant upbeat self.

"So, are you at liberty to say where you are going and what you will be doing? On second thought, maybe it is better that I don't know. Who knows who the next villains will be that will try to pry information from me about you? It is better for me not to know anything about you and your doings."

Naki smiled. He knew Ryu was right. It was better if his friend knew nothing of what he was doing, considering his last venture was a shameful failure.

Both were quiet for a moment, and they knew it was time for Naki to leave. Naki bowed to Ryu, turned and left. Ryu stood still for many moments ... long enough for Naki to disappear among the buildings.

Eventually, he picked up his naginata and continued his practice, his heart heavy.

Chapter 22

Saburo, Kenta and Mikio had been at post since the Hour of the Hare, 5:00 am. Eight hours had passed, and Joshi, Raiden and Hana had not relieved them. The pass to the main compound had been quiet. Perhaps everyone overreacted to the attack on Naki near the entrance. Perhaps it was just coincidence. Perhaps the secret entrance was still secret. Where were those three, thought Saburo. Joshi and Raiden were responsible and Hana mostly so, so where were they?

Kenta suggested he go look for them. Saburo agreed. Kenta disappeared into the woods. Saburo looked at Mikio. Was all this extra precaution necessary? It had been weeks since the attack upon Naki. The watches were very dull; they could be engaged in some other business.

Only moments passed before Kenta dropped to his knees between them. Three arrows protruded from his back.

With the little air he had left, and with the rest of his life energy he exclaimed, "They're dead, all dead!" and died. Seconds later Saburo and Mikio were dead as well.

Zatoichi stood over them smiling smugly, satisfied he

had eliminated all the watches posted at the secondary and tertiary access points; now, control of the main gateway to the compound was entirely his. There would be no warning. They would just march in and commence with the destruction. No one would come out. Zatoichi could not wait to begin the killing.

He still had to be careful; they were ninja. Even though he has the advantage of surprise, and has them surrounded and has cut off any chance of escape he had to be careful, and he was. He selected Oda Nobunaga's best samurai for the mission, four hundred of them. The Lord Unifier of Japan suggested this himself, the offer extremely magnanimous. Then again since it was such a dangerous and critical undertaking, it was wise to choose the best for the job to ensure success.

Zatoichi was aware that Nobunaga kept appointing him perilous tasks, perhaps hoping that he might die during the execution of one of them, yet he lived; moreover, he flourished, and he would continue to do so. Furthermore, this assignment naturally was his. After all, it was he who ferreted out the ninja nest, so he was very pleased he had the command of this mission, and he hoped he would be the one to kill Naki and that stupid girl.

The sun set and the night wrapped itself around the mountain rocks, towering trees, and the huddled houses. For the denizens of the enclave it was another day and night of discipline and regimine. It was just another night.

Zatoichi saw things differently. For him, this night would be spoken about for hundreds of years. He would be immortalized as the samurai that destroyed a famous ninja clan. A clan that had for hundreds of years succeeded in thwarting the plans of the ambitious, a clan that perpetuated the constant fighting among lords of the provinces. He, Zatoichi, would be the one who began the eventual eradication of all ninja clans until they were just a memory.

The Hour of the Tiger could not come soon enough. Hundreds of horses would wind their way down the narrow mountain path into the village under a full moon. Hundreds of samurai would descend ropes and vines in the moonlight and climb down rocky inclines into the community as the ninja community slept.

The hour arrived, and Zatoichi almost giddy rode into the village. His euphoria, however, did not blur his ability to absorb the clever manner in which the clan hid in the mountains, the distracters, the camouflage, and the redirectors that enabled them to hide secretly for so long. Zatoichi filed all the family's furtive deceptions into his spiteful mind; certainly it would be useful at a future time; he knew what he learned would prove valuable sooner or later. His vanity and self import were thoroughly inflated; he felt empowered.

The warriors in his command reveled in the irony, samurai surprising ninja. Horses plodded down the narrow mountain path, hooves clothed in cotton to dampen noise to prevent an unwanted alert. All guards had been dispatched, so he, Zatoichi, felt the approach would be free of danger. He knew the layout of the complex and gave his men explicit directions as to where they needed to ramify once inside the mix.

Despite Zatoichi's relatively recent influx into Nobunaga's inner circle of influence, established and veteran samurai did not hold resentment towards him; rather, they admired his astuteness and audacity; they respected his ferocity. They followed him unconditionally, much to his predilection.

It was light-dark, the moon full, the night sky partly clear; it was quiet; it was a time for surprise.

Zatoichi, leading, broke through the camouflaged façade into the complex proper. For a moment, he paused in the middle of the compound and there in the light of the moon he scanned the layout, where the important buildings might be, where arms were stored, where persons of importance slept. He immediately recognized the abode of the *Chunin*, it had a more polished appearance than the rest of the buildings; even in the dark, he could tell.

Motioning to the troops behind him, he gave silent signals for attack. The *Chunin's* home was first, concurrently with the building housing weapons which he also managed to detect. His mind raced to figure where that Nakamura creature might be. He assumed it was within the long dark barracks presumably housing the men. That building would be next and the various little abodes which apparently housed smaller ninja families would be the final flame.

He found it incredibly appropriate to set fire to the village exactly the way they set Kyoto aflame. Thousands died, horribly. So shall they. He gave the signal.

Thirty flaming arrows flew towards Konnyo Tomoki's home. Sleeping deeply, desperately trying to recover from his malaise, he heard nothing of the thump – thump - thumps which drummed his residence with an irregularly unpleasant percussion. He at first felt nothing of the heat from the flame which licked at the dried outer structure and straw roof of his home. Eventually, noise, heat and smoke seeped inside awakening the *Chunin*.

His mind raced. Why was his home afire? Despite his delirium, he answered his own question.: the compound was being attacked, so he slipped through the floor, to a tunnel that surfaced well away from his home in the woods. The effort nearly killed him.

Sai! She was not in the house. She was with Naki in the barn. She might be able to defend herself. The others ... will die without defending themselves; some will die defending their lives; others may escape; there were plenty of secret passages. These villains are not aware of them all. Hidden by the night and the forest, all he could do was watch. Indeed his suppositions were correct. Many did die, ingloriously, without the opportunity to die sword in hand.

Hisao –san, ancient, wise, humble, generous of knowledge, died without defense. His abode set apart from the rest in deference to his status and prestige was unfortunately an obvious tactical target for initial strike. It was a house of importance just like the Junin's, but he did not escape. He was not as clever as Konnyo-sama; he rushed outside and was immediately cut down. He received a noble number of arrows to the chest; seven stuck the mark; falling, he realized too late what was transpiring. More flaming arrows struck his home burning it to the ground.

Many of the clan's men and women, scores of them piled into the central compound; swords, bo sticks, bow and arrow ready to repulse the assail, but alas to no avail. Zatoichi planned the attack well. Men were pre-positioned and ready for all possible retaliatory action. He knew what to expect; he knew what he was doing, this Zatoichi.

Nevertheless, he did underestimate this particular clan. Not every one of the denizens chose to enter the open compound to be slain by arrow, yari or sword. No, many expected such an attack and prepared. Escape was the ninja's best defense.

Zatoichi was not aware of all the devious inventions and escapes the Tomoki clan had put into place well before hand, long ago, in preparation for such a prospect.

Many, like Tomoki Konnyo had getaway routes. They disappeared into the mountain side, and from positions overlooking the valley compound they were able to scrutinize what was occurring, and together they conspired to retaliate.

Zatoichi never expected the lush mountain foliage enveloping the steep slopes of the enclave to erupt with such vengeance and vehemence. From the North, South, East and West corners, they came silently, swiftly, lethally ... retribution.

Before Zatoichi knew it, he had lost one hundred men. They were everywhere and nowhere; fleeting silhouettes, darting in and out of the darkness, illuminated momentarily by the raging glow of the compound. They would strike, arrow, dart and shuriken. Samurai fell like rain, until Zatoichi gave the signal to coalesce into the center of the square, back to back, preventing ambush assaults. The stratagem worked. Now the ninja clan had to attack a unified and ready front ... a circle... which they did but to a diminished degree of success. The fight was difficult. Many more ninja died; the samurai were skilled. Eventually, without a sign, signal, or order of any sort, the ninja vanished ... gone. All that was left was a clump of shadowy samurai bathed in the orange glow of the flames, ready to fight, but lacking an opponent. Zatoichi quickly realized they retreated leaving him the compound to do what he wished.

With celerity, he razed the rest of the buildings. The valley glowed; the flames leapt high into the sky, lighting up the dark clouds overhead. Suddenly, as if the intense heat below burst the seams of the clouds above, rain began to drench the wildly burning holocaust below.

For a moment, Zatoichi wondered if Nakamura was among one of the dead. He hoped so. Since the rain would extinguish the fires he decided to return to Kyoto believing he had inflicted sufficient damage to the ninja hideaway, leveling it, blackening it, essentially eradicating it out of existence.

———◁《◉》▷———

During the onslaught, Sai awoke, first. Stirring Naki, she motioned for him to follow her to the barn door. Opening it slightly, she looked out upon the compound and saw her father's house ablaze, as well as the rest of the compound. She was neither surprised nor disturbed; her father, she knew was safe, the emergency plan in place since the day she was born. This was the way of the ninja. Go with what is given, make the best of it, prepare, adjust, and move on. She didn't worry about the rest of the clan. They were capable, ready to die if need be. She must save herself and Naki.

Both retreated to the back of the barn and bolted through the door crossing the babbling brook; however, once outside, they both realized ... horses... they needed horses, so back into the barn they dashed. Leading all the horses out the door, horse heads barely clearing the passage way, Naki and Sai mounted Jun and Aiko and escaped along a rarely usued path. Tomoki Konnyo was correct; Zatoichi did not know all of the routes in and out of the village.

The burning compound lit the sky with a ginger hue illuminating the clouds above and the road ahead. Naki and Sai bathed in orange light rode furiously. They didn't know where they were going, only away, fleeing to safety. Sai knew they were headed east towards the coast, but that was as much as she knew and the coast was days away. Naki knew Jun could negotiate the dark carroty mountain road, but he wondered if Sai's horse was equally competent; it was and Sai was safe. Both rode well out of danger.

Zatoichi, however, had been clever. He had placed men along all the roads leading out from the compound, including roads leading east. There, just beyond the night's red glow, five large armed and amored men waited, patiently.

They watched the two riders approach. They were ready. Who else could they be but ninja fleeing the holocaust? They blocked the road with their horses and sat, katanas at the ready to eliminate the vestiges of the Tomoki clan.

Ever so intuitive, Jun reared almost throwing Naki to the ground. Sai's steed instinctively responded and stopped. Shadows in the distance. Naki and Sai prepared for the worst. Both sides of the road were hemmed in by the mountain's steep slopes. There was no escape; an encounter was imminent. Sai looked into Naki's eyes and they spoke of concern, love, commitment and determination ... they would extract themselves from this situation, somehow ... he had faith. They remained still. Reaching for weapons they they readied themselves. The shadows approached quietly, menacingly.

Sai blurted out, "Naki, I love you."

Naki responded in kind, "And I you."

The dark specters materialized ... five samurai poised to kill.

Sai and Naki were ready to die, together.

For a singular moment, the antagonists faced each other, still figures in the night.

The samurai, feeling smugly confident attacked first.

Naki and Sai were prepared, but not for what happened.

Erratically, the lead samurai's horse reared throwing its rider to the ground. Panic spread to the other horses and they became wildly intractable ignoring the pulls and tugs of their riders. The horses wanted to run, but their masters wouldn't let them. Consequently, chaos ensued with much rearing, and neighing and uncontrollable spinning. The samurai struggled to manage their steeds but were unsuccessful. The horses were terrified. Since the road ahead wasn't an option nor was the road behind they bolted left and right up the steep mountain sides throwing their riders off their mounts, each landing heavily, painfully upon the steep mountain slope.

Unexpectedly, the road ahead for Naki and Sai was clear. Then they saw the cause of the mayhem. The massive black hulk of a monster cat became visible; its yellow eyes staring, momentarily directly upon the both of them, then snarling it turned and bolted up the mountain towards a samurai recovering from his fall. The creature launched itself into the air, claws, fangs bared ready to grip, rip its prey apart. The dazed samurai having just risen was taken down again; this time there was no getting up. The cat impaled its fangs into the neck of the hapless human. With a vicious tug of its royal head, it snapped the samurai's neck and he was dead. The rest desperate to live fled up the mountain into the night.

Naki and Sai did not take long to take advantage of their break and they shot forward leaving the chaos behind.

<hr />

The morning sun rose as if nothing had occured. It ascended at the same time, shone with the same luminosity, was covered by the few scant passing clouds as it had been for eons. It was oblivious to the lost world of the Tomoki clan. It poured its rays upon the land encouraging life to flourish in spite of the devastation which occurred during its absence.

Tomoki Konnyo remained ... on the mountain ... hidden. He watched his clan, family, yield to Oda Nobunaga's villainy. He had no idea how his village was discovered or who his immediate enemy was. His understanding of the reasons how his village and his life were destroyed were agonizingly deficient. He lay in pain, in ignorance; he was unable to move, to kill someone, to do something to defend against the atrocities being inflicted upon his people; no sword rose in retaliation, he was humiliated, humbled, defeated.

Barely surviving the night, he stumbled down the mountain into the valley, horrified his people had died this way, so ingloriously. He descended from his place of refuge into the charred corpse filled yard, his clan's communal congregational arena, traditionally a place of life, filled with laughter, cleverness, skill and imagination ... now a tomb.

The eerie silence was broken as he stumbled downhill, cracking twigs and rustling foliage. Even the birds paid homage to the dead by remaining quiet. The stillness overwhelmed him. His body was already ravaged and now his soul was suffering unimaginable pain; he knew he was not long for this world. He just didn't know how soon his end would be.

The arrows were silent. They were accurate, into his heart and his lungs, lodging frontally and arterially. Tomoki Konnyo crumbled, falling to his knees, ploughing his face into the ashy remnants of his compound's yard. He joined his bretheren; his pain was relieved, for that, he could thank his executioners.

They were samurai left behind, hiding, waiting, just in case ninja mysteriously appeared ... after they all seemingly disappeared. Zatoichi correctly assumed ninja would materialize and when they did into dirt they would fall. And so, Tomoki Konnyo appeared, stumbling clumsily falling into the trap. He was shot well; as he dropped blood gushed readily from the wounds, profoundly vermillion. Five arrows stuck in his lifeless body, two mashed, broken, beneath his corpse, the three jutted from his back, deathly still.

Chapter 23

Abbot Kossa heaved a heavy sigh, Tomoki Konnyo dead ... the village annihilated ... hundreds gone. The Abbot forced himself to control his mind, but found it exceedingly difficult to do so. For the first time, his resourcefulness was completely fettered. He wrestled with how to cope with this calamity. He tried to console himself with the thought that their suffering on this earth had ended.

What benefit could he extract from the destruction of the Tomoki clan? What could he derive from this heinous act that could bring him understanding and clarity. He could not answer this, and his myopism disturbed him. He had faced so many conundrums, so many challenges in the past and was able to unravel so many of them, but this was different: this was too personal; he was connected to Tomoki Konnyo, to Sai, to Naki. They were his secret family and they were dead. Could he follow the practices he so easily taught others in times of trouble? He had the troubles now. What was he to do?

Answers eluded him. He felt ineffectual. He was entirely

frustrated. He needed to meditate more; perhaps the answer would eventually come to him as it had so many times in the past.

With every faith in the power of the mind calming the soul, he resorted to the cuts of the *Kuj- in*. They will work to reveal the answer. What answer would he conjure? The Abbot waited.

Inspiration was not forthcoming. Why did a solution evade him? The Abbot was distressed. How things had changed? Surely, an answer would manifest itself ... surely it would.

The Abbot was in a quandary; his dilemma immobilized him, and for the first time he did nothing.

—— ◉ ——

Nobunaga planned the assault well; it needed to succeed; nothing but victory would do; he was adamant about that.

Since Zatoichi had succeeded so well in destroying the ninja, he was now in charge of the annihilation of Mt. Hiei. Each of his successful ventures placed him closer to his aspirations of power and prominence. Moreover, this assault was sweet and ever so satisfying, deliciously vengeful. Thirty thousand men were positioned and ready.

The monastery, the inhabitants, never really appreciated him, some did, but most didn't and now, it was time for him to repay their ambivalence and disdain. He would be ruthless. Not a soul would survive. He would make sure for he was like that, merciless.

The base of the mountain swarmed with black clad men, ants, intently grim, teeming, black- clad pismires swarming, busily preparing a horrific infestation. Gun squads rehearsed firing the arquebus, loading, firing, reloading again, over and over, their efficiency honed to a devastating degree.

It was his suggestion to station fifteen thousand men at the mountain's base completely encircling it. They were to remain there waiting for inhabitants that might try to flee from the annihilation above. The objective: complete immolation.

<hr />

The sun rose. Sleepy souls engagaed in early morning rituals.

Gunners and archers moved up the mountain ramifying into the pocket communities along the mountain's lower roads.

Arrows, sounding soft whirrs and dull death thuds, struck down innocent victims tending to mundane every day duties. Strangely, they were the lucky ones, dying suddenly, quickly.

People who lived at the base of the mountain were neither armed nor skilled in the fighting arts. These simple souls died with little resistance, essentially slaughtered.

Surprisingly, for Zatoichi, the first half of the mountain's population was eliminated without a significant loss of his men. Pathetically, the killing became tedious, laborious, lacking in thrill, a seemingly endless extermination of men, women, children and even animals.

Smoke was everywhere. Sounds of gunfire rose to the upper reaches of the mountain where there were others not so defenceless.

The top half was where the elite warrior monks lived. They were fierce and formidable. Unfortunately, they were not prepared for Nobuinaga's incursion. They had been outmaneuvered. Zatoichi, knew where the arms were stored and managed to remove them before the assault on the base of the mountain, leaving them defenseless. Constant volleys of musket balls, nails, and sundry lethal matter followed by a shower of arrows downed scores of monks with every volley. Ironically, the incessant barrage of firepower was a tactic they, themselves, devised, and now it was being used against them with savage efficiency.

They were ready to die, but seeing as their sacrifices were ineffective they scattered and fled into the surrounding woods hoping to muster a counter offensive.

<hr />

The monks were spread out hiding in the mountain's forest. They had no leadership, no weaponry to counter the muzzles of the Portuguese arquebusiers. Their only defense was their bodies, which they were willing to sacrifice.

Their fearlessness is what concerned Nobunaga. Only their consummate destruction would suffice, and that is what he intended. They would pay for their invasions upon Kyoto, assaults upon the castles of loyal regents, for their political interference and blatant disregard for the true power of Japan. They would be quashed.

The summit is where the Abbot resided. For Zatoichi, the destruction of the temple would be supremely satisfying. The damned monk thwarted him. It was only his brilliance and his audacity that helped him recover and rise to his present and appropriate stature.

The monks would pay for not believing in him. The Abbot will die, but this time by his hand, outright, not surrepticiously.

The ascent to the top was only hindered by pockets of attack by raging monks charging out of the woods trying in their disunified way to protect the temple and the Abbot. Their assaults only slowed Zatoichi, and he reached the top by late afternoon.

Inside the Lotus Hall, the Abbot sat stoically composed amid his closest advisors and protectors, including Ryu. The Abbot had grown fond of the hulking mass of mirth and wished for Ryu to be by his side when he faced Zatoichi. Each man surrounding Abbot Kossa was a forceful entity, explosive and deadly. If the Abbot had any chance of survival it would be through these fierce and loyal men.

Zatoichi entered the hall alone. He paused for a moment, glared at the Abbot and his ten men, and smiled smugly. The Abbot remained composed as Zatoichi advanced upon the dais. Not a word was spoken. Thirty of Zatoichi's samurai poured through the open door behind him and spread out around the hall.

Ryu looked at the Abbot who now was the epitome of composure. At that moment, he realized, he was going to die defending the venerable Abbot. His alarm abated and he coldly settled into a resigned state of mind ... accepting the inevitable.

He assessed the situation quickly, without regret that he was going to die. He focused on how many men he could kill before he finally succumbed. He just hoped he could kill Zatoichi before he died. He would have liked to see him dead.

Violence erupted within the Hall of Contemplation. Zatoichi and his men rushed the eleven who had formed a circle. Fierce cries as well as the discordant clangs of finely honed metal resounded through the hall.

The defensive circle broke apart and small groups skirmished about the temple. Flashes of light glistened, almost rhythmically as metal swirled through the air catching soft shafts of sunlight streaming into the hall. Splashes of crimson rained upon ornamental decorations and glistened in the sun; floors, walls, statues, and sundry artifacts decorating the holy Lotus Hall were splattered by thick streams of ruby red blood.

Bodies littered the hall floor. More of Zatoichi's men than Abbot Kossa's, but the monk's casualties were starting to mount. Ryu was beginning to tire, his breathing labored. He had already sent five men to paradise, but men kept presenting themselves before him apparently oblivious to the formidable force of his sword. Despite being stout, Ryu had the speed of a lithe young warrior; men before him died quickly. Dispatching two samurai with seven strokes of his sword, he found a moment to rest and catch his breath. When he looked up, Zatoichi with his katana raised loomed over him.

The blade arced downward from left to right. Ryu deftly deflected it and retreated in order to place distance between him and his nemesis and to give him more time to regain his wind, but he slipped on blood still gushing from his most recent victim. Ryu landed on one knee; nevertheless, he managed to ready himself for Zatoichi's attack which didn't come. Instead, Zatoichi stood, lording over the kneeling monk, smiling. "Now, I shall have the pleasure of finally killing you as I should have done before."

Ryu said nothing. He stood up and prepared for battle. He was tired. He knew this might be his last battle, but if he died he would inflict as much damage as he could.

Attacking with all the seething rage from his humiliating failure to control the monastery, Zatoichi slashed heavily at Ryu who was barely able to resist the heavy blow. Sensing the weakness, Zatoichi mercilessly rained a cascade of fluid strikes, down and to the left, up and to the right, down at the head. Ryu's counter strikes weakened with each blow; defensive maneuvers were getting sloppy; his blade was getting heavier, and Zatoichi's was getting closer; one slash would eventually connect and he would fall. Luckily, Zatoichi winded himself with his violent flurry and needed a moment to recover much to Ryu's relief. Both large men panted heavily, gulping in as much air as quickly as they could in hopes of reviving first.

Ryu looked about him and realized they were the only two men standing. Everyone else was dead or dying; even the Abbot was prostrate on the floor in a pool of blood. Zatoichi scanned the scene and then gave Ryu a sardonic smile. Despite not being completely ready Ryu attacked, slashing, hacking, and whirling about. One swipe connected. It caught Zatoichi on the mouth, just the tip of the blade but enough to slice a gash from the corner of his mouth across his cheek almost to his ear.

Zatoichi reeled away and took a knee. Ryu couldn't belive he would survive. He advanced to deliver the final blow ... across the neck and off with his head. He took a step closer to end the fight, unfortunately one misstep too close. Zatoichi swung about and struck Ryu's knee, nearly severing his leg in half. Ryu fell. Zatoichi rose and without hesitation cleaved his neck and left clavicle imbedding the blade deeply into the body. Blood spurted voluminously ... and then it ... stopped ... Ryu was dead. Zatoichi, hovering above him, slid his blade out of the lifeless body.

Blood from his wickedly severed mouth streamed heavily mingling with the massive pool of Ryu's issue. Zatoichi loosed a roar of pain, relief and triumph, but immediately regretted it. Savagely ripping a fallen monk's garb, he fashioned himself a cloth and applied it against his wound pressing the gaping flesh closed with the rag; he wobbled out of the temple.

It seemed that the summit had been vanquished. The Abbot was dead. The attending monks were dead. There was an eerie silence about the mountain. Stillness perverted the air. There was nothing left for Zatoichi to do but burn it to its rock base.

The temple at the top was first. Then the rest of the mountain, systematically annihilated. Shrine by shrine, temple by temple, settlement by settlement; voracious, insatiable flames consumed a world a thousand years old.

Whoever managed to survive was eventually discovered and summarily killed. No one escaped. Thirty thousand men, women and children died at the hands of Zatoichi and Oda Nobunaga. The holocaust rose to the heavens in a vicious homage; the smoke high above the flames, and the gods took notice and decided to right decades of wrong; it was imminent.

Chapter 24

Winter passed and the denizen of the village were grateful that it was a mild one. The spring sun enticed dormant bulbs to flowering bloom. Purple irises and yellow daffodils poked out of the moist ground contrasting delightfully against the patches of snow melting at the base of shady pine trees.

The sun shone warmly upon the newest residents of the little rural community. Naki and Sai stood on their porch looking out over the collection of little cottages below. The villagers, friendly and exceedingly hospitable had greeted the bedraggled and gaunt strangers with acceptance when they arrived five months ago. They knew they had nothing to fear from these creatures from the southern provinces that were in desperate need of refuge. The elders of the village instinctively sensed a uniqueness emanating from these two, their comportment different from the rustic behavior of the majority of the village. Everyone belived they were in the company of gods or royalty, someone special who had suffered tremendous loss and was now in need of their help. The village was more than willing to extend its hospitality.

Indeed as time passed, Naki and Sai ingratiated themselves with their hosts teaching esoteric medicinal practices which proved life saving several times for members of the community who had become sick or had injured themselves. Without Sai's wealth of knowledge about such remedies they would have died or been maimed for life.

Naki instructed the men of the village in new forms of self-defense; he taught them tricks they would never in one hundred years have learned. The village took on a new sense of self-worth and confidence; the village quickly came to cherish the new couple.

Naki and Sai had married, not formally, but spiritually. Since they were orphaned - in a sense – due to the annilation of Mt. Hiei and of the ninja compound, they had no one left but each other, for which they were entirely grateful to the gods. The demons which plagued them ... Sai's disenchantment with her demanding heritage and Naki's hellish dreams ... seemed to fade. Sai was no longer resentfully resigned to a commitment which she had found increasingly difficult to continue. Even though she missed her father dearly, her obligations as the Chunin's daughter no longer preoccupied her. Instead, she focused on helping Naki and the villagers, something which she found pleasurable and something at which she was entirely marvelous.

Naki no longer had the dreams; they disappeared. His feelings of despair were supplanted with those of hope. He was happy. The Abbot, Ryu, the monastary, all prized memories, were honored, but what he lost in them he gained in a woman who thankfully loved him and whom he fiercely loved back. Life was as he hoped it would one day be; the sun shone every day, overcast or not.

———⟨⟨◍⟩⟩———

Over the ensuing year, the valley provided a plentiful bounty ... more than the villagers needed. The mountain rice grew so well there was sufficient surplus to trade. New and wonderous items, some practical, some luxurious, were hauled to this remote little village. News of the village's prosperity spread through the various mountain communities.

In the closest neighboring villages, speculation, as to why this particular little village had suddenly become so prosperous, turned to the newcomers, those two with special knowledge of medicine, martial arts, and agriculture. It was determined they were the reason for the valley's unexpected success. Who were they? Where did they come from? When inappropriately asked by curious visiting neighbors, they discreetly and ever so politely redirected the conversation so as to not have to answer questions clearly. They were masters of this, Sai especially; she made these visitors feel shameful about questioning them about who they were and where they came from? The inhabitants of the little village had simply given up inquiring, long ago, and just appreciated the benificence bestowed upon them.

Not everyone was so respectful, however. The supersticious in distant villages concocted tales of the village being cursed or blessed by the presence of gods. Something supernatural had occurred in the sleepy little village by the river. Skeptical minds determined the strangers to be demons and that a catastrophe would befall them.

Despite the storm of speculation, Naki took to improving the men and the young boys, in the art of fighting. They became fit, robust, and skilled. They learned to fashion weapons of steel. Somehow, Portuguese guns appeared in the village from a battle somewhere to the south and quickly they were being reproduced by men who were willing to learn the ways of the new world.

Naturally, neighboring communities became concerned about the prosperity and the military strength of their previously docile, impoverished fellow citizens. Imagination and resentment spun wild speculations of what could occur if the village were not checked and kept in its place.

Word of its military strength spread south, far south, to Kyoto, in fact, to Oda Nobunaga's chamberlains who discussed the matter briefly before moving on to more pressing military engagements. The little village was a curious anomaly, nothing of consequence, but something which needed periodic attention to make sure it did not somehow pose a threat of any sort in the future.

<hr />

Another year of peace and prosperity blessed the little village which was now not so little. Its population doubled to over four hundred able bodied men who were skilled in the use of bow, sword, bo-stick, and arquebus. The little village became a destination point for those who wished to share its prosperity and opportunity, and indeed there was plenty of both. The jealousy expressed by neighboring villages was judiciously mitigated when the little village shared its knowledge and expertise. These thorps in turn began to prosper and the surrounding communities became allies. The northern communities coalesced into one accord and developed a sense of confidence in their abilities to defend themselves against an incursion. They were aware that for the time being, Oda Nobunaga's interests lay in provinces south of them, but if he continued his expansion, which was moving slowly, but expanding north nonetheless, they could defend their autonomy.

Naki and Sai had become leaders in the community. Their knowledge, wisdom, kindness secured them a home on earth and a place in the universe. They knew this was where they belonged and where they would continue to live. Sai was with child, in the early stages, and, the village along with the surrounding communities rejoiced. Naki, despite his youth, had become a voice of wisdom among the elders; he was consulted on matters ranging from martial arts to village defences to settling disputes amongst the population as if he were an arbiter who had lived among them for scores of years.

In times of quiet reflection, Naki could not quite believe the turn of events. Such dramatic changes occurred so quickly, and yet what replaced his old existence is what he had been seeking, unconsciously, his whole life. He loved Sai, more than he could fathom. He was to be a father. He was respected in the community. His former taciturn self transformed

into an almost larger than life garrulous presence who captured everyone's attention and respect. Naki had become
dynamic and powerful. He sometimes envisioned himself
like the Chunin, her father, athough he chastised himself for
such whimsical thoughts never wanting to believe that he
could ever become the man he was; however, the change in
him was remarkable. He secretly knew that Sai had much to
do with his transformation, and that was one of the reasons
he loved her so.

She was dearer to him now than he could remember;
perhaps, it was because he was so happy. He recalled the
admiration he developed for her when he realized she was
not simply an impudent, empty-headed girl, but a woman of
immeasurable talent and deep devotion. Her teaching him
family secrets, and constantly encouraging him to excel mo-
tivated him, and when she celeberated his successes his pride
quietly rose along with his appreciation of her. When his ob-
sessions led him to dangerous foolish adventures, and when
the consequences of his actions brought about disasterous
results, she never judged, but only loved in a way far too wise
for a soul of her verdant youth; she was remarkable: humble,
beautiful, intelligent, kind almost beyond this world, and she
was his, and she was having his child.

Things were too good, and dark thoughts began to form
in the light of all that was agreeable. He wondered ... could
he cope if he lost her ... could he cope if he lost the people
he now loved, and the new life he had constructed. His world
had been destroyed once before, could it happen again? The
threat was still out there, albeit south of him, but still there.
It has not disappeared; the danger is still real. Just because

he has enjoyed almost two years of peace, prosperity and freedom from the horrifying visions which dominated his former life does not mean that the monster could not return to plague him. Nobunaga was still campaigning and for the most part succeeding in conquering the provinces. What was to stop him from one day sending an envoy to his village demanding they ally or die? Would he pledge allegiance in order to save Sai and the surrounding communities? Could he? What was he to do? He knew deep in his soul a battle was yet to come.

He didn't share his concerns with Sai; though, he knew she knew of them. She probably had the same thoughts and kept them from him. They were not mentioned. The ninja village and the monestary at Mt. Hiei were never mentioned. They were ghosts of the past. This life was their new concern, this life and that of their baby.

He tried to relieve his anxiety with the assurances that the men of the village were well armed and numerous defenses had been constructed to thwart an invasion, yet had the ninja compound not been well fortified? Had the monastery not been a bastion of resistance for hundreds of years? How did they fall? Naki's intuition suspected that the cretin he tried to kill one time, Zatoichi, was the common element in all the disasters, for sure. He knew the mountain and the monastery intimately, and somehow, he discovered the location of the clan's compound. It was he who was responsible for Naki's misery and ... inadvertently his present happiness. Could this fiend possibly endanger his new life? These thoughts plagued him.

Wisely, he chose not to ignore the premonitions. He

alerted the neighboring villages to post a watch … a vigilant watch. He had never asked them to do such a thing in the past, and gratefully without a whisper or a grumble they set a watch. Pigeons were readied; message paper, pens and sundry items were set: everything was prepared willingly. Basically, he placed the mountain on a state of alert based on a premonition.

"Fumio, I have put everyone on edge. Everyone thinks an attack is at hand. "

"Yes, Nakamura-san we are all ready."

"But, I truly do not know if we are in danger."

"You are wise to be cautious. If you are wrong, no one will take offense."

"If I am wrong I will lose some of the faith people have in me."

"Please, Nakamura-san, do not concern yourself so. It is better we are ready than to be caught off guard."

"You are correct Fumio-san, but I do not want to create fear when there is no need, yet. I wish to be ready."

"We are."

"It was long ago, I felt the same foreboding I do now. I was a boy; I ran and hid. Oda Nobunaga's men attacked our village and slaughtered everyone. I survived."

"Yes, because you sensed danger, as you do now."

"Yes."

"So, when they come, we will be prepared, and maybe we will have an advantage since they will not expect resistance. If they do not come, then we will have practiced what to do when they come, and they will, there is no question about that. Everyone knows Nobunaga's ambitious plans to unite everyone under his banner will one day come to our communities. No one is resentful that you charge us to be prepared. You are not taking time from our duties; we have plenty to eat, thanks to you; do not concern yourself about inconveniencing us; it is for our own good."

"Thank you, Fumio-san."

"No we thank you Nakamura-san. Since you and Sai stumbled into our village we have become blessed. You bring with you blessed chi; the gods smile upon you both."

Naki grinned and wished it were so.

⸺◈⸺

Zatoichi was beyond friendly frontiers, deep in enemy terrain. If he were discovered penetrating these northern mountain passes, he would be killed; destroyed before he could exact the vengeance he so passionately sought. Zatoichi knew that Naki survived the destruction of the camp and was somewhere in these hills; Ito Nakamura, that irkesome little weasel, Naki.

Since the destruction of Mt. Hiei, life had been very good for Zatoichi; campaigns were successful; he managed to avoid pitfalls; moreover, he gained respect, authority, power and wealth. He got what he wanted, and now, he wanted revenge. How dare that impudent little bastard threaten his life … his life! Zatoichi's life! Not only did he embarrass and inconvenience him with that pathetic assassination attempt, but he also thwarted him in overthrowing the Abbot at the monastery, an unforgiveable transgression. The little shit must pay for his offenses, that bastard son of a fucking eta. He and all he holds dear will die ... horribly.

Truly, it was the need for reprisal that drove Zatoichi not so much the pragmatism of defensive reconaissance. For some reason, the thought of Naki merely living, let alone succeeding in anything, drove Zatoichi beyond reason, to madness. He dreamt of his immolation. Never in his life, had he been as preoccupied with someone as he was with Ito Nakamura.

Zatoichi did not reside within the realm of introspection, and he did not wonder why he hated the young ninja so much, and why he would risk his reputation, his life, and the life of his men to foray into hostile territory. Unfortunately for him, his abnormal preoccupation began to worry his men, as they knew they were in danger and the mission could prove disasterous. Even though they were obliged to serve this maniac to their death none felt obligated. If the mission was to go badly, to the man, they would abandon their duty and let him fend for himself. None feared the reprisals which could ultimately befall them should they contravene the bushido code. They all believed Zatoichi to be an abomination and no one would suffer should they abandon their oath.

Zatoichi was oblivious. He was too preoccupied with his own interests and causes to concern himself with his men.

Naki felt disquiet. Zatoichi felt enervated. Miles apart their souls intersected. Zatoichi palpably felt victory and redemption. Naki felt fear, loss.

Dusk drew to a close and darkness fell upon the troops in the woods. A runner slipped into Zatoichi's tent with news: the bastard has been found, his village not far away.

The news ignited Zatoichi's face with excitement. At last, retribution ... he tried to kill me, and now I will kill him and those who champion him. Zatoichi was titillated. He went to sleep comforted that his vengeance would shortly be satisfied.

Naki on the other hand slept restlessly. Something was wrong; he couldn't explain it. Scouts were dispatched, directed to scour the surrounds, looking for ... things out of balance, and they found it, in abundance: hundreds of men, heavily armed and only an hour away. Racing home, they sounded the alarm. The moment was upon them. They would live or die according to Naki.

Weapons were retrieved from the armory; plans were executed. They were ready.

Zatoichi wasn't. His men were lethargic, exhibiting signs of apathy and smatterings of rebellion.

Zatoichi sensed the shift in energy, and it disturbed him. His fleeting feelings of euphoria dissipated as if they were blown away by a malevolent breeze leaving him confounded. Always a leader and always in control, he felt suddenly feckless. It frightened him. He could fail. He could die. He didn't like it.

Nevertheless, he pushed forward, angrily, ignoring all instincts that his actions were folly, such was the nature of his pride.

Naki and his villagers were not so arrogant. They were living on the thin edge of fear. Their senses were attuned to instincts of survival. Zatoichi's were not. He was about revenge; Naki, luckily, now, knew better.

Early in the morning, before the sun rose, Zatoichi and his

disgrutled horde rose and marched. By mid-morning it would be over he gloated. The sun would be up and Nakamura's blood would be on the ground. Grumbling, his men loped along hoping that their master was correct that this would be an easy fight and they would soon be home, but deep in their shared hearts they knew better: they would not survive.

Their fears were soon realized. They were not ten miles ouside the village when the arrows began to rain.

Groans … anguished cries … . Men ramified into the protective woods. Zatoichi was suddenly left alone with very few men upon the road; he was livid, oblivious to the pointy storm showering him. Standing firm with an authoritative voice, he bellowed for them to return, to re-assemble, to resume attack. A few did, obsequious and dispirited, more afraid of Zatoichi than death from a storm of arrows. Then it stopped. Some of those that fled returned, poor warriors for the battle ahead; he had lost many men and their zest for the fight.

But then Zatoichi paused, why did they stop firing? Why did they not just wipe everyone out there on the road? They are not equipped well enough, he reasoned. They don't have enough weaponry to stop them. This heartened him and to the dismay of his men he continued on. Somehow in his twisted mind he envisioned a victory. Naki and Sai dead at his feet; he could imagine nothing sweeter. Nothing would stop him. He roared an animalistic resonance echoing a reverberation of sheer hatred at the thought of being threatened or thwarted. His viciousness manifested itself to such a degree that his troops could not deny him; they were entirely servile, unfortunately.

Thinking, he had an assembly of men who would ultimately stand by him, he marched onward determined to wipe out the village.

Naki hadn't lost anyone in the first salvo. He pulled back and regrouped. The first attack was more reconnaissance than an all out assault. Naki wanted to test the timbre of Zatoichi's men, to see what they were made of, and now he knew. Naki was confident he could eradicate the scoundrel and his pathetic invaders from his mountain. They were still miles away from the village and he knew the mountain better than Zatoichi; there would be plenty of opportunity to annihilate him. The thought now saddened Naki for some reason; he had changed, not so eager to kill anymore, death, even Zatoichi's disturbed him, but Naki knew his immolation was imminent,. He had a family to protect, a village, a mountain.

Zatoichi was smugly satisfied that he could decimate the village and finally put an end to the irritation named Ito Nakamura and Tomoki Sai.

Naki positoned his men on both sides of the road. He positioned his men there to resume a shower of arrows upon the unwelcome guests threatening the village.

Marching recklessly down the mountain road without thought of what might lay ahead, Zatoihi wanted to reach the village and kill everyone. His men knew that somehow his mind had been weakened; it had become cloudy and dim. Unfortunately, his rage had not subsided and it still subjected them to his will.

Naki positioned his men on both sides of the road. Zatoichi would be ... engulfed. It was time to add heat to the arrow onslaught ... fire. Naki hoped a mountain flame roaring before them, moving towards them, would send them back to the hell from which they came, Naki was sad to have to resort to such extremes.

Zatoichi was relentless. He marched forward ignoring defensive precautions; he was brutishly offensive envisioning the death of everyone in the village. He was mad, and the men knew it.

It was noon, and the sun bore down upon the troops; the sun evaporating their vigor. Suddenly, the sky glowed brighter somehow. Sparkling jewels descended from the ledges and cliffs above the road. They glimmered and flamed, a myriad of gems descending, descending with lethal potency.

For the second time that day death struck; soldiers fell like pine needles upon the road. Again the troops fled for the woods. Again Zatoichi was inflamed beyond any reason he happened to retain. Fire and smoke confused the entire conflict. This time, his men abandoned him entirely. No matter how much he hollered and bellowed for them to return, they did not. He was, this time, finally left solitary upon his horse, in the middle of the road engulfed by smoke and flame.

Then the rain of fire stopped. The flames died, and the smoke cleared, and the air was hazy but clear enough to see that in the middle of the road, stood Naki, sword in hand, a barrier, blocking Zatoichi's advance. There was no getting around him ... only through him.

Zatoichi stood facing his nemesis. Delighted at the curious turn of events, Zatoichi's enraged and addled mind calmed and turned coldly calculating. Intoxicated, as if he was under the influence of strong saki, he felt deliriously happy that he was at last on the verge of satisfying his vengeance. A wry smile spread across his ugly scarred face; blackness clouded his soul; he was going to enjoy this; he was not in his correct mind, but he did not know it. He got off his horse.

Naki stood his ground ready to reenact their first encounter in the courtyard of Mt Hiei, but this time with real weapons. As he recalled, he won.

Zatoichi envisioned it differently; he saw the boy severed and bleeding beneath his feet.

Zatoichi struck first. Naki deflected the blow easily. It did not possess the same strength as he remembered in Kyoto. It was weaker.

He struck back. His blows were quick, light but focused. He knew where he wanted to strike, but Zatoichi somehow managed to counter them.

Naki retreated and scrutinized his opponent. For a moment he considered signaling the archers to end Zatoichi's pathetic life, but that would rob him of the satisfaction of killing the miserable wretch by his own hand. The demons within dictated he should end Zatoichi's life, and for the first time, Naki was pleased with his demons.

He readied himself. There would be no mistake. To accidentally die by the hand of this villain would be a travesty. No! Zatoichi is supposed to die; he will die; anything but Zatoichi's death would be a mockery.

Naki struck this time, strongly ... incensed with the thought the outcome could possibly be something other than what should be.

Zatoichi, masterfully, staunched the blow and countered with a punishingly heavy one to Naki's shock and surprise.

Naki faltered,; he was confused. Zatoichi was fat; he should be slow; his rich life should have made him soft and weak, yet he wasn't.

Zatoichi sensed Naki's confusion and rallied, applying several severe strikes knocking Naki backwards.

Sweat began to trickle down Naki's brow stinging his eyes. What was happening? Why was this not an easy win? Then he realized if it was easy it would not be as satisfying, and so he gathered his muster, focused his chi and attacked with vigor and confidence.

This time Zatoichi retreated, shocked, somewhat, by the ferocity of the youth's assault. Each knew the battle would be pivotal; the outcome would be definitely death for one and serious injuries for the other.

Naki's men in the woods knew better than to intervene. Despite their reverrence for the young man they knew this was his battle, his war and to intrude would be to disrespect him; however, they did descend from the mountain to watch the fight between two gifted swordsmen.

The remainder of Zatoichi's men who were hiding in the woods also crept closer to witness a fight that would be passed on to future generations. The previously opposing factions were indeed so close to each other there in the woods they could have reached out and touched one another, yet they ignored one another focusing rather upon Naki and Zatoichi. Strangely, all the men were secretly supporting Naki. Zatoichi was truly alone in this struggle and death would be his reward whether he overwhelmed Naki or not, if not by the hand of one of his men then by the arrow of one of Naki's.

Zatoichi realized this when tumultuous cheers erupted as Naki was showing an advantage. The silent woods suddenly became a clamorous copse of encouragement for the young man. However, this realization of his impending fate, his ultimate doom, only served to inflame Zatoichi's hot hatred and energized him at a time when the fight was taking its toll on his vigor. He responded with power and renewed violence. He reasoned that maybe if he won decisively and with a sense of artistry and elegance respect from both groups might save his life, and so he rallied and exploded upon Naki with an inner strength he did not know he had.

Naki was forced to retreat and stop to catch his breath. Zatoichi would not let him and pursued, katana slashing down hard upon Naki's and the counter blow. The clash of the metals sent strong waves of debilitating vibrations into Naki's forearms, paralyzing them momentarily. The next blow he would not be able to block with his sword; he knew it. When it came, all Naki could do was to get out of its way, so he stepped off to the side and the blade swished down narrowly slashing him. Feelings had not returned to his tingling arms and hands yet and so Naki's only defense was to evade. Strike after strike had Naki moving left, right, down and back. Then a thought lightening quick hit Naki. This was the way to defeat Zatoichi. He is powerful and skilled, but fat and easily winded. Make him strike so many times he won't have the energy to lift his sword.

This tactic infuriated Zatoichi to madness. He would swing, and Naki would dodge, and he would miss and curse. "Fight me you coward. You know you can't win,; feel my blade and die." Naki remained silent and continued his dance around Zatoichi's deadly blows. Naki knew that his next strike against Zatoichi would be the final one. He could see it; it was just a matter of moments. And then, it came. Zatoichi paused just a little too long at the top of one of his swings, for a breath. It was long enough for Naki to lunge forward and to smash him across his metal chest plate, a strong blow which shook Zatoichi to the bone whereupon he paused again. Naki dropped to one knee and focused on an exposed patch of flesh, not plated by armor at the back of his knee and he hacked. Zatoichi fell like a giant cedar tree. He dropped forward on his hands and knees, but in true warrior fashion he did not remain in that vulnerable position for long. He tried to rise, but he didn't have a functioning right leg and he dropped to his knees, exhausted, arms hanging limply by his side, his sword dangling from his hand. Naki circled him and faced him head on, looking down into the eyes of the man he was about to slay. Zatoichi opened his mouth about to say something, but Naki wouldn't let him. He plunged his sword through a small opening between the plates that protect his neck. Instead of spewing insults, Zatoichi spewed blood, large quantities of it with every beat of his heart. The splatter stained Naki and covered the once gleaming armor Zatoichi wore. He remained upright on his knees for a moment. The blood that gave him his life erupting from the gash at his throat took a moment or two to drain. There was time for a few last thoughts to pass through his mind before he died, since his throat was cut, he could not speak, and so his last moments were silent and the last thing he understood, and the last thing he heard was a fly buzz before he died. He fell, face first into the dusty road, and there he lay.

BLOOD SHINOBI

A cheer rose from the woods; Naki's men rushed forward sweeping him away. Zatoichi's men clambered out of the woods and surrounded their fallen leader. No one spoke. Eventually, they all turned and began their march home, leaving their leader in the road; relieved that they could return home claiming their leader died and they were forced to retreat, a minor shame but a forgivable one.

Flies continued to buzz around the body before they were joined by carrion birds.

Chapter 25

Exhausted, physically, emotionally, Naki let himself be carried off by the villagers. Eneravated, he wished only one thing: to be alone with Sai, but honorings precluded any such notion, and he unselfishly celebrated with the villagers long into the night. Not one person died. His people were saved, and any further threat from Nobunaga was now very unlikely, for Naki knew it was Zatoichi alone who was pre-occupied with their village.

All Naki wanted was to wrap his wife up in his arms. Oh, how he longed for her skin, her firm flesh and the peace that only she could bring him. Far too long, had he sought vengeance; far too long, he had been plagued with horrific visions; far too long had he been enslaved by hell, and now finally he believed he was free. No, he had not killed Oda Nobunaga; but he did kill Zatoichi, who theatened his new life. Naki somehow understood that Nobunaga would die ... soon without his intervention. Truly, his nemesis was Zatoichi who was now nothing but bone on the dusty road.

—————⫸《◉》⫷—————

Sai lay naked, waiting, longing for his touch. Naki, finally at home, undressed and slid into bed beside her. Her soft supple skin excited him; her breasts were full, her belly swollen; he was excited; he so wanted to make love to her, but he was too tired. At last, he knew true peace and was genuinely happy. Happily, he was whole, uninjured, alive, and lying beside his most precious pregnant jewel, life sparkled glistening like a gem.

—————⫸《◉》⫷—————

He slept long. Sai was up hours before him, quietly bustling about. He was sore. The fight depleted him, but not as much as it depleted Zatoichi. He wanted to smile a smile of smug satisfaction, vengeful retribution, but he felt sad instead. He had trouble understanding how human life meant so little to so many. He was soon going to be granted the greatest gift, the gift of life, boy or girl, it didn't matter. He could not fathom how ruthless people could so callously snuff the precious endowment of life. He felt pangs of grief for the lives he had taken. They were brothers, fathers, and sons to someone … to somebody. He realized his quest for revenge had obscured the deeper sensibilities he had been granted. He realized, at that moment, he was not placed on this earth to kill Nobunaga, but he was here for a greater purpose. Was it to love Sai? Was it to raise his child? What was his purpose? He had been struggling with this question his entire life. He understood that it did not revolve around Oda Nobunaga. His purpose was superior to such a mundane task as revenge. He knew he was destined for greater glory. Maybe not in an enduring historical sense, but in a truly meaningful way that made the world a genuinely better place. His miniscule contribution was for the greater good as the Abbot once told him. His purpose was to fulfill a greater good, whatever that might be. And with these thoughts, he was satisfied. He was going to have a child and nothing was more important to him than that.

He or she was a part of Sai and him. The revelation confounded him. It stupefied him. The miracle of life intrigued him more than the notion of death with which he had for far too long been preoccupied.

From his cot, he watched Sai move. She was beautiful. Her body was full; her skin was radiant. She was the embodiment of everything Naki could have possibly desired, and her deepest beauty was that even though she fully recognized her hold over Naki, she was not corrupted or tempted to abuse her power; she was not manipulative; she was entirely without guile. Her love was pure.

<hr/>

She was due; he was nervous; Sai's pregnancy was out of his charge; he hadn't any influence. He prayed wholeheartedly that all would go well and that he would soon hold a healthy child, but as he was now wise, wise enough to understand that life does not attend to the wishes of the dreamer that it has a will and a destiny of its own; he was terrified.

Sai assured him that she was fine. "The delivery would go well," she told him; nevertheless, he was nervous. He refused to believe that this good fortune which had recently blessed him was not an illusion waiting to darken, to turn malevolent, to devilishly torment him and suck him back to hell. He panicked, momentarily. He desperately longed for peace. He had enough of darkness, revenge, and death. He wished for life, love, growth, beauty, creativity, for light, for heaven on earth. He knew it was impossible to sustain happiness forever, but maybe for a moment, a brief fleeting moment, life could be sublime, be worry free; he prayed, oh, how he prayed, Sai and the baby would be fine.

The mid-wife was summoned. During labor, Sai remained stoic and did not cry out. Naki was not allowed near Sai. She had the village women to attend to her and assist with the delivery.

Naki paced the garden outside his home listening for … anything … anything to divulge how things were going, but Sai was unbending about being quiet, despite the pain, so he heard nothing. Her attendants were equally quiet as the delivery was to be a subdued and passive affair; Sai had eaten mochi and eggs, and when the labor pains arrived, she felt energetic, charged and ready to deliver a healthy baby.

Naki, the typical expectant father, continued to feel totally at a loss, out of his element, a situation out of his control which he didn't like much. The women ruled the roost; this was their domain; however, somehow, somewhere in the disquietude of it all he felt assured the women with all their experience would soon produce a healthy bawling baby and a beaming wife. So, all he could do was pace, which he did vigorously.

Then he heard a cry, his child's cry. He embraced the sound. He dashed into the house not waiting to be invited. Sai was beaming, cradling a black haired beauty to her breast, a little girl. Sai shone. The baby burbled. Naki smiled. A brilliant sun added to all that was golden this glorious morning.

Epilogue

Years passed, and Naki and Sai enjoyed their serenity: more children, happy children, gloriously oblivious to the secrets their parents kept from them; no ninja legacy no weapons, no poisons, only a carefree life filled with sunshine, butterflies and beetle bugs, an idyllic pastoral existence. The cycle had stopped.

The dark shifty shadow of ninja machinations faded into memory, a memory written on parchment, bleached by the sun, letters no longer black, significant, only fading grey, indisctinct, marked by vaguery rather than recollection.

———≈())≈———

For Nobunaga, on the other hand, his trials did not grow fainter; they remained a dark quintessential essence delineating, distinctly, the destiny he chose: treachery, murder, vengeance, hubris, and arrogance; these were his horrific companions, his constant cohorts accompanying him, nightly, haunting his dreams, never giving him a moment's peace. Oh, for a moment of respite, a lull from the hatred, a second of genuine sentiment, trust and peace. Impossible! Too much blood had been let for such a moment to actually occur. He accepted the inevitable suffering, restless nights filled with horrifying spirits.

———◦⦿◦———

Akechi Mitsuhide was a talented general and poet. He fared well; he was successful; he was efficient. Not only did he overpower the castle of Hatano, but he also did it bloodlessly, and then he presented Hatano Hideharu with his brother in person to Oda Nobunaga, all without violence. Unfortunately, for Mitsuhide, Nobunaga could not have been more alarmed: to Oda Nobunaga, Mitsuhide was a threat; he was too triumphant. He could pose problems.

Out of jealousy, the forgiving demeanor, which typically characterized Nobunaga's successes, disappeared. Darkness and hatred conspired to cruelly condemn the two trusting brothers to their death; these brothers who gave themselves up, throwing themselves upon the mercy of "The Great Unifier", to save their lives, counting most assuredly upon Nobunaga's munificence, shockingly discovered they made a fatal mistake. Hatano and his brother were dispensed a hideous and public execution which shocked the country. Hearts hardened, especially Mitsuhide's.

He was unfortunately held responsible for their deaths,

and so, in retribution, his mother was heinously murdered by Hatano's retainers.

Akechi Mitsuhide lost his mind, literally. Visions of her death had been graphically reported and these images tormented him. He swore revenge upon Nobunaga.

Oddly, Nobunaga was unwontedly insensible to the hatred he had engendered; normally astute to the ramifications of his actions, he was,this time, insensible, and it cost him dearly.

———⊶«◉»⊷———

In the spring of 1582, a year after the Hatano Hideharu incident, Nobunaga returned from a victorious conquest of the Takeda clan. His losses were infinitesimal; theirs were overwhelming; smugly he gloated; his victories were becoming easier. It would not be long now, and Japan would be his.

Unfortunately, news of a new conflagration erupted, a threatening blaze burned in the west, and he needed to douse it.

He sent his most trusted retainer, General Hideyoshi to contend with the issue, but alas, he needed assistance, and Nobunaga would not deny his favorite retainer help, so he sped him all of his personal troops, leaving behind only a small contingent of men to protect the fortress, Kyoto. Uunconcerned that he was was unprotected, that night he supped sumptuously and entertained royally.

It was a glorious gastronomic affair: salmon, tuna, squid, sweet shrimp and sea urchin; music and entertainments spun magical moments for his dignified guests, and a copious amount of sake was provided.

Diplomatic ties were forged easily during the convivial congregation. Nobunaga could not have been happier with the outcome. He had not only secured some provinces in the south, but also fortified the difficult northern territories. That night he went to bed drunk, happily dreaming of a unified Japan under his rule.

He awoke, painfully to find that he had been spitefully betrayed.

Akechi Mitsuhide was to have taken his forces to aide Hideyoshi with the contest in the west; instead, the avenging General diverted his men to Kyoto. Surrounding the castle, taking advantage of the minimal reinforcements guarding it, he set it afire.

Initially, Oda Nobunaga succeeded in overcoming the conflagration, fleeing the blaze. Honnoji Temple was completely aflame; however, during his escape he unfortunately ran directly into Akechi Mitsuhide and his men. Forty Samurai blocked his way. He knew he was doomed. He had no protection, five against forty. Nobunaga conceded; he succumbed. He knew his time on this earth had come to an end at the hands of his vengeful general, Akechi Mitsuhide.

He supplicated himself and asked if he could die honorably. Akechi Mitsuhide conceded.

Nobunaga withdrew his short sword and asked his personal attendant, Mori Ranmaru, if he would be kind enough to be his second?

"Hai', whispered the grieved man knowing that shortly thereafter he would be killing himself as well.

Nobunaga knelt on the floor before Akechi Mitsuhide. Without hesitation, proudly and spontaneously he plunged the blade into his belly and with vigor ripped left and right. His bowls emerged, maimed and bleeding; stoically Nobunaga suffered the pain and indignity but not for long, for his own katana came swinging down decapitating his head from his slumping body.

The head thumped and the body toppled after it; Nobunaga's terrible tyranny changed hands.

———— ((()) ————

General Hideyoshi was infuriated by Mitsuhide's treachery, and swore to avenge Nobunaga's death. To add to Hideyoshi's umbrage, Mitsuhide was officially titled Shogun by the Emperor who recognized Mitsuhide's claims that his lineage was worthy of the title. Hideyoshi acted quickly and only thirteen days later he faced Mitsuhide at the Battle of Yamazaki.

Mitsuhide, in spite of being granted title of Shogun, did not have the forces to defeat Hideyoshi's superior numbers. Mitsuhide, not wanting to fight within the walls of Kyoto took the fight south, between a mountain and a river, feeling that would be most advantageous for him and his inferior number of troops.

Unfortunately for Mitsuhide, Hideyoshi secured the mountain first eliminating hist advantage. Furthermore, Hideyoshi cleverly employed the use of ninja, that night, to strike fear into the souls of Mitsuhide's soldiers, to weaken their spirits for the morning fight. Ninjas set fire to the camp; killed many of their leaders; decimated any sense of confidence which might have had sway over the battle; Mitsuhide's troops were destroyed before the battle began.

In the morning, Mitsuhide sent his feckless troops across the river and up the mountain to face Hideyoshi's men, but they were driven back by the infernal new technology, the devastating arquebus.

Adding further to Mitsuhide's misery, Hideyoshi sent flanks left and right to quell the attack on the mountain. Mitsuhide's troops were surrounded, so in order to save himself, he fled the fight …. the battle of Yamazaki was essentially over. Two hundred men remained foolishly loyal to Mitsuhide, and were soon destroyed.

The General fled … to the town of Ogurusu … where he was unforutnateley captured by a band of vicious bandits. Foolishy arrogant and haughty, despite his precarious position, he was defiant and unwilling to comply with any of their outrageous demands, so General Akechi Mitsuhide, Lord of Japan, vanquisher of Oda Nobunaga, was summarily executed by an unpleasant and surly, peasant youth, curiously, named … Naki.

CPSIA information can be obtained at www.ICGtesting.com
Printed in the USA
LVOW132024210313

325358LV00001B/1/P